Chapt

Prolegomenon

I was 17, deep in a natural wood and aimlessly inch-worming towards three years as a manic-depressive psychopath when I met Hadi-Alim and Eleazer. The wood and I were harmoniously sentient, whimsically communicating through unambiguous acts of associative thought and relishing in our bi-kingdom connectivity.

So too I'd formed a fine relationship with the squirrels and deer, whose homes I was welcome to intrude, the deer coaxing grazes of their hyper-paletted noses. The instant I caressed one of 'em they'd seduced me into an eternity of affection. The squirrels were sprightly and feared nothing, hopping up and perching beside me where-and-whenever I'd take a seat. Every so often a chipmunk would dart straight for me, leap, and I'd grab her up, stroking her striped back as we commuted. Should I begin to read or write a rejuvenated troupe of seven gnats would appear, rippin' concentrics around my head, shootin' stars about my papery goods. In that moment I was on the approach to Morla, most always my destination, trudging thru the mushy field that leads directly up to and above the crusted folds of his kvetchy head and neck. Suctioned in place, often for years at a time, nothing at all to do but think up syntactically obnoxious commentary and wait for the opportunity to employ it, a bad, sad and lonely prophet, obese and supersaturated with hopeless lament, essentially dead and buried in quicksand activated by apprehension.

As someone who spends an unhealthy amount of time alone and parallel to the ground, I can assure you that the mind goes to black places of utter nothingness when isolated for too long. As loathsome as I become after but a few hours quarantined with my neuroses, I can't fathom the existential nightmares he's been forging down there. Well aware that I am nothing more than a local simpleton he'd be compromising his mandate by emerging to sneeze on me. If he wasn't so stubborn faced he could conjoin with every other animal in town and accept my companionship. I could play him some rock 'n' roll and tell him the 3 or 4 jokes I know, infuse his miserable, isolated and tragically eternal life with a bit of pleasure. I've long been and remain more than happy to befriend him, but not once have I felt the gentlest rumble whilst atop his mossy, unkempt shell.

The one pleasure Satan affords the poor guy, glued to that eternal coordinate of his, is the suck of hubris from the world's bravest warriors. No qualified guerrilla travels a path that directs them but precisely at him, the colossal fucker is keen to know each is on approach be they thousands of miles away. But he isn't really the rotten curmudgeon he portends to be. As invariably cranky as is his behavior and as much as he seems to destroy each of these young dudes' will, all comers depart with their capacity to prevail intact, craftily veiled insights sublimated in by ol' Morle to benefit their quests. His snarky attitude isn't authentic, he feigns narcissism to mask his depression.

I hadn't planned much for this particular saunter, only to climb up and onto his carapace and rework lyrical bits of a song I'd been writing about cunnilingus. Accomplishing all that much was never the plan or point when I visited this well familiar place, most commonly by my lonesome. The local bluebirds and honeybees, reincarnations of thousands of Russian, Italian and Armenian women who each needed to exist precisely as they had so that I too could in turn approached adoringly with stamen and regurgitated worms should my tummy growl and knew of my pleasures to include walking, climbing, sitting, writing, reading, smoking, blasting a Walkman through giant headphones on holes three and four and most recently intertwining with young ladies, oblivious to be fucking me atop a giant snapping turtle.

My casual pace kept my feet less than a flattened foot from the meat and potatoes of my body and as my left waited for my right a crumpled scrap of faded ochre came to rest on the forest floor in front of me, so impeccably timed and placed that it straddled my belly button, brushing up against my bare big toes. Visibly as worn and weathered as the pantherines and brontosauruses below, the tatter's aroma was delightfully wind-swept. Picking it up I felt and began to see that razor-thin slits had been fashioned into the coarse cloth. I raised up with it but sunlight drenched the arborous expanse and exploding paint seared thru my face, my eyes were glazed over by a temperate itch while dwarf stars and rotating rings flashed gold and rose, overpowering the tight squeeze of my lids. As the last of this quick trip dripped from my throat, all malady having leaked out of my head, I re-raised the cloth, eye-leveled. I then discovered that its abrasions formed a series of boxy letters and flipped it right-side up, spacing in sensation before I could read not ten of the document's characters whilst terror and elation bee lined my skull and neck, each set on dying or killing the other.

It read:
Dearest Rupert: My companion and I are suspended a substantial ways above you, enjoying the simplicities of the wood you've made a second home. Don't strain your neck attempting to locate us, we're sneaky up here.
My appearance resembles that of a man. My wonderful cohort is a male Asiatic lion. We'd quite like to float down and speak with you, neither of us has aggressive or deceitful intentions, rather quite the opposite. I assure you that despite our appearance and largess you will not be overwhelmed by your interactions with us. If indeed you'd like to meet us, simply remain where you are whilst we make it all the way down. Thanks so much. --Hadi-Alim

I rejoiced in the notion that there may be more to this world I found so unbreachably under-stimulating, overloadcd on excitement and tortured by the wait. I planted myself in the soil, uprooting my heels only as I first heard the wildcat's bassy breathing. Wanting somehow else to ready myself, I inhaled two giant tokes of preparatory fresh air as they descended. As the chubbier molecules of the second slipped back betwixt my lips Hadi-Alim and Eleazer came into visibility to my left. As they did so every mobile resident of the forest congregated behind me and, guided by the big fella's deeper than deepest baritone, formed an avant-garde big band,

producing as such a tune that I'm sorry to say subjugated Ornette Coleman's finest hour to a mere footnote. Once the animals situated themselves each became silent, as the latest comers tapered off Eleazer's sonic intensity began fading away as if an early Kinks side and then held in perpetuum at mezzo piano, demonstrating in a single sweep his super-earthly capacity within the eight basic and 4,203,315 labyrinthian elements of music.
With a good eyeballing of the pair my body warmed as from a hypodermic takeover that gratified my every corpuscle. Concordantly one of the few things I'd been wholly sure of, complete godlessness, slowed metronomically and slipped out of my ear once it's momentum had been exhausted. Fortunately it fell dead down on a patch of dirt rather than bounding into the adjacent flora where it would have been more difficult to retrieve.

"It's so nice to meet you Rupert," Hadi-Alim began, extending his hand and I mine, wholly securing two of his fingers as we shook.

"It's nice to be meeting you as well," I responded, disappointed with my mirrored reply. Rotating my scrawny self clockwise by about an hour and a half I added "and you." Eleazer's tongue took a beach ball sized lap around his mouth in reciprocity, bending each of his psychedelic whiskers as it passed them by, after which they vibrated at sound speed, unleashing monsoon sized saliva speckles as they resettled .

"Rupert, throughout the several millennia of our existence, you are the first person I have ever spoken to, the first to be aware of us in any way, basically," continued Hadi-Alim.

"Is that right?" I wondered why me, and why now.

He was the illest looking dude I'd ever seen. I decided he was incapable of cruelty nor would he conjure or expel a disparaging thought. Further along in our interaction I came to know this wasn't fully accurate as he had no problem sullying complete wack-a-doos.

"I feel like I may've been a poor choice."

"No bud, we're sure you're a good one. Rupe, Eleazer and I are six-thousand, seven hundred and thirty-four years old. During that span, we have aged near precisely at the rate of seventy-six and a half to each foregone year of a human life. Effectively, we've just had our eighty-eighth birthday."

"A very happy birthday to you both."

"Yes, thank you," Hadi-Alim grinned, never before having been issued this conventional sentiment. Eleazer transmitted handsome appreciation with a loosy goosy nod of his elephantine head.

"Which one of you is, like, god or whatever the fuck?"

"Both or neither of us seems like the safest bet. When we were born, in concert to the zilli-second, we were the size of newborn bunnies, and equally unaware that we'd been gifted history's most useful opportunity. The day we turned four I awoke with recollection of every instant since our births. I knew matter of factly that 5:43 post meridian marked the moment of our arrival, not much of a revelation as we'd done little more than cry, giggle, stumble and fuck around in this rectangle prior to that early morn. A confluence of design and happenstance dictated that Eleazer and I should live co-equally. We are pacted to each other, really we are one, I think; we had no say in our togetherness, though if separated I doubt either of us would make it another day."

He paused, offering me the opportunity to interject.

"Alright," I dribbled, initiating a lengthy intermission whilst I foraged for a conversation piece. The silence would have made any other freshly familiarized crew of folks uncomfortable, though we three carelessly appreciated the gentle way of the wood long enough for a three-toed sloth to lumber cloudways from a jungle floor until within the sturdy, canopied abode of a neighborly family of diana monkeys, upon intertwining limbs strong and healthy enough to house simian after simian by maintaining a steady diet of fat, nutritious, equatorial raindrops.

As his harmless claws took hold of the ungurahui's eldest tributary I'd gauged Hadi's vibrations well enough to get my shit together a little and asked "how were you able to remain safely on your platform when you were bunny-rabbit sized little babies?"

"There're walls all around us, three are made of one-way glass, as is our floor. The fourth, which now faces you, is archaically futuristic, forged from invisible bricks and mortar. We were amply cradled."

"Ok, good. How did you survive without someone to give you like food, baths, warmth, you know, baby shit?"

"Well our body heat stays at a comfortable temperature no matter the climate and we don't need nutrition to survive. Nor do our bodies require any bathing or grooming, the only exception being the maintenance as I see befitting my face hair, head hair and 20 odd nails. Otherwise, we aren't the sort of perfect creatures men have invented to soothe their souls. In truth Rupert I don't feel much more capable or disciplined than they. I have no inkling as to why we gain and are stripped of powers as we venture, simply we try to best utilize what wiggles in.

And finding we can accomplishing things we couldn't previously doesn't distinguish us. Y'all engulf sophistications and strengths, there's just a little ridge separating your perspective from mine maybe. You and I are of similar intellect, though qualifying this I have had a bit more time than you have to figure shit out. But I often deal with existential uncertainty, wonder what makes people behave with deceit. I'm really good at math, I can't imagine that would inspire very many. I don't know if I can reign over the world and I'm sure I don't want to. The major differences between us are an invisible flying cubic rectangle and a big ol' lion cub. What with the stockpile of technologies, licking their lips and waiting their turn to destroy, I'd say our circumstance are antiquated more than anything else really."

"I guess everyone's deprived of pure bliss by their own set of particulars…So we somehow shook hands thru an invisible brick wall though?"

"Yes but we didn't collaborate in a magic trick, Eleazer and I attached a little hinge to these four bricks upon deciding we'd like to meet you, thru which I could shake your hand, a long hankered commodity." He sort of wiggled and figure-eighted his left arm about the space in pointing it out, from my hip to his and about 8 feet goin' across. "You can throw your, fuckin', book bag on the thing there if you want to."

"Yeah ok thanks. It made me feel like a baby grabbing just two of your fingers but I imagine that played into my enjoyment of it. Why don't you guys have anything in there?"

"I guess our experiences serve as our possessions. We've seen every inch of this place, another perfect example of just how on par we really are with y'all. Anyone with a library card, or without one, can take a look at the whole thing, learn everything about it. While we were young my shalwar kameez grew along with my expanding body, and as you can see it is now a bit roomy. I've repaired small rips incurred over time and added some supportive stitches to its three buttons when they've loosened. Eleazer has always elected to freeball it. Once I knitted him a Chanukah sweater, I dressed him with it as he snoozed but he ate that shit off himself the moment he woke up."

"I'm not really much of a consumer either, but you must've wanted to take a closer look at a few things throughout all these years, no?"

"Yeah, we have been, a few. Since say the infancy of the United States, all we've tangibly possessed are a pair of scissors, needles and thread, checkers set, sewing needles, yarn, a hammer and chisel, brick glue and a hinge, a bushel of Georgia peaches, an Atari, a Nintendo, razor blades, for a few overnight hours Picasso's Guernica..." Hadi-Alim tilted his head skyward, brought his hands to his hips, his brainwaves provoking squiggly contour lines that added superfluous distinguish to his forehead; he took a reflective glance at his feet and re-affixed the connection between our retinae..... "I think that's it. You have to eat, so you need food, your body heat changes and your clothes soil, so you need a bit of a wardrobe, detergent, shampoo, deodorant, toothpaste. Beyond that, your life would scarcely change if you threw all of your possessions in the river aside from your es-335, Grunge pedal, Blues Cube, records and turntable no?"

"Yeah, I'd be fine as long as I had that stuff. That and pictures of my family and my bears. And Smurfs. And Onyx's paintings........ When you come to desire a thing, how da ya go 'bout gettin' it?"

"Nowadays Eleazer likes to gank them from a megalo, eatin' em and shitting on their Mercedes' in the process, proliferating our one and only tradition."

"What if they don't have a Mercedes?"

They all have one Rupert. Believe it or not I've never stepped beyond our enclosure, when we want something Eleazer bounds down to the earth's flexuous epidermis and ganks it. We meet remotely and back into the secrecy of the sky we go. His ability to slink makes a mockery of the ghostly advance that's served every feline since the Miocene. Occasionally he flashes me a certain expression indicating he's a leap away from satisfying an ancestral urge, to stalk, choke life from and devour a member of his innumerable kingdom, most often a peripatetic water buffalo, elephant or hippopotamus roaming from town to town, allowing sweet Eleazer to juice them as they wander the forests and grasslands separating the hamlets of humanless jungles and crocodile holes.

Much like your way of eating the halves of your egg everything bagels with vegetable cream cheese and sweet munchee, biting around the outside, circumnavigating the secondary exterior created when you do so, finally savoring the topping concentrated center in a single bite, Eleazer devours his treats in a similarly obsessive sequence, his impulse towards a five bite progression: chest, reproductive organs, head, torso, and limbs. When all the good stuff is in his belly he spits out the pressurized bone fragments like sunflower seed casings. Yes I know lions eat the bones but he doesn't have a ravenous pride to compete with, and as I mentioned has no need for the nutrition, only the hunt. It's funny, he started eating people like 900 years ago, as far as forensics have come the cops still have the same no fuckin' clue what to make of the scenes he leaves behind.

I'd prefer he resist this evolutionary impulse though when you have but one true friend in the entire universe you learn not to nag him or muddle with his predilections, and it's the only convention of his fearless species and its ancestry he can perform; he's never been able to commiserate with other lions, even for a simple, satisfying laze in the sun. Safely situated in our enclosure and when acquiring or engorging his is a stately demeanor. Amongst his kind he'd be transfixed by their ways, losing the intellectual caution he otherwise maintains. He understands this, and as his primary instinct is to remain beta to my alpha he's horrified by the notion of compromising my trust in him. Could it be, every lion would bask in the fuzzy feeling of his supremacy over the wilds as it soothed their souls like raw, delectable Afghani heroin. They would be relieved of suspicion, of ambush, and each potential prey would become as safe as they'd be in a butcher's shop, mortified to exhaustion, mentally necktied by the knowledge of such an inescapable beast."

"He would be the guy," I agreed, momentarily gazing up at a resting cardinal while pinching my lower lip with my thumb and pointer finger. "How did he get Guernica in here?"

"He's more cunning than you're probably imagining. And by multiples, to my knowledge, the most powerful animal to ever toe this place."

"Oh, holy shit, alright," I accepted jerkily, taking a wobbly step backwards from the seemingly uncaged Eleazer despite his docility since their appearance. "I'd like to know what happens to be your coloring."

"My skin is citrine yellow, my hair was phyto-velvininal Bengal tiger orange until it key lime greened over. Eleazer's fur is manganese violet, his mane's palatinate and Carolina blue."

Hadi-Alim dominated my attention, as Eleazer hadn't spoken, but the cat was incomprehensibly spectacular, very much the more radiant of the two. The confidence that positioned him and his sphinxoid stoicism made me wonder when and to what he'd begin speaking.

"And how big are you fuckin' guys?"

"Well at my tallest I was nineteen and a half feet tall. Today, straightening my spine as best I can I stretch to seventeen feet, nine and a half inches. At my most virile I was four-hundred ninety two pounds. Since reaching maturity Eleazer's been forty-six feet, eight and a quarter inches long, from the tip of his nose to the top of his tail, and when he was a primed blend of power and exertion he weighed twenty-nine hundred and seventy-three pounds."

"Hadi, conjoining your experiences and observations into as nonpartisan an opinion as possible, what do you think of this dirty little planet?"

"Well Rupert, I'd say it can be one Hell of a place. It could also be a Utopia. After Eleazer and I gained cognition, we spent millennia zip-hovering the globe and watching as eclectic, intuitive communities cultivated soily waterways, soaking in the milk of their locales. Wheels bounded in all directions as pockets of people initiated each other and communally apportioned their spoils. Greedless men shared joyous embraces whilst negotiating and finalizing their arrangements with not slippery but rather authentic smiles on their faces. People everywhere were overjoyed by the pleasures available to them. They feasted on maize, legumes, boar, venison, fire making them taste far better than ripping into them raw. They became less and less like animals, using bowls and utensils rather than their deceptively less and less grimy hands to eat. When silver was discovered and people far and wide got a look at it, whether they could obtain it or not, the Indian Ocean sprung a girthy erection so extensive that the cirrocumuli were ejaculate in suspended animation.

As there weren't yet any sophisticated science, institutional finance, no sense of space time, vortexes, down to the shape of the earth, imagine living your entire life knowing the planet was a goddamn Frisbee, the most comfortable choice people had was to devise fairy tales that obscured their cluelessness. When people chose religion, they pushed away from each other as seamlessly as they'd previously unified. I believed someday scientific proofs would revoke the notion that eyes in the skies were monitoring people's behavior, each set having decreed steadfast rules to be held as absolute; antithetical to sound reasoning religion would get dropped, people would cease living as minions and the moral would do their best to uphold the Golden Rule, as their current state of being was the only one they were gonna get.

But life is horrifying and mainstream religions continued to amass membership, people refused to accept that one day, any day, they were gonna be nothing but an assemblage of cold skin and entrails rotting away in the dirt. And a more devastating inevitability to accept, after all being dead is pretty fuckin' easy, was that everyone they loved would be evaporating too, that once there was no more blood flowing through their brains they had nothing further to experience or produce. They'd disagree, but the most notable arrogants and megalos are made from the same old decomposable cells, so posthumous notoriety doesn't do them personally, or a-personally, any fuckin' good. Since dawn the teensiest proportion of humans have done such good prior to their departure that it has everlasted, and I assure you none of them were thinkin' of themselves whilst accomplishing their noble deeds.

As devoutly as many are wired only like 19% of people on mainstream religion believe there's any sanity behind their repetitions. Look at the folks who assert the universe is 5,000 years old. Really? I could dig a few feet into this forest floor and find rocks many times older. Eleazer and I are fuckin' older than that. As I interpret it there aren't many mentions of Spinosaurus in the Old Testament. Seems something folks would've made a record of.

The question was this: would I want someone telling Eleazer and myself how we should live and what we can and more to the point cannot do? We're old sons of bitches but humanity is far older. Such nerve it would take were I to take hold of what undeniably were freely fulfilled lives. I worried it would freeze mankind, create a massive open air jailhouse. Why wake up only to have your life lived for you? Those who currently do so are motivated by 72 squeaky clean pussies or a cloud shrouded eternity with their lost love ones or Elvis or whoever the fuck, four out of five perpetuating a self-righteous lie, the fifth a straight up loony toon.

I couldn't reveal myself, all I could do was watch as the world developed and look for things to appreciate about it. I suppose I could have wished upon the UY Scuti that people would change for the better but then I'd just be another cookie cutting believer, blind hope is precisely what maintains religious fanaticism. I bit my toenails and spit them down upon those whose drive was towards connivery, to impede progress, to murder, to lie eyeball to eyeball. But those were their choices to make, not mine. And what nerve I'd be employing were I to conclude that I possess a most powerful dominion. Perhaps there's some dude twice as old and half my age zoomin' around alongside a 7,000 pound hypercolor Khorasani Fighting

Dog. Or an ancient little girl barefootin' the universe atop a 20 mile long platinum blue whale with a chameleonic underbelly. It would be short-sighted for me to rule out the possibility. If they are out there, they haven't made themselves known to me. This allows me to stay true to my decisions with pure peace of mind.

I can't shut the fuck up Rupert, should we switch gears a bit?"

"I'll leave that up to you Hadi," I said, exhuming a wad of stale phlegm from my larynx like an old Chinese lady. "I usually avoid dictating to 18 foot tall men and 3,000 pound lions, and I don't know how cuz my brain's fucked but I'm pretty sure I could repeat every word you've spoken. "

"Well, your brain has had an ally. Moments before unhanding that letter I released a pure and harmless dust, I believe mine is the only sack, it corkscrewed your way and swooped below back up and into your nostrils. Quicker than a speedball it's tiny molecules coursed your veins. Had I not dosed you you would have had a bit of trouble interacting with us so effectively."

I entertained the idea of asking him if I could have some more for later but let it be. Mightily aware of the superdrug swimming relays 'round my extremities my attention shifted briefly from entirely on the fellas to mostly on the dope. I felt an orchestra of pulsations, drawing mad applause from the packed audience of my nervous system.

"You've been patient while listening to my rambles Rupert so why don't you shoot me some more of the questions you'd like answers to."

The thoughts inside my skullbones as unified as they'd ever been, I got my little brain birds in a row. "Are you immortal, Hadi?"

"Best guess no, we are not, I have no precedent to go off of. As centuries have passed our appearance has changed, our joints ache at times, our sleep schedule has shifted, our eyesight has become clouded, and as you can plainly see we're quite relatively 88."

"Well you guys look awesome to me, and plenty capable. With respect Hadi, aren't you kinda fuckin' up my free will a little bit right now?"

"That's right Rupert, just a little. A time came when we were stuffed with knowledge though but a textbook understanding of life's essence. We coveted real wisdom and pined for a way to obtain it. So we mulled, and we stopped. Mulled again, stopped. We then chose to admonish our overview and began to study individual lifespans, wanting that a sharper focus would yield an understanding of the human condition. This was about 3,000 years ago. As we got a few dudes and chicks deep, we were positive that one life can be well more rewarding to observe than entire civilizations come and gone. Whereas before we could only see people when unobstructed by a thick wood or a man-made structure, we began to see our selected subjects through any impediment. Further we became cognizant of his or her thoughts and able to acutely monitor the actions of folks playing substantial roles in the life and psyche of our person. While earlier we may have spent days hovering over St. Petersburg, looking at the top of the same shearlings hour before hour, we were now inside the mind of Raskolnikov. Though the world is constantly changing, human life will forevermore be plagued by a revolving kill show. The hoarders on both ends of every gory money suck will just wait 20 years after slaughtering each others' babies before reinstating commerce. I couldn't watch that shit anymore. When on holiday we'd travel not to Rome or Jerusalem but rather to the Colombian Amazon or Tanzanian Plains. The more devoid of sprawl and warfare our brains became, the freer we felt. We'd spent such wasted time focused on the predictable, the locations and the people affected differed but not the outcomes. Should we study someone sadder than the otherwise accumulated global population we'd come to understand the circumstances engineering their despair."

"What decides how you pick a person?"

"It's very simple. We sail way high up into the atmosphere where a carnival wheel the perimeter of Pluto is slotted out with the names of every newborn baby in the world. I give it my best spin, it clicks at a spitfire pace for a few days and begins to slow, to the pace of a cheetah, a locomotive, a bicycle, a streetwalker, a resting heartbeat, a slug, and before long it loses its last bit of momentum and snaps into place, revealing the appellation of our newest intrigue. When our person passes on I spin again, cold and robotic as a sad psychiatrist, and we soak in the alliteration of a fresh moniker."

"So," my tone was aggressive as this explanation was a painful disappointment, "you wouldn't be here and I would never have had what 'til now I thought was the tantamount privilege of meeting you had I not won a baby carnival name lottery?"

“That’s correct, Rupe. But you did win that lottery.”

“And having never approached anybody before you come at a subversive, self-sabotaging, suicidal piece of shit like myself? This was decided by some crazy randomness too?”

“You forgot self-deprecating,” Hadi addended wryly.

‘Fuck you god’ got all the way to the tip of my tongue but I sucked it up and back in.

“No Rupert, no, we had to approach you, were urgent to meet you. Your sense of self does not dictate how we feel about you, it doesn’t define your worth as we see it, and value it. The transgressions that make you hate yourself so much would have dissipated into the past if you’d allowed them to. I’m sorry Rupert, that was a terrible way to put it. If it was easier for you to let go of foregone torments your perception of self would be vastly disparate. You’re only 17 Rupert. You will do good, find peace, and put a little print on this hopeless globe, and maybe it’ll keep when the thing explodes if you can come to see yourself as we do.”

“Thank you Hadi, that is a beautiful notion, but I feel sick having heard you say it, like when I lie to my parents, disappoint the people I want so achingly to please; knowing that they hold to faith in me deepens my depression, because I know I can’t do it, and I wake thinking about that every day. Now you’re another person to whom I get to demonstrate that I’m a fuckin’ zero.”

“Rupert I know you feel this way. But just as much I know that you are a sweet, wonderful kid at heart. It just comes out of you in a singular and thereby a fashion unrecognizable to most. You have such a compassionate soul Rupert, you have always been compelled towards helping those who need it the most. If we thought you were a fucking zero we may've passed on being here. You know, when you were three years old and attending Tom Thumb there was a little girl in your class with a laundry list of physical and mental disabilities. By the end of the first school day you were her protector, you hugged and kissed her, pushed away any child who tried to take advantage of her weakness. Few have your empathy, far fewer at three. You don't credit the positive things you do and let your indiscretions unnerve you. You don't have to be perfect Rupe, not even close."

"I don't remember that."

"Your mom told you about it a couple of years ago but I guess you'd forgotten. It's ok. Listen Rupert, after deciding to approach you my brainstem spawned a bold request. I've spent my life but an endless, nameless, faceless spectator. As such I haven't made a single mark of my own. You've inspired me to do so. Since Eleazer and I began this path 3,210 years ago, we'd observed every moment of 65 lives before landing on your name. I'd like to write the story of your life, Rupe. I figure once it's done it'll mysteriously appear on the desk of an overpaid, overfucked publishing magnate under a silly pen name on its way to every shelf the universe over."

"...I mean, yeah, you can. Only what if you're wrong about me? How will you feel if I do precisely nothing and you're left with worthless nonsense? Would you hate me for it?"

"No Rupert, I wouldn't hate you if you climbed up here and beat Eleazer bloody."
Eleazer pretended he hadn't been listening and faked one Hell of a yawn, affording me a peregrine eyeball's gaze at his mouth machetes.

"All I ask is you don't alter your actions because I am chronicling them, retain your free will, please live as you desire to. After we part I won't advise you nor offer you any help. Joining Eleazer in *sui generis* to my existence will in itself be useless. I promise you Rupert, if you can steer clear of blaming yourself for everything, remain calm and seek out solutions when you face adversity, one day you will reach the greatest of heights."

"And in obliging I give you carte blanche to chronicle all of the horrific, anarchistic, morally borderline and private peculiarities you witness?"

"I'd prefer not to falsify the thing, but if there's something you'd like me to leave alone it's a request I'll uphold."

"You know what, fuck it. I don't care who knows what about me. If people have a problem with how I live they can form a human ball, roll themselves into the sea and let a blue whale fuck the crevices between their bodies."

"That's good Rupe, fuck all the hypocrites. With an ashy, twenty foot long whale dick."

"Just promise me this. Please don't leave out any of my most triumphant carnalities, if some qualified opportunities arise…just let the world know I'm a good fucker."

"You have my word Rupert, I'll be as filthy as I can. Is it alright if I inject a bit of color here and there if it feels right?"

"You may, as long as it doesn't run contrary to my expert approach towards slamming a pussy."

"Of course not, you just make sure you slam away whenever you have the chance."

"That's one way in which I hope to never self-sabotage. Hey, Hadi, why with the relative lifespan of a dude and a cat has Eleazer survived, aged alongside you?"

"Another question I can't answer with certainty Rupe. Perhaps he has fought mightily against the spectre of death because he refuses to leave me without companionship. Or maybe his longevity suggests that we're immortal after all."

"Well I hope that your second hypothesis rings true, if that's what you'd prefer. Hadi I honored your request, so I'm gonna present my own."

"Do the monkey bud."

"Speaking to my 17 years, growing up with my baby bro, Onyx, and this parlay transcend all else, and your superdust has enabled me to remember every word and nuance of our congregation. As such, I'd like to write a preface to your book, chronicling this brief yet lush experience."

"Yes Rupert, I think that makes perfect sense. If I'm gonna tell the world about you, you have every right and reason to do the same in turn."

"Word. Thanks."

"You're welcome pal. Another request your way if I may?"

"What can I do?"

"Eleazer just ate the christ out of some motherfucker like 8 hours ago. Would you gather the materials I'll need, a couple of spiral notebooks and a few pens?"

"I will, of course, is it cool if I get them to you in say, a week, so I have time to write my prologue and leave that with you too?"

"If you feel that gives you enough time."

"I doubt I'll give much time to anything else. So I'll meet you here next Saturday, 7:06?"

"Well, no. I don't wanna compromise your will any more than I have already. I'd enjoy to but can't meet with you when you bring the supplies, could you please just place them here and we'll come grab them after you've headed back and out of the wood. I promise going forward I'll call on you once more."

"Ok, yes, I will," I answered, blue that this was about it but comforted by the thought of seeing him upon another place and time of his selection. I was sure that Hadi knew best and this way of doing things was in no way a slight to me.

"Rupe I'd like to give you a bit of advice before you go. Happiness is to whittle down the people you spend your time with as far as you can to the people you love and who in turn love you. Shower them with affection and recognize their beauty every chance you get, cook meals with them, travel the world with them, grant them patience and embrace their flaws. This will create an album of sweet memories in your mind. Only those who truly love you and have earned your implicit trust will tattoo soul-soothing recollections in and on your brain and its stem. Should they perish they'll remain precious in your consciousness and continue to provide love and support as they adoringly did before. In turn you will give them the same gift, you'll remain in their thoughts and hearts until Earth reconstitutes. But be suspicious of friendship Rupert, people use up their love on their families, those born even with love to give. I believe D'Shaundrius and Casimir love you, but the list ends there. The rest are liable to leave you ruptured in the dirt if it best serves them. Actually Rupert I should tell you that when you were born I gained a new ability, to understand not just your thoughts but also those of the people you love and who love you back. So really I know they are the only friends who love you."

"I see. I thought the list was longer, but if I guessed two of course it would be them."

"I'm glad you see that, and I'm glad I acknowledged it. One last thing before we part Rupert. May I have that letter back so I can re-stitch it to my pant leg?"

I balled it up, rolled a rubber band off my wrist, lapped it around tightly and threw it over the wall into his brassy yellow catcher's mitts with fingers, this was more dramatic than slipping it through the opening in the brick and avoided the preclusion of an 88 year old man hunching over to grab it up.

"Oh and I almost forgot. Have a great trip, and put that shit in your sock before you leave your house."

"Thank you, I will. Well fellas," I said, sighing, "this was unequivocally the greatest venture I've made into this wood, and as you know I've eviscerated a couple of fine hymen atop old Morla ova there. I thank you both heart and soul for it."

"I assure you it was as delightful for Eleazer and myself."

"Bye you guys."

"Take care of yourself Rupert."

At that moment Hadi-Alim's magical opiate de-intensified in my cells. Morbidity returned to my thoughts but not as thickly as was typical. I began walking away, knowing that I'd start to cry if we extended our farewell. The animals blew me their kisses before scampering a thousand ways away and after taking a few steps from Hadi and Eleazer I threw up my right arm in a backwards aloha. I levitated home from the wood, dissecting the experience that couldn't possibly be elbowed or hip boned into the recesses of my brain for as long as climbing moons and ascending suns tempered my yet to be written future.

I was stoked to find the house empty when I got home because my mom has the sharpest ability to recognize when I'm high on one thing or another and my mind was so stuck on the encounter that I would have had no shot at explaining my silly face. As was a Sauerstein family requisite I found a note on the kitchen counter informing me that she and my dad had departed about 17 minutes earlier to have dinner with some old and dear friends and that Benny was sleeping out. Still I tiptoed upstairs to my bedroom, Pavlovian since substance abuse had become a hobby. I've always been a poor sleeper, analyzing and brooding over the consortium of experiences that compile when I decide to live a day. It was far earlier than I'd ordinarily attempt to catch some z's, but I felt drained from the intensity of my conversation with Hadi and Eleazer. That said I knew there was no sense in attempting to shut it down, I was zonked but my synapses were coked.

And so I decided to elaborate upon Hadi's most modest request, opening my closet in search of an unwanted article to rebirth as a saddlebag for the solicited materials. My eyeballs centered in on an ill-fitting pair of dark blue jeans that I never wore as they were too monochromatic and goofily short. I ripped them from their hanger which shot at me after whipping violently around the bar and devised a practical order of operations as I continued, next rifling thru my big bag o' pens and identifying the fattest and most reliable dozen. I then wobble-stepped my way up the stairs to the loft and stole three pristine spiral notebooks from the dayless file cabinet where they had been hibernating in perpetuity.

Back in my bedroom I took great care in measuring and sewing a pouch and strap appropriate for storing the gathered goods, first constructing its frame, inclusive of a twelve by nine inch internal pocket. Opposite the flap I securely sewed twelve equidistant sheaths, each a cozy home for a solitary ballpoint. I then snipped at a slab of grey foam I'd snatched from the garage, reconstructing it into two eleven and a quarter by eight and a quarter inch sections which I glued to the front and back of the internal pocket. My task was structurally complete once I'd cut and reinforced two slits through which I slipped a blue and a purple button. I slapped it with a few shades of oil paint in denigration of the material's tackiness, hung it up to dry, and that was that. I was pleased with my creation, useful and effectuated sans blueprint, suited I thought to the man for whom it was devised.

I must've passed out upon finishing the project, the next thing I recall was the gentle reverberation of my mom's voice encouraging me to wake up as it had become three in the afternoon. I blathered like a cranky junky readying his morning fix, marble mouthing a palette-less chain of syllables whilst endeavoring to revisit the phantasmagorical delight I'd gotten high on as the day before had dusked. During the week's course I fucked off high school, smoked one-hundred and seventeen joints, railed amphetamine salts with quantified abandon and micro-dosed LSD-25, painstakingly making 39 revisions to this tale. I had it ready 51 minutes before I'd assured Hadi I would get it to him, leaving me ample time to sod past my plant and animal friends and drop the anticipated goods for the two most radical motherfuckers the world has ever unknown.

Chapter 2

Juvenility

I met her in Hawaii, in the good ol' summertime of '65
She was so fine, with her long blonde hair hangin' down to her clit
In her blue bikini, she said that she would like to be a star
In the movies, Oh Hollywood gal won't you be my pal?

Hey Bab, Hey Bab, Hey Babro
She's Swedish sunshine
Hey Bab, Hey Bab, Hey Babro
She's Swedish sunshine, she's Swedish snow

Then she flew to Stockholm, to study at the old academy
Mr. Bergman, I can almost see the steam on the silver screen
Why the sudden changes, from Hollywood to European scene?
It's the weather, all the Hollywood producers just tryin' ta seduce her now

(extended refrain)
-Mark Lindsay, featured

Rupert Isidoro Sauerstein, Esquire was conceived in Brooklyn, born in Manhattan, and raised in the sugar sweet suburb of Yorktown, 29 miles north of the Bronx border. Six days before he turned three his baby brother

Benjamin was born and soon joined him at home. Any way you might turn in the Sauersteins' white colonial, which sat on a quarter acre of equal parts rolling and smoothed out grassland at the fork of two upward slanting, winding cul-de-sacs, you could find photographic evidence of Rupert's adoration for the little guy.

His mom Kayiane and dad Isaac doted on their two boys and upon each other, as a foursome they basked in a shared love and happiness. They'd met while students at Brooklyn College, where he had gravitated away from her best friend towards the genuine object of his enamor. Growing up not once did the boys hear their parents argue, there isn't a more symbiotic couple to be found. At least once a week Isaac would return from his job in the city with flowers for his beautiful bride. Kayiane, who was interning at Seventeen magazine when she and Isaac met, was and is a delightful woman and a supremely proud mother. She would tell you without hesitation that the most wonderful years of her life were spent when her silly and precocious redheaded boys were babies. When Benny began nursery school Kayiane took a part time job in the mornings and every night at or within minutes of 6:45 the Sauerstein four would sit down for one of her balanced, delicious and lovingly prepared dinners, the unanimous favorite and renowned staple of her repertoire starting with stuffed artichokes and culminating in breaded chicken cutlets, rice pilaf and steamed broccoli.

When Rupert was one and a half his maternal grandparents Giuseppe and Miriam left Sheepshead Bay and moved into a condo within a sprawling retirement community, their unit a mile plus home plate to the right field foul pole in Yankee Stadium from the colonial on Timberlane Court. The boys enjoyed spending time at their grandparents' house just as much as they did their own. They'd simultaneously pounce onto 6' 2" Giuseppe's lap and watch golf with him on his rocking chair. They made fishing poles and dipped them into the vast, unfishable lake behind the condo, where they were sure to see a scampering muskrat. For years they marveled at a majestic, wide-winged Siberian crane who habitually perched herself upon an instinctively selected rooftop coordinate opposite what was really a small pond. Rupert adored that motherfucker, she shaped herself straight Pterodactyl whilst she soared the skies at a perfect parallel with the sloping earth. Miriam took them for nature walks that had them on the lookout for lions, tigers and bears. They'd stop and pick peppers and tomatoes from their plot in the community garden, studying someone else's harvest of sunflowers which seemed to brush up against the clouds. Their final point of observation was most always a twelve foot long, semi-ovular rust painted bridge at whom's apex the boys would perk up on their tippy-toes and examine whichever creatures decided to stream past.

By three years and nine months Rupert had examined every accessible inch of the family home. Kayiane was never more than a whimper's distance away and Rupert was a cautious boy with good dexterity. She afforded him the freedom of discovery. If ever he hurt himself he was tough about it.

As is a near universality amongst small children Rupert parented a stuffed animal, clutching him proudly and protectively all around the town. His was a gentle looking sepia brown bear, a foot long from the cropped crown of his head to the plush claws of his feet. He aged more quickly than Rupert himself from all the suffocating squeezes and runs through the washing machine to clean off spaghetti sauce. Rupert cleverly named him Teddy, Isaac and Kayiane were so concerned about how he would react should he ever misplace him that they had purchased a backup facsimile of the pacifying little fellow. Inexorably one funny Friday Rupert's detective work led him to the uncirculated clone as he'd pulled a chair over to the washer and dryer, climbed up, and sifted through the contents of an overhanging shelf. 'Mommy!' he elated as his mind blew. Kayiane came around the corner from the kitchen to find Rupert upon the chair, holding Teddy's pristine brother high up in his right hand and issuing her a most expressively jubilant gaze, sharing the miracle, sure she was finding it as revelatory as he had. She laughed for days envisioning Rupert at that moment, his pose and the tickled shape of his baby face. And so from then on Rupert had both Teddy and Freddy, one to cradle under each of his chubby arms.

Whilst Rupert elaborately anthropomorphized his beloved bears he never found himself inclined to concoct an imaginary friend. He did however enjoy a recurring dream that fits into the same sort of psychological classification. Behind the Sauerstein home lay a vast brick patio. Beyond the lip of the patio was a black locust that the boys jumped at from the deck and climbed until, as with most every childhood activity, they grew disinterested. A second benefit of this location was that it shaded a portion of its mortary neighbor. In these dreams it would always be summer and Rupert would always be wearing his favorite Crayola consistent shorts of blue with thin red and white side stripes and his favorite slubbed grey Yankees t-shirt. As he sat Indian style beneath the locust's cover he'd look out at the gargantuan weeping willow that lived near the far left corner of the plankwood outlined backyard. With passage of a brief bit he'd wag his tiny right pointer finger towards his Jimi Hendrix curls, aligning it with the hidden trunk of the willow. Out from under the ground-grazing spinach linguini leaves would then bound a triceratops with the temperament of an ebullient teenaged retriever. He'd lick Rupert from the top of his neck to his hairline, turn 90 degrees opposite the locust and the boy would climb upon his back. From there, they'd whirlwind to Avenue J, zip to Disney World, run a monkey in a horserace, canoe to Hong Kong, fly to Mars and eat knishes, whatever fantasy had seeped into Rupe's imagination that day. The dream recurred between ages 3 and 6, more than 100 times, though the activity within the dream was never duplicated.

Alongside Freddy, Rupert's other transcendent household unearthing was to be found in the living room, across the first floor from the kitchen, within the middle of three cabinets at the bottom of a floor to ceiling stained oak shelving unit. When he pulled the cabinet doors apart from their center he inhaled that distinct musk and gathered himself for a perusal. On its insides the cabinet was stuffed with thin, square books. It was early afternoon on a May Saturday and Isaac joined Rupert a moment or two into it, having heard his rustling.

"Daddy, what are these?" he was most curious to find out.

"Those are records, sweetheart."

"What do you do with them?"

"They play music, you put them in here," Isaac directed his son's attention towards the turntable that rested in an open space atop the left hand cabinet, "they spin around and around and you listen to their songs."

"Can we do it?"

"Of course, would you like to choose one?"

"Yes," Rupert responded matter of factly.

Isaac had been the lead singer and rhythm guitarist for a raucous and inventive rock outfit called The Blue Wails in college and had impeccable taste in music. The quartet garnered minor local notoriety with the 45 "Lick that Girl/Oh 19!!!" in 1969 though by '71 they'd graduated and amicably disbanded. Rupert sifted for a bit until withdrawing Evolution by the Hollies.

"Maybe daddy can we hear this one?"

"Sure, that's a good one. You have to be careful with them or they might not work as well next time. Try your best to only hold the edges. Pull out the paper sleeve with the record inside it and find the opening. Stick your fingers in and slowly take it out. Look at one side. Do you see a 'one' or a 'two' on it?"

"I see 'two' daddy."

"Ok hunny, that means that it's the second side of the record. Flip it over and tell me what number you find."

"'One' daddy. I should listen to this side first?"

"You got it sweetheart. Before you can listen, you need to turn on this silver box called a receiver by pushing this button here." Rupert depressed. "Good. Now lift the plastic top of the record player all the way up and it will stay up by itself. Can you see the circle in the center of the turntable that's the same size as the record?"

"Yup," Rupert was intoxicated with excitement, his knees swiftly pumping forward and back.

"Ok great, do you see the little silver nub sticking out of it?"

"Uh-huh."

"Why do you think that's there?"

"So you can stick it through this little hole in the record?"

"That's exactly right Rupert. So check that the side with 'one' written on it is facing up and carefully get the little nub to go through the hole."

"Did it daddy!" Rupert proclaimed upon securing insertion.

"Way to go kiddo. You can pull the plastic top down if you want. Can you find a button that says 'play' on it?"

"Yeah this one."

"Good boy. Press it."

There was motherfuckin' light. As Rupert watched the arm lift up and swing recordward, heard that spectacular crackle, and "*Then the Heartaches Begin*" began, so too did the boy's lifelong obsession with rock 'n' roll, the truest spirit of 'em all. He listened to record after record until bedtime and popped up at 5:27 the next morning to continue. Kayiane and Isaac woke to the sound of "How D'You Ride" at 5:31, flashed each other a stone-eyed smile and let their sweet boy do his thing. Benny, a perpetual rock of a sleeper, remained unruffled in his crib as the music brightened his dreams.

Among a bunch of other beauts he delighted that satin weekend in his introduction to Alias Pink Puzz, Rolled Gold, Love Man, Vincebus Eruptum, Live at the Harlem Square Club, 1963, No Way Out, This is Fats, Derek & the Dominoes in the studio and the three Experience albums. Isaac had gotten his kind hands on a copy of Electric Ladyland with the original jacket in 1972 and was psyched to buy it for $4. Rupert made his choices entirely based on the coolness or lack thereof of the album art. Kayiane's albums were incorporated with Isaac's in far lesser quantity and most of the '60s Stones records were there in duplicate, outside of that Kayiane had softer taste than her rollin' husband. Rupert disavowed Peter Paul and Mary, Simon and Garfunkel and other sorts of stupid looking malarkey, though I'll note that shifting ahead fourteen months a neoteric perspective prompted him to throw on his mom's Laura Nyro records and he dug on them.

The weekend following that most enlightening one he discovered that the cabinet below the turntable was just as stuffed with lp's along with three lunchbox handled cases full of 45s, inclusive of two copies each of all four Blue Wails singles, *"When the Devil Comes 'Round ta Getcha/Mango & Guanabana Pie"* (January 16, 1968,

375 copies pressed), *"Whoa Mama!!!!/I'm Livin' but I Ain't Givin'"* (July 16, 1968, 650 pressings), *"The Succotash Smash Parts 1&2"* (December 20, 1968, 1500 pressings) and 7,500 copies of *"Lick that Girl/Oh 19!!!!,"* which first hit the shelves on April 22, '69, his daddy using his Jaguar to make his penis look gigantic on the sleeve.

Rupert went down every strange road he desired each weekend the family was at home going quite a ways forward, in '87 he caught a bad case of Appetite for Destruction and in late '91 eardrummed a combo that obsessed him more than any other since or before. By age 22 he re-immersed himself in '52-'77 and his brain eventually served as a squishy encyclopedia of balls-out, good time shit.

During the following year, more accurately right around the time Rupert started kindergarten, two other obsessions emerged.

On the second Monday afternoon in August, 1984, Kayiane, Rupert and Benny could be seen walking through the expansive A&P parking lot in Mahopac. Rupert held his mother's left hand and Benny sat in a shopping cart trying to bite the fingers on her right. Next to him was her disintegrating Venetian red coupon holder. She and Isaac saved every penny they could for the boys' college education.

Embarking upon their conventional rounds, they reached the cereal aisle and the inevitable debate between Kayiane and Rupert began. She was steadfastly health conscious, the only cereals she'd allow were Crispix, Chex, Cheerios, and Kix. Rupert would plead for Trix or Lucky Charms but they never made their way into the cart; he hadn't yet had his first real jolt of refined sugar, as far as his mother knew. I suppose that while when an adult repeats the same behavior over and again to the same effect it's qualified or dismissed as insanity should a child do so it's out from nothing other than pure, sweet optimism.

A few feet from the Sauerstein crew were a stunning dark skinned young woman and her two daughters, one Rupert's age and the other, dangling her little legs in the cart, Benny's. Both toddlers were behaving with extreme rambunction as Kayiane began rolling towards the registers and the other mother towards the refrigerated foods. Rupert nor the little girl his age followed, rather they stayed put and transfixed upon each other. The girl approached Rupert and they came button nose to button nose. Rupert grabbed the shelf behind him with both fat fists as the girl swung her right leg across her left. She wore a pale blue strappy dress, bequeathed by the hippies to future generations of little girls, splattered with gemstones. More than any other garment this type of dress accentuates how adorable a little girl can be. That her hair mushroomed up into two fuzzy puffs compounded her preciousness.

"What's your name?" the bold little lady initiated.

"I'm Rupert. What's your name?"

"Onyx. Are you nice?"

"Yes I'm nice. Are you nice?" Onyx shook her head that yes she was too.

"I like you," she admitted without hesitation.

"I like you too. I like how you say words, I like your nose, I like your dress, I like your skin, I like your shoulders.

"Well I like the curls in your hair, the dots on your skin, I like your nose, you're tall, you're just a handsome boy."

Having known each other shy of a minute they bent delicately at their waists and kissed each other's lips. Not a moment later their moms darted 'round opposite ends of the aisle, closing their eyes and taking deep, reassured breaths as they spied their babies. Each yelled their child's name and the two families congregated.

"What are you doing sweetheart? You know better than that. Do you know how upset I get when I don't know where you are?" pleaded Kayiane.

"I'm just talking to Onyx mommy," Rupert bent the truth.

"And how about you little girlie?" Onyx's mother followed in a thick West Indian accent.

"Talkin' to Rupert."

"Well you will not leave my side in public ever again, isn't that right?"

"Right momma."

Both children feigned humility, far more fascinated with each other than remorseful about ditching their moms. The ladies exhaled truncated breaths, order having been restored.

"Oh boy," said the statuesque woman, "that is not like my Onyx, she usually stays pressed to my hip."

"I know, Rupert is terrified of losing me, I can't believe he did that," quipped Kayiane, blowing up her son's spot. "I'm Kayiane, Sauerstein" she extended her hand.

"Xaviera Graham," Onyx's mother said as they shook.

"It's nice meeting you," said Kayiane, both ladies' vocal tone having returned to sweet mommy mode, indicating to Rupert and Onyx that they were off the hook.

"Yes, likewise," Xaviera returned. "Your boys are just adorable."

"Oh, thanks, your girls are gorgeous."

"Thank you too. Who is this precious little one?" Xaviera inquired, gently tugging the itty right foot that swung from Kayiane's cart.

"This is Benjamin," replied Kayiane, stroking his hair from front to back.

"Hello Benjamin baby," Xaviera enthused as he beamed her a charmed smile accompanied by a stimming of his raspberry lips.

"And this little darling?" inquired Kayiane, taking careful hold of her soft, tiny left hand.

"This is Amoya."

"Hello beautiful, you are too much!" Amoya gazed curiously up at Kayiane.

While the moms continued their little babying Rupert and Onyx kept at soaking each other in, not once taking their eyes off of one another.

"Do you live near here?" Kayiane inquired of Xaviera.

"Um yes, yes we do, not far a'tall. Curry street? We moved here from Treasure Beach, Jamaica just two weeks ago."

"Well that makes us neighbors, we're on Timberlane, the third left after you turn up Curry."

"Oh that's so wonderful, we haven't yet met anyone here, and we run into you and you live just down the road!" Xaviera hugged Kayiane enthusiastically, joyful to know such a nice girl from the neighborhood. She turned towards Onyx and Rupert for their perspectives. "Are you excited to be neighbors?"

"Yeah," the new couple tried to play it cool though their eyes were as wide as the setting sun and their bodies wanted to gyrate from the thrill of great news, each tipping off this impulse.

"I think my Rupert may be a little smitten with your Onyx, and vice versa."

"I'd say there's no doubt about it. Onyx, what do you think of sweet Rupert here?"

"I like his hair and his dots."

"How about you baby? Do you like Onyx?"

"I like her shoulders and her nose and her skin."

"Well if it's ok with your mommy you're welcome to come play at our house Onyx,"

"Right now!?" she wished away.

"Maybe not right now sweetie, but soon, ok?"

"That would be wonderful," added Xaviera. "How terrific this is, I feel so blessed to be meeting you Kayiane."

"Oh Xaviera that is such a nice thing to say." The ladies hugged once more. "Why don't you take down my phone number and we'll make some plans."

"Oh yes, let me do that," she fished thru her purse, fingering a pen and a scrap of paper, biting the cap off the pen. "Ok baby."

Kayiane rattled off the number and after scribing it Xaviera read it back to be certain.

"That's us," confirmed momma Sauerstein. "This really is great, there are a bunch of young families in the neighborhood you can meet, I'll have my husband Isaac barbeque for us, I'm privileged to be the first to welcome you to town."

"Thank you dearie."

Excited to know that they'd be seeing each other again though too young to conceptualize the future, Rupert and Onyx embraced.

"Bye Onyx."

"Goodbye Rupert."

"Ok well call me soon and we'll get together."

"Absolutely. Thank you again Kayiane, so much."

"Don't be silly, it's my pleasure." She looked down at Onyx and gave her a little wave, thinking on what a breathtaking little girl she was. The two toddlers rattled around in their metal seats, each far away in the abstract geometrics of the supermarket's color wheel nirvana.

"I guess we should finish our shopping and get these crazy children home, but I will most certainly call you."

“Sounds great,” Kayiane concluded. They began to part ways, reversing their previous trajectories; after they’d each taken a few steps Kayiane stopped and spun towards Xaviera. “Is Onyx going into kindergarten?”

“She is. Rupert as well?”

“Yeah. Who does she have?”

“Ms. Goodridge?”

“Rupert too.”

“Morning or afternoon?”

“Mornin’.”

“So you two are not just neighbors but you’re going to be in the same kindergarten class!" Kayiane made the realization as clear as the Caribbean for them.

‘Holy fuckin’ shit,’ Rupert thought.

‘I’m gonna kiss him every day,’ imagined Onyx.

“Neither of you have a reaction to this news?” Both children shrugged. “You two are sneaky I think. I’ll call you soon Kayiane.”

“Ok Xaviera, you better.”

The two trios continued their tour and Rupert and Onyx were able each to put one eyeball on the other as they cornered the aisle in concert.

Inside the span of one little month Rupert had his first kiss and got his first hit. Neither Kayiane nor Isaac were particularly athletic or in the slightest the sort of parents who chose their childrens’ activities for them. The previous fall Rupert had played soccer, which at that age consists of the ball making its way into a herd of kids representing the entirety of both teams until someone squibs it out of the scrum, the first child to reach it trips over it and cries, this repeats until the ball angles off into a net, the parents clap and everybody goes home. One season of soccer was indeed enough for Rupert, but he was curious enough to try other sports and he accepted Kayiane's offer to pile baseball on top of Teddy, Freddy, Onyx and rock 'n' roll.

What well determined his relationship with the game was the coach he drew, Sal Amante, a Santa Claus sort of a man, robust and wonderful in his way with children, though unlike the conclusion Rupert had reached regarding Old Saint Nick prior to his fourth Christmas, having asserted to Kayiane that 'he couldn't go to all them houses and eat all them cookies in one night', coach Amante truly existed. The eight teams in the league were allotted field time for one practice and one game a week, though Coach had been granted permission by Sal Jr.'s elementary principal to use his school's field for an additional weekly practice. He made it clear to the parents that there was no pressure to bring their boys to the extra session if it didn't fit their schedules but all of the parents really liked Sal, were glad to have him coach their children, and appreciated his willingness to devote so much time to teaching their boys how to play. As such, all practices were thick with bright eyed baseballers.

Rupert had watched occasional Yankee games prior to becoming a player though this didn't translate to much of an understanding as to what to do on the field. The team practiced six times before their first game and Isaac played catch with Rupert after work, never having baseballed before attending to his first born's newest interest. It was liquid acid clear to Coach Amante that Rupert was chemically inclined towards their nation's pastime. He was one of the youngest players in the league, a month and a half from his fifth birthday, but the little motherfucker could ball.

Having had a solid think on the ballplayers' skillsets Coach put Rupert at first base, which at that age is a vital position. Nearly every ball stays in the infield and commonly heads towards short so logic suggests placing the most steady handed player at first and the second most in the hole as fielding a dribbling ground ball with your body squared to it is marginally easier than keeping a foot on the bag and adjusting to the unpredictable course of the ball as it crosses the diamond. Rupert was glad not to be all the way in the outfield but had no idea that his coach had pegged him as such a prospectus asset.

The first game of the season Rupert and his mates were the home team. In the top of the first a couple balls got booted but no runs scored, he and the shortstop connected on two groundouts and Rupe snagged a loopy pop-up that had discovered the foul grounds. Third up in the bottom of the first, more excited than nervous about his first opportunity to do the damn thing he bounced the ball towards third, reaching safely though disappointed that he hadn't gotten a better piece of it. As the game progressed he grew multiply comfortable and discovered that he really enjoyed hitting, being on the field and sitting on the bench watching his teammates' at-bats. And spitting. When the lineup turned over and he made his second appearance he looked at the first pitch, a rarity amongst nubile, free swingin' little dudes and chicks. His coach was on the mound, as children of 4 5 and 6 trying to throw strikes would be a chaotic folly.

"Good eye Rupert," remarked Coach Amante. Rupert wondered which eye he was referencing but congratulated himself on having received the compliment anyhow. The second pitch came in waist high on the outer half and Rupe laced a line drive that zipped directly over and beyond the first baseman's grommet before he had reacted to it. It hit chalk and rolled to the adjacent field's third base bag, angling away from the right fielder all the way.

"Touch 'em all kid," Coach said, circularly waving his right pointer finger. Rupe didn't know what in fuck the guy was talking about but he threw the bat 20 feet towards the visiting team's bench and started beelining around the bases, halfway around third before the poor goof in right had the stitched up orb run down. The pound of his left foot on home plate was a sensation akin to that first sizzlin' record. He envisioned himself playing the game until he'd grown too old, a time which would never come. He wouldn't always be the best player on his squad but never did he have a coach who put more faith in a teammate's acumen or ability in the clutch. Coach Amante's wife Louise, herself a terrific person and benefit to the team, kept stats all season, and handed each player a detachable hole-punched stat sheet at the post-season pizza party. Keeping in mind that many grounded and flown balls which would yield putouts in a league of more seasoned players were recorded as base hits, in ten games Rupert effectively won the Triple Crown with a line of .891, 14 HR and 37 RBI.

Benny turned out to be a better athlete than his big brother and as they grew they lived outside, throwing each other grounders on the driveway, pitching to each other in the backyard and seasonally sleighing its slope, slowed by the easterly flatlands before they could ram the knotted metal fence and carve their faces all to shreds. At the top of the driveway to the left of the exdent where the boys placed first base for infield practice Isaac planted a rather handsome and well-constructed basketball hoop with a squared plexiglass backboard, drawing in neighborhood kids for pick-up games more afternoons than it didn't. When nobody rolled through they played one-on-one or 'Harlem Globetrotters,' which involved them walking to the foot of the driveway, discussing a series of fancy passes to be executed on approach to the basket and culminating in turn with tangle-bodied circus shots.

Should it rain the boys would unfold their ping-pong table or architect miniature golf courses a hole at a time using the abundant lot of geometrically diverse wooden blocks which Oscar and Nava had purchased for them before Benny could eat spaghetti, the very set found in any properly funded American nursery school or kindergarten classroom, employing their toys and contorted bodies as obstacles as the ball made its way towards the cup sized circle Isaac had knifed away from the carpeting, the happiness of his boys far more important than the state of materials in their home.

Kayiane was delighted that her sons so loved being together and enjoyed such a variety of physical activities. She hated television, it ranked somewhere closely behind bigots and weapons on her list of things she wished to stricken from the earth. The boys were endeared to and allowed to watch PBS, The Cosby Show, The Wonder Years, Alf, Who's the Boss?, Diff'rent Strokes, Sesame Street, Mr. Roger's Neighborhood, He-Man, Thundercats, The Transformers, baseball and basketball games. They could watch network television for up to an hour per day and PBS, the only channel they were allowed to watch without Kayiane in the family room with them, up to 2. Her greatest concern above even mind-numb was the baleful manipulation within the advertisements. She would not have her boys grow up to be consumerists. She was so vigilantly against the nature of capitalist exploitation that as commercial breaks began she'd turn the volume off and engage them in conversation or have them go across the room and toss a tennis ball back and forth with her. She knew she couldn't shield them forever from corporate rape but at least she could for now, she hoped that by doing so it would lead them to disavow materialistic tendencies on down their roads.

On the weekend and throughout the summers the boys were free to watch their modest but quality collection of movies on VHS, the thrill rides within kept them up late ninja kicking, boxing, swinging for the bleachers or running past stone naked laser beam eyed ladies should they view one on a school night. They owned Rad, Karate Kid I and II, E.T., The Neverending Story, Dumbo, Pinocchio, The Natural and Rocky I-IV. Themes of good sportsmanship, honesty, compassion, forgiveness, redemption and justice coursed through the collection, excellent concepts for the boys to familiarize themselves with though not an all too accurate representation of the world outside. It's a momentous conclusion that a boxing match should terminate a forty-five year political jerk-off though it's about as likely as someone providing concrete evidence that their god is more akin to a black hole than an Aesop fable.

While these young and innocent days were filled with an abundance of sweetness for Rupert and the Sauersteins as a whole, they came with a heavy hit of sour. Isaac's parents Nava and Oscar still lived in Brooklyn as the boys grew. If it was entirely up to Nava they would have moved in right across the hall from Miriam and Giuseppe but Oscar was Brooklyn to the bone and he preferred to stay that way. This however didn't mean that the boys got to see them much less often than they did their mother's parents. At least one weekend a month Nava and Oscar would cruise up to Yorktown and nearly as often the Sauerstein four would take a ride down to Midwood. The boys loved being in Brooklyn, it was so interesting and in such contrast to the Jefferson Estates, consisting only of Timberlane Court, Stonewall Lane, Juniper Drive and its tributaries. Just the same they loved waiting at the top of the driveway for Oscar to rev his big ol' Lincoln on up.

As Rupert's been told and as I've bared witness, Nava was such a doting grandmother that while some throughout history may have equaled her in that way, none has surpassed the fervency with which she loved her grandchildren, as it was of maximum capacity and came from a great woman with the heart and soul of 200 good ones. There wasn't a time Nava visited or was visited by Rupert that she didn't present him with a little plastic Smurf, he arranged them atop his dresser so as to please his sense of aesthetics and they are now accumulated inside a plastic marching band drum which sits filled to the skin in the Sauerstein garage. Rupert was Nava and Oscar's first grandchild, when she got hold of him she wouldn't consider sharing, just hugging and kissing him all day long. Contrary to what one might surmise no one in witness to her adoration objected to the misallocation of baby-holding time, experiencing the intensity of her love for him was more of a pleasure to the extended family than cradling him themselves.

At the time of our encounter and through to this day Rupert has two favorite photographs. One is of Benny at two years old, shirtless on the patio, a cartoon animal decorated kiddie pool in partial view at the bottom left of the frame, baby bro looking up at the camera and squinting just a bit against the sun with an expression of complete tranquility, of knowing nothing but. Many times Rupert has sat staring at that picture, reminding himself of how extraordinary his life had been and trying to convince himself that it could once again be that way. The other milli-moment in time that speaks so profoundly to Rupert was taken in front of his grandparents' house on 13th Street. A young and relatively svelte Oscar stands, from Isaac's photographic perspective to the right of Nava, who has baby Benny secured by his tush with her left arm. She is beaming at him and he has his head turned to take a peek at Oscar's wide and adoring grin. Rupert stands centered in front of his grandma, his left arm raised and his fingers interlocked with those of her available right hand. Rupert's expression can only be described as that of a four year old who'd just enjoyed the most mirthful thing to've ever been uttered or enacted. Thank not god but rather Aristotle and Alhazen for the camera.

Shy of a month after that picture was taken Nava lost her life to an undiagnosed heart ailment. The most vivid memory Rupert has dating prior to his fifth birthday is of being in his bedroom playing with a Tonka truck as Isaac walked in wearing a mien more somber than Rupert had ever seen upon his father prior to that moment. Isaac walked over to Rupert, gently moving the truck aside whilst he got to one knee as to level himself with his son.

"Sweetheart," he said, "Grandma Nava has passed away. Do you understand what that means?"

He didn't, but his face metamorphosed sullen in pained empathy for his father.

"What daddy, what does it mean?" he asked as his eyes welled up with tears.

"It means that she went to live in Heaven, and we won't be able to visit her there."

"How come?"

"Because when people go to Heaven no one can go visit them, but they can watch us from there, and they can still love us, and we can still love them."

"Ok daddy. I really love you."

"Rupert I really love you too, so so much."

Isaac squeezed his son tightly. During the brief, woeful discussion he was on the verge of broken-hearted tears, only able to hold them back through the strength he mustered in guardianship of his son's innocence. Rupert loves his father in a thousand ways, that moment stands alone in his memory as the most profound show of his bravery, his nobility. They both miss her deeply still.

The Saturday after their chance encounter Xaviera gave Kayiane a buzz. The Sauersteins had nothing on the docket for Sunday and Kayiane asked if she'd like to bring her girls and husband over for a barbeque, a proposal gladly accepted.

"Hold on a second, I wanna mess with Rupert," Kayiane told her new friend. "Rupert!"

"Yes mommy!"

"Are you playing records all day tomorrow or do you want Onyx to come over for a barbeque and you guys can run thru the sprinkler?"

"Is she gonna wear a bathing suit?!"

"Oh lord," reacted Xaviera. "These children have activated each other's libidos. She's gonna want to wear her blue bikini."

"Hold on. Rupert!"

"Mommy!?"

"Is it ok if she wears a little blue bikini?"

"Yes she should. She doesn't need to wear the top if she doesn't want to!"

Kayiane sealed her mouth with her elbow and listened with three molecules of jealousy to Xaviera's unencumbered laughter through the handset.

"She's probably gonna wear the top!"

"My Onyx can do whatever she wants!"

"That's right baby. You think about all girls that way ok?! But still she'll likely wear the whole thing!"

"I would never tell a girl what to do mommy! I would punch a boy in his face if he told Onyx what to do though!"

"Fighting is never right sweetheart, you know that!"

"If someone messes with Onyx I won't give a shit what's right or wrong mommy, I'm just gonna hit him!"

"Rupert stop it!" Each word continued to come clear on the other end and though the discussion had coursed curiously it warmed and entertained both Kayiane and Xaviera. "Can you believe the things coming out of my little guy's mouth?"

"Oh dear Kayiane I can't quite figure what to make of it. Your sweet Rupert is cursing and talking about punching other boys but it's all in the name of protecting my little girl."

"I'm glad that gorgeous daughter of yours will have a protector in my Rupert, but I should probably talk to him about his diction and violent intent. That little beauty fires up his synapses."

"I'm sorry baby."

"No, no please, believe me, I'm proud of his feminism and chivalrous valor more than anything else right now."

"Oh good Kayiane I didn't know what to think!"

"I'd rather he not curse or fight but if he must I'm glad it's motivated by defending Onyx's sanctity."

"Oh lord!" giggled Xaviera.

"So you still wanna let my sex-crazed four year old see your little supermodel of a daughter in a bikini tomorrow?"

"I grew up in Kingston baby, da boys start seducin' da girls right out da womb down dare."

"It's not much diff'rent in south Brooklyn hun."

"Lordy lordy. Babies are always liable to surprise you aren't they?"

"It's really so true. My Benjamin's favorite thing is stalking human flesh like a swamp tiger and I now know that Rupert is a pimp." Kayiane sighed and asked "you wanna come over at 4:30? My husband Isaac will have the grill fired up."

"Yes dearie that's perfect. What can I bring?"

"You have any real Jamaican rum?"

"Indeed I do."

"Well I will see you at five then."

"Ok baby. Thank you so much for inviting us."

"I wouldn't have if I didn't want to hang out with you Xaviera. Don't think of me as a white girl that you have to be extra polite to, just think of me as your friend, ok?"

"Ok Kayiane. You're one of the good ones. I'll see you tomorrow with my naked daughter and the rest of my family."

"I look forward to it. I'm gonna go stitch up the penis hole Rupert just cut into his bathing suit."

"It's up to you baby. I'll see you."

"We'll be here. Goodnight Xaviera."

Ok goodnight Kayiane."

Kayiane was too charmed by her son's protective instincts to scold him. She didn't really care about the cursing, there isn't an age clause attached to y'all's freedom of speech. Should she have put a moratorium on it it wouldn't have lasted long anyway, a couple of years later Rupert would lead a force of Charlie, Hank and Benny into grandma Miriam and grandpa Giuseppe's kitchen, 'Appetite' cassette jacket in hand, and ask Kayiane and his aunt Miriam if they were allowed to listen to songs that say the word 'motherfucker.' They couldn't say no to those faces.

She'd become a little troubled in hearing her gentle son express a desire to act violently, but she quickly recognized that it was the one appropriate type of violence of which he spoke, a necessary violence, the protection of an innocent someone in distress. If a strange man were to grab or fondle her she'd want Isaac to knock the motherfucker out if it was the last available defense, and if the guy's skull split in the process it'd thusly become more appropriately constituted. His infatuation with Onyx yielded for Kayiane alien insights into Rupert's super-ego. Thinking a bit deeper into it she assured herself that he'd provide the same protection for Benny should someone try to do him harm, and that assuaged her every mitochondria. She walked into the family room, dropped herself on the couch and both of her boys cuddled up on her.

The two families sat in such copacetic harmony at the barbeque that if someone should have joined Eleazer and me in observance that day they'd have presumed to be watching old friends. Isaac and Xaviera's husband Zane took to each other quickly and the guests were treated to flank steak, shrimp kabobs, pork loin, corn on the cob and potato salad. Onyx did in fact wear her blue bikini though Rupert wasn't sure she had as when the Grahams arrived she was in an Aureolin dress that bow-tied at the back of her slender, silky neck. On the front of the dress, which frilled above her knees was the jet black silhouette of a giraffe. No longer in symmetrical puffs, her hair was left to roam free, drooping over her ears and rising high up into the sky.

Rupert's penis' brain forced him to consider pulling the tie undone, but he would never do something so disrespectful to Onyx. In fact he had cultivated a sophisticated understanding of how to treat her and a good read on her body language though this was only their second time together. When she wanted to take off the dress and start messin' around in the sprinkler she asked Rupert if he would untie it for her. 'Damn,' he thought, chubbing up. After dinner Xaviera took Benny on her lap and Kayiane Amoya on hers. Isaac and Zane slipped around the corner of the house and smoked a joint. Noticing that their daddies had gone somewhere and their mommies were focused on their little brother and sister, Rupert and Onyx snuck in a couple kisses as the sun went down. They walked towards the patio and Rupert said "mommy we're gonna get a jar."

"Ok hunny be careful."

"We will."

Onyx and he went thru the screen door and into the kitchen. Rupert grabbed a pencil, sawed off a square of aluminum foil and located a cleaned and de-labeled Ba Tampte jar, poked a few holes in the foil with the pencil, replaced the pencil in its cup as well as the aluminum foil in its cabinet and back outside they went, catching 6 fireflies between them, keeping them contained and oxygenated with the foil. Rupert insisted that Onyx take them home with her when the Grahams departed at 9:46. The parents had cleaned as they ate and drank, Isaac twice checked to make sure the propane tank was turned off and they got the boys right to bed as they were headed to the Cape in the early morning. It would be an eternal two weeks for Onyx and Rupert before they found themselves sitting side by side en route to their first day of kindergarten.

Isaac woke the boys up at 6:00 and after they'd finished bouncing down and against the stairwell wall and back and forth against the hallway Kayiane had bacon, scrambled eggs, toast and apple juice waiting on the table for them. They mangia'd and went back upstairs to shit their brains out and grab pillows. The family was on the road by 6:37 and Benny was asleep on his brother's lap, who was also out, before they hit the Taconic.

They roused about 15 minutes from their destination, three and a half hours after they'd departed, and began observing the quaint, clean, sandy roads and charming houses they had happened upon, having moments before crossed the canal onto Cape Cod for the first time. An older gentleman named Aaron, a colleague of Isaac's who the boys were yet to meet, having seen pictures of him with his charming wife and adorable sons, offered up his one story beach house in Sandwich so that they could enjoy the simple pleasures available all over and along the pseudo-peninsula. It was the first of many consecutive summers that the family would seize the kindly opportunity as the boys loved it there. Disney World, Roseville and the Cape were the places the family most enjoyed visiting while the boys were still just that.

The family took three trips to Disney World and one to Disneyland, the last in April 1993. Barring an unpredictable accident, who's ever had a bad time at Disney? Rupert loved it so much there that he would later wonder if his opinion of the little suicide case would be any less ferocious if it was called Hitler Town.

Here is the shortlist of activities that the Sauersteins would partake in during each visit to the cape, though none of them got old and each trip found a way of distinguishing itself despite nearly identical itineraries: elaborate miniature golf courses, whale watching, seafood restaurants where if you were really patient you could eat while sitting above the ocean, walks through rustic and charming town squares, a whole locality of cool looking gay people, tiny movie theaters, a chain of stores that exclusively sold thousands of wacky t-shirts and warm strangers mellowing together on a litter-less beach architected by Frankie Wright, sequestered by sand dunes and nature trails. The Cape Cod sun scorched a little more softly than the New York and Florida ones, a relief to the boys' pale, freckly skin.

The simple little summer home's shower was 'round back in a wooden enclosure and though Kayiane asked him not to Rupert couldn't resist running naked around the house after he'd cleaned himself up. At home the boys bathed and showered together, sword fighting daily, until around the time Rupert entered second grade. At 5 and 2 they started playing a game wherein they'd exit their bedrooms and rest their bodies against the banister as Rupert yelled "Maaaammmeeeee!"

"Ye-es?!"

"Weeeehr noo-oood!"

Kayiane would slowly and deliberately stomp towards the stairwell while the boys ran giggling either back inside their rooms or into the bathroom before she could catch them in their nakedness.

The morning after they arrived in Sandwich Isaac went out to get bagels, cream cheese, eggs, apple and orange juices before Kayiane woke the boys. He also picked up a fat mouthed fishing net for each of them. They were certain that the juvenile bamboo sharks they caught with those nets were newborn great whites. When the boys came to the table, far more refreshed than the morning before as it was three hours later in the day, Rupert began his dialogue with "what the Hell are these things?"

"They're bagels silly, "Kayiane informed him.

"Are they bagels for babies? Baby bagels?"

"No they're just smaller than the ones from grandpa's house." Though they occasionally bought a baker's dozen in Yorktown, most of their bagels were purchased at what very likely was the best bagel shop this side of the Old City of Jerusalem, around the corner from grandpa Oscar's house on Avenue J. They'd keep a few days' worth in the bread box and slice and freeze the rest.

When Rupert thinks about the shop's aroma his taste buds drip from the recall of its exquisite bagels, bialys, cheeses, knishes, half sours, rugelach and blintzes.

"Ok whatever this is a bagel," Rupert conceded. "Where's the sweet munchee?"

"I don't think they sell it on Cape Cod hunny," Kayiane told him.

"Why are the vegetables in the cream cheese in big chunks instead of little slivers?"

"Hunny, not all foods are made exactly the same way in every place."

"Uh-duh." Rupert pretentiously prepared his bagel and took a bite. "What!? Mommy why did you trick me this is disgusting!"

"I know hunny they're not very good, try to eat that one and next time we come up here we'll bring grandpa's bagels."

"And grampa's sweet munchee?"

"And grandpa's sweet munchee."

"And grampa's vegetable cream cheese?

"Yes, just eat so we can go see some whales."

"Ok, but just so you know I'm only gonna eat it cuz it makes me go see whales."

"That's fine with me sweetheart, just eat it."

Rupert had learned the valuable lesson that the farther you stray from Avenue J, the lesser the bagel ye shall receive. He made a good decision to eat the putrid thing because the humpbacks and bowheads they saw that day blew his mind, a whale tail in his face was double the thrill of hitting a home run and half as fantastic as kissing Onyx.

They returned home the following Sunday, the boys sleeping just as soundly on the way. Rupert was thrilled that half of the time between the barbeque and the first day of school had elapsed. Kayiane called Miriam to let her know they'd gotten home safely and Miriam asked if she could have the boys for a night or two before school started. Having just spent a week on vacation with them Kayiane was happy to hand them off and she and the boys made the quick trip over to their grandparents' house in the morning, She sat chatting with her parents at the kitchen table while the boys painted the wooden fence that bookended their small back patio with water.

"All done gramma," Rupert reported as the boys came inside, their t-shirts wetter than the fence. Kayiane took Benny's off and asked Rupert to do the same, grabbing fresh ones from their overnight bag.

"Thank you dear, the fence needed a good painting."

"Well we did it real good."

"I wouldn't expect anything less, you boys are the best fence painters I know. Say 'we did it very well sweetie', that's proper grammar."

"We did it very well sweetie, we tried extra hard cuz it's your fence."

"I appreciate your supreme effort."

"You're welcome."

"Benjamin sweetheart, did you also try very hard?"

"Yef ganma, I dood."

"Thank you so much dear."

"Wecum ganma."

"Alright, I'm gonna get going," informed a spent Kayiane.

Giuseppe and Miriam stood up to give their adored younger daughter kisses and hugs; in their eyes she was still just as precious as Rupert and Benny were to her.

"Kisses boys."

Benny ran, jumped at his mother and she grabbed him up, hugging him while twisting from side to side. Rupert walked over and with Benny still in her arms she bent down so he could give her a smack on the lips. "Get home safely mommy," he insisted.

"I will baby don't worry. I'll call later to say goodnight."

"Ok mommy. I love you."

"I love you too. Have fun and be good for grandma and grandpa."

"I don't think they could ever be bad in my eyes darling," Miriam interjected.

"These two? They're always stirring up trouble. They're sillyheads if ya ask me." antagonized Giuseppe.

"You're a sillyhead too grampa," Rupert struck back.

"I got the silliest head in the whole town Rupert, that's why I love you guys so much."

"I love you too grampa."

"I know ya do pal."

With that, Kayiane kissed her boys one more time and headed out.

"Gramma?"

"Yes dear?"

"Do you still have those little wood blocks with the letters and the holes?"

"I just bought some more the other day. What would you like to make?"

"A necklace for my girlfriend."

"I didn't know you had a girlfriend! What's the lucky girl's name?"

"Onyx."

"I love that name. How long has she been your girlfriend?"

"Um, like a mumph. She just moved here from Janaica."

"Oh my, how're things going?"

"Good. I kissed her three times."

"Oh goodness dear, does mommy know that?" Kayiane had detailed the story of Rupert and Onyx to her but Miriam delighted in his version.

"Nope," in fact Rupert was correct that his mother knew not of the kisses.

"Don't worry, I'll keep your secret. Is she pretty?"

"Um, no, she's beautiful."

"Well that's even better. What would you like the necklace to say?"

"I want it to say 'I LOVE YOU ONYX LOVE RUPERT.' I'm gonna give it to her on the bus and then I'm gonna kiss her again."

"That's very nice dear. Just don't kiss her in school because little boys and little girls don't kiss in school."

"Even if the teacher isn't looking?"

"Yes dear, even then. Would you like to go get the basket."

"Yes I will gramma." Miriam kept a large wicker basket filled with crafts in the room where the boys slept.

"Bennnnneeee," said Giuseppe bassily, snapping him out of a daze to take a look up at his big ol' grandpa. "You wanna sit with me on my chair and watch some TV?" Miriam aligned with her daughter's opinion on television but Giuseppe was a bit looser about it. And besides, one of the best things about grandparents is that they let you get away with the most stuff.

"Yef ganpa. Cooka?"

"Just a couple ok? Are you gonna tell mommy?"

"No ganpa."

"Good boy. Can you go get them by yourself?"

"Yef," said Benny as he turned and speedily waddled towards the kitchen. Giuseppe stored Milanos in the cabinet beside the fridge for when the boys visited.

"Thanks big guy," Giuseppe said to Benny as he grabbed him up upon his return.

"Wecum ganpa."

When Rupert returned with the basket, Miriam asked "do you think you can find the letters yourself or shall I help you?"

"I can do it myself. How do you spell Onyx gramma?

"O-N-Y-X"

"Thank you. I can do it myself, but I wanna sit right next to you."

"That works out well because I want to sit next to you, too." Rupert decided to make the necklace out of purple, green, pink, red, yellow and blue, each word spelled out in its own color, a blank white block substituting as a space between them. Miriam cut a length of stretchy string just the right size for a little girl to wear loosely around her neck and tied one end enough so that it would secure the blocks. She helped him lay the characters out in a row. Rupert carefully put a dot of glue between each so they wouldn't roll around, as suggested by his grandmother who, though certainly this wasn't the most indicative display of it, was a brilliant woman. The task was complete once Rupert triple-knotted the ends. Miriam said "this is beautiful. Onyx is going to love it. But I'm a little jealous."

"Why gramma?"

"Well if Onyx is going to get a kiss I think grandma should get one too."

"Come here."

She leaned over and he put one on her.

Finally, the first Monday in September arrived. The bus stopped at Onyx's house before it did Rupert's, climbing aboard he spotted her afro peering over the second seat beyond the bus driver and sat beside her.

"Hi."

"Hi Rupert."

"I missed you a lot."

"Me too."

"Here," he gave her the necklace.

She read it and said "this is I love it. Would you put it around my neck please."

"Of course I will sweetheart."

As anticipated by both, they shared their fourth kiss. A boy sitting across the aisle saw them and said "ewwww!"

"Pffff," Rupert excommunicated his immaturity.

The kids were giddy as they got off the bus, feeling so grown-up and excited to meet their teacher. Crossing the threshold of the main entry their sensorium went berserk like stoned teenagers walking into a mall. There they met their principal Mrs. Sharper, since she'd earned the position at the beginning of the previous school year she would stand by the front doors every morning (and afternoon for the second kindergarten crew) and greet the children with warm words and big smiles. Rupert described her to Kayiane as 'seven feet tall with purple shoelaces.'

At the door to their classroom was a sizzlin' hot caramel skinned young woman, wearing a long thinly strapped blue cheer dress patterned with provocative canary yellow tiger footprints. Ms. Goodridge was Barbadian and had moved to the states at 17 to study as an undergrad at NYU, moving on to Columbia to earn her masters in elementary ed. While if each girl born in Barbados was as gorgeous as Rihanna every earthly pussy-baller and lesbianizer would overcrowd Bridgetown like a Tokyo subway car, Kela Goodridge mesmerized as or more deeply than the Satanism and Illuminati rumored seductress with her creamy, sun-splashed skin, painfully arousing figure, paralyzing face, and that adorable fuckin' button nose. All the burned out and busted up teachers shot hateful, envious laser beams at her as she'd strutted towards her classroom that morning. When they found out where she went to school they hated her even more, until they got to know her and discovered she was a doll and comprised of not an atom's narcissism. What they'd truly come to envy was what a remarkable educator little miss brains was. As the children walked in she tussled their hair, pinched their cheeks, said things like 'hello beautiful' and 'good morning darling.'

Once every student had twirled and karate chopped in she said "sit where you'd like for now sweet children, and please give me your attention so I can learn your names and determine what makes each of you special. Do you know what is wonderful? You are big boys and girls now, big smart kindergarteners. This is your first day of school and guess what? It is mine too. You are my first class, which means you will always be in my heart and my thoughts. I don't even know your names yet precious ones, but I love you all with my entire soul. By the end of the year you will all be so smart that you'll probably be smarter than me. That is my wish for you."

Along with her teaching acumen miss Kela Goodridge held an undergrad degree in psychology. She'd graduated with a 3.93 at both NYU and Columbia, only missing out on a 4.0 because she wouldn't have dinner with a professor at each school, both downgrading her to an A-, just subtle enough not to garner suspicion of unethical behavior; had they graded her without concern for consequences both would have flunked her on the disappointment of not having had her for a meal. On par with grandma Miriam, qualifying for the wisdom that only time and experience can provide, she was a brilliant individual, every statement, question and action complexly calculated. By the end of the year she had each student, smartest to dimmest, on at least a second grade level in every of the district's academic subjects, most of which weren't part of the kindergarten curriculum. She came from an obscenely wealthy family and spent more on the children during the year than she took in as salary. She could do whatever she wanted to, live in selfish, jobless bliss and travel infinitely to every inch of the map, but above all else she coveted the opportunity to enrich young minds, and that sincerity had in a few spare moments created an incredibly warm and motivational atmosphere in the classroom.

"So ok my sweet ones, first I need to learn your names, and then I'd like to give each of you a hug. Who'd like to go first?"

Every child shot a hand into the air aside from Rupert and Onyx. Rupert could feel a distasteful energy emanating from his love. He knew he needed to freeze it right away. He grabbed her hand and whispered "You know what? You are seventeen times more beautiful than that teacher. Remember what your new necklace says. You are the only girl I ever wanna kiss."

A bit misguided, the notion that the stunner at the front of the room would try to steal her Rupert away from Onyx, but love can get the mind swoopin' through some gnarly loop-de-loops, even at 4 and 5 years old.

"You promise Rupert?"

"Yes I do, I promise. The way I felt when I met you in the stupermarket I won't never feel again."

"I believe you. I love you."

"I love you more than the earth, Onyx. Do you know why Ms. Goodridge is really here?"

"No, why Rupert?"

"She was sent here to show you that even though there are many beautiful girls in the world, no matter what for me you'll always be the beautifullest."

Onyx was rather comforted by this sentiment and rested her head on his shoulder, one of the most pacifying things she'd learn to do.

"And what about you handsome with those big red curls?" Ms. Goodridge said, bringing the two out of their hypnotic swoon.

"Um, this is my Onyx and I'm Rupert. I'll hug you but only if me and Onyx can hug you together."

"You and this gorgeous one, yes? How long have you been boyfriend and girlfriend?"

"Since fa'eva missy," Onyx interjected territorially.

"I see baby. Where are you from with that nice accent of yours?"

"Treasure Beach, Jamaica."

"How wonderful. Rupert you are from Treasure Beach as well?"

"Yup."

"Oh how lucky for you to both come from Jamaica and be placed in the same kindergarten class. Rupert, I want you to say only if Onyx and I can hug you together rather than me and Onyx."

"Ok, can Onyx and I hug you together?"

"Good work, mister. Well I'm waiting, come here you precious Jamaican lovebirds. I adore triple hugs."

As they approached Rupert told her that "lot of people hugs are nice. Me and my...my mommy, my daddy, my brother and I like to do body hugs."

"Well that's a very special thing for your family cutie-pie."

As she grabbed each of them up with one arm they grinned temple to temple at one another behind her suckable neck.

"Ok beautiful children that's all I need to learn from you today. Since it's our first day of school we need to have a party. I have music, fresh and delicious pineapple, guava and Barbados cherry juices in the icebox, snacks and prizes for each of you. Let us all, just this once, go outside and get crazy. How does that sound?"

The children went bananas as if the Giants had won the pennant and out they squeezed through the back door of the classroom to the adjacent blacktop, twistin' the mornin' away. Having reaffirmed their devotion and absolved Onyx's jealousy, she and Rupert were able to benefit fully from the fact that Ms. Goodridge would soon develop into the best teacher in the Americas and not become torn apart because she was already the sexiest. Kayiane and Xaviera noticed their children getting wiser by the day, and after Xaviera met Ms. Goodridge while picking Onyx up for a dental appointment she and Kayiane brainstormed ways to keep their husbands away from parent-teacher night.

Come the following July Onyx and Rupert were despondent upon learning that they wouldn't share a first grade teacher. Their classrooms were positioned directly across the hall from each other and to be so close but have their faces blocked out by two thicknesses of pocked plaster they may as well have been drawn and quartered. During the doubly-long school day the only time they spent together was four lousy minutes each way on the bus, and the bus driver had issued them a no kissing warning during the very first bumpy ride of the year. At recess, Onyx wasn't about to play kickball or football, nor was Rupert about to hopscotch or jump rope. He would keep a protective eye on his love from the baseball diamond or adjacent soccer field as she played with the other girls on the basketball court.

Desperate for some alone time, they pleaded with Kayiane and Xaviera for a sleepover. Reluctantly, they agreed. After lights out they disobediently used a Glo-Worm and Lite Brite so they could see each other well enough to philosophise and kiss. Kayiane left the door open just enough so that she could peek in while still creating for the children a sense of privacy. When she checked on them 45 minutes later she found them making out with a hand down each other's pants. "How are you two doing in there?" Kayiane asked as Onyx scrambled for Rupert's bed and Rupert to the cot.

"We're fine mommy."

"I bet you are."

When Xaviera came to pick Onyx up in the morning, Kayiane relayed to her the pornography she'd witnessed. They stepped slowly down to the basement, planning on the fly as it were, whereabouts it wreaked of prepubescent carnality, and the little subverts were busy co-creating a Lego mansion. Xaviera yielded to Kayiane, who began the discussion.

"We need to have a very serious talk you two."

'Ahh fuck,' Rupert thought, knowing well what it'd be about.

"I saw you doing things last night that you cannot do."

"Like what?" Rupert played dumb.

"You both know what," added Xaviera firmly."

Neither child admitted they did.

"You may never touch each other's special places, or we won't ever allow you to be alone again," she asserted.

"Onyx's special vagina?" Rupert asked.

"Yes," Kayiane responded in her sternest tone.

"Rupert's special penis?" Onyx made sure everyone was on the same page.

"You already know the answer to that missy."

"Yes momma."

"But mommy it's just a vagina, everybody's got one," rationalized Rupert.

"You don't have one," Kayiane stated what she thought to be the obvious.

"Yes I do, I have Onyx's."

"No, that is for Onyx to use for pee-pee, and not for you to ever touch."

"And the same goes for Rupert's penis, it's for going pee, and nothing else," Xaviera held firm with Kayiane against early adult tooth sex.

"Ok, we didn't know that," Rupert lied.

“Is this ever going to happen again?” queried Kayiane.

“No mommy,” Rupert hoped he was lying again.

“And you little girlie?”

“Uh-uh momma.”

“This was your one and only sleepover, and when you have eat-overs you will remain in our sight the whole time,” asserted Kayiane.

Both nodded in concession.

“Ok missy, let’s go home.” The moms decided not to tell their husbands about the debauchery. Kayiane and Xaviera were so intensely in love with their children that their pacifist, weed smoking husbands, neither of whom was any less protective or in love with his babies, sat at the extreme leftist edge of their momma bear suspicion spectrums.

Having ruined their opportunity to ever sex each other up Rupert began breaking his brain, sifting for a new lovemaking arena. They couldn’t so much as sit together at lunch as each class had an assigned table and some churchy little Young Republican fuckface dimed them out when he had pulled his t-shirt over his afro and sneak-sat beside her the second day of the year. He came up with this during an Otis Redding marathon the following Sunday: first, Onyx and he synchronized their Swatches. Second, they’d ensure their mothers continued to make their lunches every day, a non-issue as neither wanted their children eating the slop served up by the school. This saved them from obligating precious minutes to standing on line awaiting purchase of said slop.

Beyond the far end of the cafeteria from where the first graders entered, to the left of the lunch line, were boys and girls bathrooms. Continuing beyond them, the hallway went past the side entrance to the gymnasium and ended with the double doors through which the children went to recess. Immediately before the doors on the right there was a little nook, 6' x 8'. Between the gym doors and the nook exercise mats were piled in droves. Before implementing his plan and divulging it to Onyx, so as not to sully himself in her honey brown eyes should he be unable to pull it off, Rupert covertly moved four thereupon unnoticeably absent tri-fold mats and stacked them slightly at an indent from the left end of the nook, parallel with the hallway, well high enough to obscure the bodies of two seated children, even if either of their afros were puffed as high as it could capably poof. Once the mats were securely in place, he whispered his plan to Onyx on the bus.

On Mondays, Wednesdays and Thursdays they would eat their lunches quickly and then alternate as the first to request a trip to the bathroom. Once the first had exited, the other would wait 17 ticks and ask to do the same, each making sure to vary the monitor from whom they asked permission. Once in the bathroom they'd hold for a count of 66, put half an eyeball on the hallway to make sure it was clear and briskly walk towards their fortress, taking two quick glances back as an added precaution whilst proceeding. With exactly two minutes left before the kids lined up for recess Onyx would cat burglar her way back into the cafeteria, Rupert'd sly dog behind a minute later. The only part of the caper he didn't share with her was that should they get busted he planned on taking the fall, telling their captor he had lied to her and said there were candy and diamonds back there. Over the course of first grade, against odds longer than the Mets winning the World Series in a given year (though that spring, summer and fall they were amazin'), the couple kibitzed undetected 104 times. They hugged, kissed and engaged in chimerical conversations, somehow repressing their thirst and leaving each other's special penis and special vagina alone.

That summer Kayiane brought the boys into the city on a perfect Friday, walking from Grand Central Station up Fifth Avenue to 72nd street and winding across Terrace Drive to see the bridge, Turtle Pond, climb to the top of Belvedere Castle and adventure through Strawberry Fields. They then took a cab from Central Park West down into the East Village for a jaunt and hot-footed it back up to midtown to meet Isaac at the Oyster Bar, where they made a clam chowder so spot on it drew the ire of every New Englander who angrily savored it.
As they strolled back up north an energized woman with glasses, a power suit and tied back bleach unblackened hair approached them. "Excuse me have you thought about having your son do some modeling?"

"I made a model of an elephant in art class."

"That's great." She didn't give a shit. "Listen here's my card I work with Elle call me soon we'll have him in for a shoot." She was a block away by the time the card was secured by Kayiane's fingers, reminding her of certain uppities she had reported to while at Seventeen.

They discussed the psychotic's proposition at dinner and didn't see any harm, Rupert was enticed enough to check it out.

Two weeks and a day later he and Kayiane walked into a second floor studio on the Upper West Side, rife with lobotomized children and unpleasantly perfumed mothers. Over the course of seven hours Rupert was put into two outfits. The first was a puffy winter jacket and pants ensemble. He didn't understand why they dotted his face with yellow and blue, he already had freckles. The second was an ankle to jawbone leather get-up, his confusion there was why he couldn't take it home afterwards, having worked his fully descended balls off all day. After they painstakingly arranged it on him and just as particularly positioned his body, he announced to the crowd that "mommy I gotta pee."

The snobs running the thing made faces and sounds of disgust but soon enough he was empty-bladdered and reconstituted.

As they left, Kayiane asked "no good huh?"

"No good mommy, I don't wanna do that again."

And you can bet your bottom dollar he never did.

Two days after the photo-shoot the phone rang and Kayiane answered in the kitchen while the boys lazed in the family room. The volume was turned up high as they watched the intense final moments of Rad. Rupert lounged facing the television at the elbow of the floral couch which covered most of two walls, Benny sat a couple feet to his right with his legs crossed upon the couch. As the credits rolled Kayiane's call ended and she turned off the television, readying herself for a difficult conversation with Rupert.

"Rupert sweetie could you sit up for me please?" she asked as she eased down between the boys.

"Sure mommy are you ok?"

"Yes mommy's fine but I hafta talk to you about something. Sweetheart, Onyx's mommy and daddy have decided to move to a place called Atlanta, Georgia."

"Is Onyx going too?" Rupert quivered.

"Yes baby she is."

"Is it far away?"

"Yes love it's very far."

Rupert processed the information for a brief moment and began crying as loudly as he could scream, absolutely magma-eyed. Benny began crying near as deeply, broken by the sight and sound of his big brother in such despair.

"I wanna move there too mommy!" he infused into his bawling, though he suspected the family couldn't move solely to follow the love of his little life.

"I know you do hunny but then everyone here will miss us."

"I know!" He cried and he cried, holding his mother tight, until the sun had begun to make its way west out of an eternal responsibility to light each sky above the heartless spheroid. When Isaac got home from a business dinner at 9:20 Rupert was asleep but still crying. Benny slept on his mother just the same, quietly, frowning.

"What's wrong?" Isaac asked, delicate though frantic.

"The Grahams are moving to Atlanta."

"Oh my poor little guy!"

Isaac gingerly peeled him off of his mother and carried him to his room. Rupert came partially awake.

"Daddy?"

"I know sweetheart, I know, I'm so sorry. You can call her on the telephone whenever you want and when you get big I'll let you go on an airplane all by yourself to visit her ok?"

"You promise?"

"Would daddy ever lie to you?"

"No you never would."

Good. You always remember that ok."

"Ok, I will."

Isaac laid him down as if his bed was a sidewalk and his body an egg. He began whisper-singing *"It's Late*" at half tempo and stroking his son's hair until his sleep restored to "*now you tell me you're leavin', and I just can't believe it's true, ohh you know that I could love you, though I know I can't be true, ahh you make me love you, don't tell me that we're through,*" giving him a long, gentle kiss on the forehead upon finishing the verse. As he did so Kayiane was putting Benny to bed and they met between the two softly closed doors, both with tears in their eyes.

"I hate it when my babies get stung," Kayiane lamented.

"I know sweetheart, I'd sit around and just listen to records with him forever if it was right. He'll be ok, we'll stay in touch with the Grahams, in a year they'll have forgotten about each other."

"I know. I'll still remember telling him."

"I know." Isaac grabbed his bleeding-hearted wife's hand as they tiptoed past Rupert's room and into their own.

When second grade started, Rupert won the consolation prize of making a best friend, having just lost his sweet Onyx to geography. A group of boys congregated to play football at recess and Rupert was one of two who got to select a squad. Among the combatants was an overwhelmed looking boy, new to Rupert. He stood a good three inches above the second tallest on the board. Rupert looked at him and asked "what's your name?"

"Me? D'Shaundrius."

"Did you just move here?"

"Yeah. We're from Harlem but my parents thought this was better."

"Have you played football before?"

"Yeah."

"Alright, I pick you."

D'Shaundrius smirked most subtly and walked over to Rupert. They shook hands and patted each other on the back. The score is loosely kept during an elementary school football game but between them Rupert and D'Shaundrius snagged eight interceptions and connected on ten touchdowns in the span of 25 minutes. The following day the collective of footballers decided that Rupe and D'Shaun could be on the same team only if the rest of it was strictly bottom of the barrel. It didn't really matter, the two could have beaten the rest of the kids by themselves. They began fixing the games, always retaining the lead but keeping it close enough as not to frustrate the other boys into retirement. Omitting the kissing, google-eying, heads on shoulders and hands down pants, they began seeking each other's company as often as Rupert had with Onyx until her tragic departure the previous summer.

Two weeks into Benny's term as a first grader the boys lost grandpa Giuseppe. They knew he wasn't feeling well but Kayiane and Isaac well understated the seriousness of his condition whenever the boys asked about him, as had grandma Miriam to a lesser degree when speaking with her daughter. They visited him once or twice a week at what wasn't quite a hospital nor a nursing home, rather a place shadowing the shore of the Hudson, near the Putnam-Dutchess border, architecturally and by its size reminiscent of Monticello. He remained there for over a month and the family believed his health had been restored upon his return home. Two nights later he passed in his sleep. While Rupert and Benny were headed for the bus at dismissal they found their crestfallen parents at the end of the hall. As soon as Rupert saw them he knew. He began running and when he got close he asked "Grandpa died?!" in terror.

"Yes sweetheart, he did," Isaac confirmed the gut-wrenching news.

"Oh grandpa!" Rupert anguished.

Benny was already with his parents, who'd told him that his strong, gentle grandpa had passed away. When Rupert reached them, the four cried together in a body hug. On their way to what was now only grandma

Miriam's house they stopped for gasoline. As the attendant pumped, Benny asked, "mommy, why did grampa die?"
While she gathered the strength to respond Rupert did so for her.

"Because he was so fun and he loved us so much, and everybody wanted to be with him, that's why grandma and he have so many friends, because they're both so great. Grandpa was so happy for so long, and god wanted to spend time with him before he got really old and couldn't have as much fun anymore. He can still see us and he wants us to have fun and be nice. And we can pretend we're sitting on his lap and playing with his hair. And we can still love him and he still loves us as much up there as he did down here."

"Rupert sweetheart, that was so beautiful," Kayiane reacted, warmed by her son's wisdom and the comfort he provided for his baby brother.

"Thanks mom."

And it was beautiful, though it didn't concretely lessen anyone's sadness.
When they walked into grandma Miriam's she sat facing out from the kitchen table in shock. Isaac and the boys told her how sorry they were and gave her big hugs and kisses, as did Kayiane, who was just as devastated. The four took a seat with her, not much spoken. Miriam dampened her despair for her boys' sake, as did her daughter. Rupert and Benny stayed with family friends across the street during the wake and funeral. During the weeks to come Rupert broke down in tears several times, pining for his comforting, community leading grandpa Giuseppe.

Throughout their youth the boys were exposed to the culture, mannerisms and accentuations of people born to plethoric demarcations, be it through watching Sesame Street and other PBS programming, playing in the pools of Disney resorts, (one time they and Kayiane were tossing a tennis ball in a Miro contoured lagoon when a pudgy Aryan fellow approximately Rupert's age drew up the courage to approach them. "I'm Sherman," he said, simply and apprehensively. "Hi Sherman, I'm Kayiane and these are my sons, Rupert and Benjamin. Would you like to play with us?" "Oh yes please misses, sank you wonderfully." Kayiane soft tossed him the ball and it hit him right between his Goebbels blue eyes as his arms crisscrossed behind it a split-second too late. "Boys say hello to Sherman." Hi Sherman," echoed Benny. "Hey man," said Rupe. "I'm Rolph," the boy's voice crackled nervously, "I'm from Shermany."), their interactions with the Grahams and with scattered others who'd migrated to their cozy corner of Yorktown or worked for Isaac's company.

Aware that Aaron, himself a born Brooklynite, was selling his many properties, strewn throughout sophisticated localities within the Americas, and retiring to Tel Aviv, Isaac was compelled to have him meet the boys during their final visit to his home in Sandwich and the summer before Rupert entered 6th grade they sailed off course a bit to visit him at his office, about 45 minutes up the coast from the Cape. They halted the car in the small parking lot at front of his building and as they sauntered towards the entrance the boys admired the bold lettering in Israeli blue and white that cascaded the archway leading to the front doors and read 'Abraham Enterprises.'

The utilitarian two story building was tastefully artful on its insides. The Sauersteins said hello to the duel receptionists positioned left and right of the entrance and walked through the glass doors to Aaron's office at their left as he'd anticipated Isaac's always prompt arrival and was positioned to wave them in. His heart was most warmed as the boys each gave him a hug and Rupert began thanking him for letting them use his house, noting how much he loved it, regaling him with an account of their cherished experiences. He and Rupert were in unmitigated agreement that the delicatessen on the Cape sucked dick. Once their charming interchange had exhausted the boys hugged and thanked him once more and walked back out into the lobby. Kayiane, Isaac and Aaron sat to reminisce at the near end of a conference table and the boys pulled out their Gameboys whilst each secretary aerosol-soaked her absurd, time period hairdo with one hand and twirled gum with the other.

The brothers plopped themselves into side-by-side plush armchairs and Benny got to playing Battletoads while Rupert powered up for a round of Maru's Mission. A spare moment or two later their attention was wrestled away from adventuring as the two ladies began discussing their plans for the soon to begin weekend. Reared by their parents to be tactful and polite, they lost all ability to be either and began laughing as loudly as they could scream, each locking eyes with one of the innocently ridiculous women as tears of hilarity streamed down their cheeks and onto their Bart Simpson t-shirts. Kayiane re-entered the lobby shortly thereafter to see what had overtaken her gelastic sons.

"Mommy!?," Benjamin whooped, "Why do they talk like that?!"

The only little dude Rupert had befriended in school prior to meeting D'Shaundrius was a fellow named Rocco Angelino. He lived a few houses down Curry, his house recessed from the main road, and Kayiane was friendly with his mother Alana. His little brother Arlo was a grade ahead of Benny and kind spirited, as they were allowed to make the short walk to each other's houses the four would ill together once or twice a week. More often than otherwise they played two on two football, be it 90 degrees outside or 19, The Sauersteins vs. The Angelinos. The Angelinos' quarter acre was largely comprised of the backyard and as it was straight flat provided the perfect venue for a game of pigskin. Unanimously they enjoyed playing their football in the snow more than on the grass, they could smash and get smashed yet were saved from injury by the frosty cotton. In late winter of '91 the four were about to begin the day's standoff when two neighborhood kids, Brad and Ray, happened by and asked to join in.

Brad Rupert liked, Ray he hated. They were both in fifth grade though Ray was Rupert's senior by two months, having done a stretch in pre-k. He had a constant puss on his face and picked fights with every neighborhood kid he thought he could take. Rupert never understood why Brad hung out with him. Rupe and Benny took Brad, Rocco and Arlo Ray. Rupert detested the idea of Benny lining up against that motherfucker but he didn't show his hand at first. Hierarchy dictated that Rupert and Rocco were field captains, assigning routes to their receivers. Rocco booted the opening kickoff and Benny secured it, instinctively taking the route with the most potential. Sure enough, when Ray got to him he clotheslined him to the ground. Rupert got on him in a palpitation and put him in a stranglehold. He'd compromised many a windpipe in foregone years championing his baby brother's safety.

"I knew you were gonna pull some shit, you don't know how not to!" Rupert's arms were a Titanoboa around his neck. "Are you gonna calm down or are you gonna leave!?"

"Calm down, calm down," he rasped.

"We'll see," Rupert said as he pushed him face down into the snow. "I'm gonna rip your fuckin' throat out if you do my little brother dirty again."

Benny was a big kid, two inches shorter than Rupert despite the three year gap in their ages but he was as mild-mannered as a grizzly cub, pure and pacifistic, his appearance and temperament both proof he was Giuseppe's grandson. The game continued civilly for a few possessions until Benny put a nasty move on Ray for a touchdown. As Benny started heading back towards the Angelinos' end zone, Ray turned back into Ray and shoved him down from behind. Before Rupert could turn the kid into pulp Benny bum rushed him, bent his arms, pressed his fists together and mashed him square in the face, knocking him off his feet. A second later slick crimson was gushing from his nose, dying his Jets jacket Giants. He laid there crying for a couple minutes while Rupert berated him, got himself to his feet and retreated home, snorting and swallowing bad blood.

"I'm sorry you guys," said Brad.

"Don't be sorry man, you can play with us whenever you want. Just stop hanging out with that kid, he's a fuckin' asshole," advised Rupert.

"Yeah," answered Brad, lamenting the fact that he had such a piece of shit for a best friend. "Alright I'll see you guys later."

"Seriously man, come by whenever you want."

"Thanks Rupert." Brad shook his hand, turned and headed home.

Rupert walked over to his little brother, put his arm around him and gave him a big kiss on the cheek. Looking at Rocco he asked "I guess that's it?"

"Yeah, that's it. Fuckin' Ray. Wayta be Benny."

They went inside where Alana had hot chocolate pipin' ready and waiting. Since that afternoon Rupert's given Benny space to speak and fight for himself, always though ready to rip throats out if his baby bro were to find himself in trouble. Two months later, the Angelinos moved to Florida and Rupert went back to having one favorite contemporary, having added D'Shaundrius to Rocco and subtracted Rocco from D'Shaundrius.

As Rupert's baseball career had progressed more and more he became a student of the game, in constant analysis on the field. He figured out which plays kids could make and which they couldn't. When on the mound he kept a mental record of where to locate his deliveries so as to get opposing hitters out, and when at the plate or on the bench he paid close attention to the spots opposing hurlers tended to pitch to. He knew his own strengths and weaknesses within the strike zone and learned the mental aspect of competition, the gamesmanship.

In the spring of sixth grade his team was primed to play in the Championship Game. The venue was an elementary school in the southern part of Yorktown, in a district separate from his own. He had a plan that day to get in the heads of the other team as much as he could. The school had a front and a back parking lot and his coach had asked the parents all to park in the back for a pregame evaluation of their opponents and pep-talk. The teams warmed up on the field and upon returning to their benches the coaches and umpires congregated in front of the mound to discuss conduct and the like. As they did so, Rupert discreetly rolled a ball against the fence protecting the opposing team's quarters up the third base line and as he retrieved it murmured "you guys are fucked, I'm gonna beat you by myself." He stared at the biggest cocksucker among them as he ground out his decree, mindfully ensuring that no one but his opponents could hear him.

Rupe started the game on the mound, slated to pitch the opening three of six frames. He threw an immaculate inning and pumped himself up for his at bat in the bottom of the first. The leadoff man slapped one up the middle and it trickled into center, the #2 hitter and fat son of the coach popped up to short. Rupert stepped into the box and said 'time please ump.' He let out a guttural scream and dug into the dirt with each cleat eleven times. He looked at the pitcher and said 'ok kid come on.'

First pitch swinging he crushed the ball high and deep to dead center, tilting his head upwards and pressing his left thumb against his forehead militarily. When the ball landed beyond the meshed plastic, neon orange fence, careening off the trunk of a pine tree, he flipped the bat and started around the bases, calculatedly letting out a 'wooo!' as he rounded first. When he stepped on home the umpire scolded "listen son you gotta take it easy."

"I'm very sorry sir," he said with convincing mock sincerity, "I haven't been hitting well lately and I was quite nervous. Please don't issue me a warning."

"Ok no warning, just calm down."

"I will sir, again I'm very sorry."

Over the next two innings Rupe's blue team doubled up to four and he gave up a two run bomb to the red team's brawny cleanup hitter in the top of the third. The game was intense from start to finish. The parents screamed for their sons and at each other. Despite Rupert's psychological warfare and play on the field, the game entered the bottom of the conclusive sixth inning with blue trailing 6-5. Rupert was due up fifth, hoping his comrades would get him there. He looked towards the mound and noticed that who else had been handed the ball but the little bastard Benny had jacked up the previous winter. As Rupert anticipated but prayed to Slade they wouldn't, the #8 and 9 hitters both fanned. From the far end of the bench Rupert implored his teammates, "come on guys we still got this, keep your heads up!"

The dependable leadoff hitter smacked one between the third baseman and shortstop, reanimating the players and their supporters. While putting on his helmet and before heading to the on-deck circle, he quietly told his team to do the chant when he made the motion. The #2 hitter lucked into one and pushed a swinging bunt towards third. It came to rest with a solitary seam grazing the outer edge of the chalk, halfway up the line. Rupert would either be the Mighty Casey or his foil. He strolled towards the plate with a short, slow gape, blowing a bubble in his Big League Chew two-thirds the size of his head. He stepped into the box, serene and prepared. The first pitch lofted in and bounced two feet in front of home. This kid was nervous as fuck. The ball went to the backstop but his teammates remained on first and second, as stealing wouldn't be allowed until travel team play began that summer. While the catcher reared back to return the ball to the tool on the hill, Rupert held up his bat and pointed it towards the left field gap, aways past which was The House that No, No Nanette Built. As he did so the team began screaming "Babe Rupe! Babe Rupe! Babe Rupe! Babe Rupe!"

The pitch came in headed for his wheelhouse, inner half and just below the belt. It met with the epicentric sweet spot of his black and gold Easton and shot out towards left center, two hopping the fence. There was no grandstanding this time, Rupe began hustlin' 'round the diamond and slid into home as the cutoff man futilely hurled it towards the catcher. Three seconds later he was at the bottom of an ecstatic mountain of ten, eleven and twelve year-olds. The players and their families celebrated on the field for a few minutes before heading to the parking lot en route to Maria's, the finest pizzeria in town, serving up not only Queens quality delicious but notoriously gigantic slices that Rupert took with mushrooms for which the owner had devised a mystical cacophony of spices. A meat-headed father and his dejected son walked in the same direction, separated by a few meters from the champs.

"You know," he said, loudly enough to get all forty-six heads to turn towards him, Rupert's being the only one he was after.

"What's up?" inquired Rupert.

"That last hit was only a triple, the game was over when the kid in front of you scored." To date it remains the most petty comment he's heard someone utter, distinguished so as it came out of an adult and Rupert was eleven.

Babe Rupe grabbed his chin with his right thumb and pointer finger. "Oh, hmmm, I guess you're right. Thanks, mister. What did your son do, 0 for 4 with an error at second? I'll take the triple. We'll see you in the fall unless he realizes it's time to take up needlepointing, and if you don't force him to keep playing hardball anyways."

Rupert found the rage and embarrassment he'd created on the dude's face outstanding, and what in fuck was he gonna do, fight a kid, the momentary hero of the forty-five people surrounding him?

"Now get the fuck outta here, we're not going in that parking lot while you're behind the wheel you fuckin' psychopath. You heard me, take a walk!" And walk he did. "Way to humiliate your son right after he suffered a crushing loss," Rupe salted as the man distanced, his cleft chin one in defeat with his pulsating neck.

The pizza party was a gas, and from there Rupert began anxiously waiting for hair to begin growing at the base of his victorious dick.

Chapter 3

Pubescence

Oh yes it's me, and I'm walkin' in the rain
I'm lookin' for my baby, her name is Ida Jane
And if she don't come back today, I guess I'll pass away

The sun is shinin', but it rainin' in my heart
Because Ida Jane, ripped it apart
And if she don't come back today, I guess I'll pass away

I believe I'm losin', I'm losin' my mind
Because Ida Jane, she can't be found
And if she don't come back today, I guess I'll pass away

-Antoine 'Fats' Domino

"Who the fuck is that?" D'Shaundrius asked Rupert as they sauntered into the Van Cortlandtville gymnasium. What the fuck they'd walked in on was a precursor to five elementary schools merging into one middle school for 7th and 8th graders, a district organized roller-skating, basketball and dancehall ruckus held to allow the soon to be classmates an opportunity to look on and size up one another. A boy standing nearby them aimed to impress by way of the coincidence that his parents had bought a home in the same corner of the district as hers and provided them with an i.d. of Apollonia Stracciatelli. The girl had enormous breasts for a sixth grader, any earthly female human or otherwise in fact, and had worn a Dodger blue, frilly shirt that exposed the upper half of them. Late 80s and early 90s pop culture would inaccurately suggest this was a case of a girl showing up in more conservative garb and changing into a whore after her parents had departed, though Apollonia's parents were as committed to blood fueling hundreds of pubescent erections as she and had proudly purchased the article to service the iniquity. A family teeming with dirty birds they surely were. And she'd been chosen to make a big orgiastic mess out of everything.

By ninth grade she was well known and oft discussed as the premier whore in and beyond the district, to the practice surfaces of every basketball, football and lacrosse team Lakeland High opposed during her tenure. Playoff berths were bonuses paid out by Satan. She embraced this queening same as would a fella who'd been distinguished as a pussy magnet, with his throne and apartment sized bed and grapes and such. One could hardly exhaust a school day without turning a corner to find her squatted with a scattering of dicks in her face.

The only disposition that extinguished her cum lust was timidity, though any boy who could mask his or came to her without it was welcome to any and all of her nine holes. When a Lakeland team hit the road her postgame routine was to wait v-legged in the home team locker room, wearing nothing but her emblematic jeweled and crusted bra and panties, jumpy for a pre-modern, post-pornographic hecatomb with the soon to be bedeviled boys, stuffing as many shafts into as many holes as time and blood flow allowed for.

A vague though pre-plotted moment would come when the coaches, who stayed behind talking about local Chinese buffets until they grew impatient would enter the body filth strewn changing room for a brief, vaudevillian scolding of their players. Once the players exited, empty in every way, the coaches would feed their inescapable hunger and eat her poisonous parts all up. She enjoyed it fat and old just as much as she did young and virile, as long as they could plug the holes. Somehow D'Shaundrius, Rupert and their soon to be brand new favorite contemporary were individually and in outspoken solidarity suspicious and disgusted by the girl and pacted themselves to never fall to her sickly seduction.

Two months into the uncomfortable piddle of middle school Rupert became acquainted with a gent named Casimir Burnakowski. A full-blooded Polishman whose ancestral transpositions had impelled his boyhood as a shepherd rooted deep in the Dutch countryside, Caz and family had made the offbeat move straight to Yorktown two years earlier. As it were, Benny and the younger Burnakowski brother Robert were the same age and on a b-ball team together that late fall into winter. Rather than go food shopping with their mothers Rupe and Caz had each decided one evening to hang around and watch them practice. Had either a less mundane option who could know if they'd have ever even known each other. The first several times they chilled together Casimir wore a crisp, white, short sleeved button down stifled by suspenders which tugged aggressively at khaki knickers skimpy like a fatso zookeeper, though, incidental as it may be, he was and has remained a trim and muscular lad.

Entering 7th grade Rupert was still abundantly outgoing, his aberrant passel of interests and good humor endeared him to 'most every lineated faction of hyper-hormonal and secretly miserable kids in his grade. Casimir, who by Rupert's supposition was hardly more Americanized upon their acquaintance than he was the day that the Burnakowskis placed themselves and their homemade barge of quilted sheep corpses in the East River was his insular opposite, speaking very softly and holding no discernible stick. They attended their baby bros' practice weekly to hang out, every Wednesday Casimir's voice strengthening and sharp wit further giving itself away; even his eyebrows, translucent at the time of their acquaintance, began displaying a notably emboldened pigmentation.

As the two grew, got laid, went to and graduated from college together, Casimir would become the more social, stable, capable pea. He'd began wearing geographically conventional clothing shortly after the two met, as Rupert had delivered a logic laced testimony to his mother Daffodil, Daffy to those fortunate enough to claim her as a friend. He and the equally guarded D'Shaundrius quickly came to share a comfortable trust and Rupert introduced Casimir to anyone he felt was worth a good goddamn.

The pecking order turns over dramatically within a two grade middle school. In one intolerable year's time the students morph from trepidatious Halifax butterflies into menacing Alaskan wolverines. On the third day of eighth grade, empowered by the expansion of flesh and follicle inside his boxer shorts and atop a mountain of quivering 7th graders, Rupert came upon Apollonia in the hallway on his way to the bathroom and she engaged him in a genital-to-genital hug. Rupert can remember precisely where they stood and the density of students co-occupying the hollow, enough so that a discourse could be well heard and humiliating whilst dozens of heads too sparse to be drowned out by talk of mix tapes and handjobs. Rupert's shield was down by his waist as he enjoyed the initially innocent mirth of their conversation, failing to administer that imperative force field he'd confabulated with Caz and D'Shaun, leaving the Queen open to lubricate her larynx and swell the hall with what she couldn't have in a desolate or gilled passage, "how come every time I'm talking to you you stare ***straight at my tits?!"***

Rupert truly thought he hadn't been as he was compulsively fearful of inciting any girl in this manner and well aware of the implications and consequences. Whether he snuck a peek or not he couldn't tell you. With Kayiane, Grandma Miriam and Onyx his templates of womanly kindness, he couldn't handle the horrific cruelty and slander which had driven her to reduce his soul to mere merchandise. Quickly he gained a reputation as a creep who spent all day drooling over titties. He measuredly ensured not to see or if so talk to Stracciatelli for the remainder of the dewy school year. Since that moment of wicked, blasphemous harlotry Eleazer and I have eagle-eyed her every action.

When high school began Rupert anticipated a spot on the school's freshman basketball team and deduced that he'd be selected as the starting catcher on the JV baseball team. He'd taken to catching for the travel team pre-seventh grade, having recognized the direct relationship between the quality of play at the position and a team's success.

Throughout the summer and fall of '93 he and his friend Greg, who lived a block down Curry on Somerston, played gladiatorial one-on-on, Greg's driveway the exclusive battleground as his father had measured out the lane, free-throw and three point lines and painted them in. D'Shaundrius would often bike through and shoot around with them, though he'd soon begin their freshman year of basketball as the starting power forward for the varsity team and there wasn't much value in his taking a turn to play against either little white shrimpbag. Twice he whipped them two-on-one but as he considered Rupert his brother he didn't wanna show him up again after that and held his visits to a purely spectatorial capacity.

Greg was undoubtedly the most competitive friend Rupert's ever had. He was also a Duke fan, and played like it. He would drill three after three and most of the time beat Rupert to 21 on the strength of converted threes, scored as two, alone. If Rupert was in the game towards the end he'd start calling touch fouls to fend off his approach. Greg knew a dozen ways to be Gerald Henderson to Rupe's Tyler Hansbrough. Pragmatic Rupert didn't mind losing to him several times a week, each time he improved and learned a little something, counting close games as a certain form of victory.

On two consecutive weekdays in October, Rupert found his stroke. He matched Greg three-for-three and on the Saturday prior had studied a microfilm on Hakeem Olajuwon at the Hart Library, his newfound knowledge enabling him to scoop and elude his shorter opponent in the post. Greg threw every cheat in his brainstem at Rupe on those two days but neither time were they enough.

After the first loss he brutalized and ruptured the adjacent screen door and its three hinges as he got to wailing at his sweet mother that she was a fucking asshole. The second time, once Rupert's clinching jumper from left of the key back-rimmed in Greg grabbed the ball and hurled it through one of four garage door windows, calm as Columbine. He then walked through the unscreened side door and into the garage, smashing window number two from the inside out. He was a smooth, groovy jazz cat revisiting the wilds to continue his evisceration. Rupert stuck around to witness the full act, and once the ball had again scudded outward to bombard the scrupulously devised half court with lethal litter he began descending the driveway, cautiously twisting his neck to relay 'alright man tough game I'll see you on the bus.'

Freshman tryouts were held at George Washington Elementary, the school's physical education teacher the head coach as well as the bench coach for the varsity baseball team. His first charge was to whittle down 33 boys, well more than half of them former students of his, to 15 or fewer. The man had a brain, demonstrating so several times during each afternoon's appraisal, though Rupert daydreamed that there must be some sort of semi-soft plastic detrimentally sequestering its lobes as often he'd slip into cognitive cunctation out of seemingly nowhere.

Tryouts went a week, every morning cuts were indicated by a shrunken list taped up in the high school locker room. The trials demanded more exertion than any Rupert had previously endured and Greg and he stunk up the Sauerstein residence with noxious ben gay every evening, barely able to climb stairs and sit at desks during the school day but willing the pains away when each afternoon's evaluation began.

On the final day of tryouts the list was already down to 15 and the boys basked in the satisfaction that they represented the freshman team as it would stand. Weary of the coach's manic idiocy and thus less willing to conclude so than the fourteen fellas one-kneeing the hardcourt beside him, Rupert busted his ass that afternoon, voraciously stealing the ball and slapping the backboard while converting subsequent breakaway layups, the coach thrice commending his efforts. Monday morning the final list of 14 squad members was taped in its place, Rupe's name having melted off of it over the weekend. He ripped it down and kicked out the back locker room doors on his way to G.W. to confront the man. He busted through and went to stand at the entrance to the gym, arms and legs tightly crossed, inviting concerned administrators and teachers to get the fuck out of his face while he waited for class to end. Before the little first graders were fully lined up and escorted away by their teacher Rupert stormed the guy and yelled "Hey!"

“What can I do for you?” he responded as if addressing a stranger.

“It’s too fucking late, you already did it! Follow me into your fucking office so we can sit and I’ll be less able to throw a haymaker across your temple.”

“Ok, so what’s the issue here?” the coach asked as he groaned into his chair, resting folded arms atop concentrated belly fat. His beloved hometown of Hazelwood provided half of the office’s decor along with remnants from a long career of high fivin’ silky haired kids.

“Why did you fucking cut me? You were down to 15 which was the line!”

“Well, ya know, I was just puttin’ the best team together, same’s I do evhry hyear.”

Rupert crumpled up the list, which he’d memorized as he power walked between schools, and threw it at him. “Open that up! Tell me how players 3, 7, 9, 11 and 13 are better basketball players than me!”

"Well, uh, they can rebound, pass, score, hard work,” he was so aloof and uninvested but were he an intelligent man he'd have identified the very real possibility that Rupert’s clenched, white-knuckled fists were primed to end his life throughout their conversation. “What in fuck are you saying? Tell me why any of them individually is a better asset to the team then I’d be!”

“Well assets are what makes a good team son.”

“If I was your son I would have shot you through the mouth as soon as I could manipulate a fuckin’ shotgun. Tell me this at least if you’re capable, do you see any commonality amongst those fuckin’ names?”

"What's that now son?"

"What if anything is the same about those five fuckheaded kids?!"

"They're all gonna be playin' fer ma squad?"

"You fuckin' redneck nepotist, I can't say for sure but I'm gonna go 89% definitely anti-Semitic son of a fuck, they all went to this elementary school where you sucked their fucking dicks for seven years. Gimme the list back. Now go rip your cock off." He stood and kicked his chair over the man's head, it clanged the wall behind him, ripping down a cork board that shed overlapping photographic baseball and soccer cards gifted to him by years of his former and in many cases once again student-athletes as it etched several lashes into his back on its way floorward.

Returning to school, he ran into Ms. Breaky and broke the situation down for her. She confided in Rupe to well knew what a dumbfuck the man was. She telephoned him that night and told him he may want to watch himself, as she'd most definitely be.

So against expectations Rupert sleigh rode the winter away with Benny, soon enough fixating on the arrival of snow admonishing warmth, anxious to put the previous season's injustice behind him on his favorite field of play.

Baseball and lacrosse were the premiere sports at Lakeland High, every summer two or three outgoing seniors would head for Division I schools to play each on scholarship. The fields were immaculately well maintained and looked more suited for a college than a high school campus. At the close of tryouts Rupert was slotted as the starting JV catcher as he'd expected. Fortunately an otherwise retired and awesome motherfucker in his late 60s named Sontolizzi Graziano, Brooklyn born, ¼ Russian Jew and not one to be told what to do was in unencumbered charge of his squad and the bench coach was powerless to redoubt his personnel decisions or democracy.

The two squads shared the field for pre-season practices and the varsity coaches seared them to the marrow on that field, addending 20 weekday hours of practice with mandatory Saturday and Sunday morning masochism. Once the season began coach Graziano, who brushed his chin with the upside of his digits at the idea of working too hard on the weekends, was permitted to rescue his boys over to the middle school field for more jovial drilling, allowing their off days to remain much more so unstripped of youthful pleasure.

Two weeks after tryouts and four days prior to Opening Day the collective of hardballers were stretching near the right field fence. Working his hamstrings, Rupert recoiled and rose as several varsity players began talking of 'niggers' and 'spear-chuckers', including the first string, Dominican varsity catcher, which perplexed the fuck out of him. Having had almost no prior exposure to such wretchedness Rupe reached a rolling boil and began "are you FUCKING KIDDING ME! You're a bunch of fucking pieces of shit! I should get half of Harlem up here to Colombian necktie you motherfuckers! You think the Peekskill team is over there (he pointed West with his left phalanges) spewing bigoted nonsense or do you think they're talking about THE FUCKING GAME!"

He turned and pointed at the coaches, who'd been chatting about hamburgers until Rupert's booming voice re-focused their attention.

"And you two fucking sympathizers. I know you hear this! And you say NOTHING! You're representatives of this team, of the district!" He began throwing each article of his catching gear at them, cleats and socks included, hitting the bench coach in the face with his mask, liberating a sizeable chunk of cells from his alcoholic nose.

Turning back towards the racist upperclassmen, he continued "I'm not playing on the same field as you fucking philistines!" They all, other than Rupert's crow-hopping friend Tony and the no. 2 varsity catcher Tim, who years later would become head coach of the Varsity, looked the word up after practice. Typically, what separates the philistines from the sophisticates is whether or not a person goes for a dictionary after being called one. Rotating back towards the coaches, he concluded "I'll go see what Breaky thinks about all this." He scooped up his catcher's mitt and commenced in a slow and casual strut towards the main office, whistling a trilled up rendition of 'Imagine' as he did so. No one but he said a word throughout his lecture nor until he was well out of sight.

Ms. Breaky was an energetic, squat woman, sweet and upbeat, the best administrator Rupert ever knew, and happened herself to hang out with a primarily brown and black crowd. She was enraged upon hearing of their disgraceful negligence and armed with a file chronicling the indiscretions of the two strictly titular educators pulled every string she could and removed them from their posts. Practice was cancelled for a week as she located a couple of hard-hittin' niggas to take their place. Rupert joined the tennis team the Monday following his screams of amplified rage and distortion on the baseball field and fit in immediately, there being a blue whale sized gap between the intellectual timbre of the two organizations.

When he was a sophomore Isaac joined what was known as the site-based team, a collective of students, teachers, parents and administrators who met once a week to discuss and resolve issues of concern to the school community. He and Ms. Breaky became fine friends which secured for his son a sort of untouchable status. She'd always been charmed and impressed with Rupert too, equally fond in fact of both Sauerstein men. By his junior year Rupert had made his way onto the list of the school's 'Top 5 Deviants,' or anyway he would have should such a list have existed. Many years later Isaac confessed to Rupert that he'd joined the site-based team in case one of his sons was stuck with a lousy teacher or trajected them self towards trouble-making. When some churchy would report him for being LSD-25'd up during school or he was found off campus buying weed, she treated him, fairly or not, with extreme leniency, a wink and a corporal tap of her pinky upon his wrist penalized his most mis-allegiant activities.

On the eighth of April, 1994, Kayiane picked Rupert up from tennis practice and needed to make a brief stop at her office on the way home. While Rupert waited for his mom to return he reached to change the radio station to k-rock, unaware that when he got there the chemistry of his brain would undergo a wretched, permanent rearrangement. As he reached 92.3 on the dial the jockey was spewing a-grammatical though painfully informative clichés.

Nirvana was Rupert's fuckin' jam, Kurt Cobain the coolest person he'd ever seen or heard. Donny Baseball had a sweet swing, Fats Domino an unmatched ability to sing all cute and joyfully about offing himself, but neither nor any other changed the way Rupert viewed or interacted with the world. When Rupert and Kayiane returned home, Benny and a friend were playing basketball on the driveway and shot poorly delivered versions of the already circulating suicide jokes at Rupert as he sorrowfully ignored them en route to his bedroom. By infinities it was the most upset he's ever been with his baby brother. He refused to go to school, rotationally blasting Nirvana's Sub Pop and Geffen albums and the 15 disks he'd accumulated from independent record stores, at that time still more than a decade from their extinction.

He'd fought against a dark though conventional and universal set of doldrums before facing that moment of disbelief, but true depression and tenuous faith settled in that afternoon with every intention of sticking around. 14 ½ saccharine spins soaked with fondness for world and self-purged like a super-saturated sea sponge yanked from the deep and as swiftly sliced from bottom to top, he was now hip to the idea that maybe he too should just motherfuckin' die. Good days were ahead, though not many, and in Rupert's mind each one dissolved far more quickly than it had coagulated.

He couldn't capably cough up a word for a dozen days after Kurt's death was discovered. The most he could empower himself for was an occasional hug from Kayiane or Isaac. To hear anyone say something about Kurt rendered him murderous, he felt he was the only one who had the right to speak of him, though he was temporarily incapable anyhow. Tennis was off, as was the rest of the school year. Ms. Breaky secretly allowed him to take his Regents Exams in a storage room adjacent to her office.

He harvested a granule of happiness in realizing People magazine, which his otherwise well-read mother held a subscription to, hadn't covered his death; he saw that vile publication and Kurt as in polar disconnect. Had he not loved his mother more than the idea of throwing the thing in the river every week before she received it he surely would have. Collecting the mail on the 27th he pulled the mailbox post from the ground and kicked it's longhouse face in upon discovering that two weeks too late the contemptible periodical had gotten around to addressing the cataclysm. As Rupert stormed inside he held the thing as high as he'd once held Freddy. He frisbee'd the junk mail onto the counter as he stormed the kitchen and wrestled Kayiane's focus from preparation of baked ziti with vodka sauce and crumbled sweet sausage. She readied herself to eardrum every decibel of Rupert's capably booming vocal chords.

"Look ma, look at Wade Newton's plastic fuck of a new wife in the photo at the top right corner! Look more closely and see the fucking shoulder puffs on her awful fuckin' dress. Dissect even more meticulously and notice that the right fucking frill obstructs a strand of Kurt's hair. And I know this picture of Kurt, look how fuckin' red they made his eyes, I'd kill the sensationalist motherfucker who smeared that shit on him!"

He fastballed the rag against the far wall of the hallway. Retrieving it he returned to the kitchen and continued.

"Wade fuckin' Newton ma! He sings like a little fuckin' asscunt!"

"He does sing like a little asscunt hunny," she tried comforting him with the gentle tone she'd used an ancient decade earlier when for example the peroxide might sting a little but it would fix his boo-boo, though as you may have deduced by now Rupert is sparsely damaged by physical injuries. The magazine never made its way into Kayiane's possession, Rupert couldn't relinquish anything that depicted him, not even that thing, and he stashed it away. When he read the article he found the words 'drugs, heroin, suicide and overdose' 34 times among its artlessly scribed captions and paragraphs. 'How did Kurt become a more misunderstood joke than me?' he sat excogitating. He wanted everything to wilt and die. A month later the magazine stopped showing up in the Sauersteins' replacement mailbox.

Since Onyx's far roam Rupert had nursed a connection with The Honorable Elijah Woodhall, neighbor to the Sauersteins since they'd moved two houses down Stonewall from him. When Rupert was nine

Elijah showed him how to throw a splitter and over the years he couriered him thru the harrowing struggles which inspired the Delta Blues. A month and change after kc'd left him fissured Elijah called Rupert on a Sunday afternoon and asked him to come over, which was unusual, unprecedented actually.

Elijah was 93 at the time of the call, and going a couple of years back from there he and Rupert had two standing appointments every week, Wednesday evenings at 6:30 and Saturdays at noon. On Wednesdays Rupert would tidy up Elijah's house, make a quick fix to the hinge on his dryer, attend to the gamut of minor household wears and imperfections. Once everything was orderly they'd share dinner, usually barbeque or Chinese delivery. Every Saturday Rupert would start the 3.8 mile round-trip to the Corner Deli at 10:15 and execute an exacted list of groceries for his dear friend and like-minded muse. The only time they'd speak on the telephone was if for some reason Rupert needed to arrive a little early or late, or if though rare he was off on a roam and couldn't make it.

"Rupert, I have something that I planned on leaving to you when I'm gone, but why wait until then when instead I can enjoy handing it off to you now and we can discuss it a bit?" Elijah bent delicately to his right and began scraping what sounded like a hard-shelled suitcase across the wood planks of the dining room floor. With every utilitarian ounce of arm muscle he then placed what Rupert recognized as an entombed acoustic guitar on the table. Inside was a masterpiece which relegated Mr. Miyagi's gift to Daniel Son to the status of a moisturizing cream and salt sandwich.

"Rupe, I've owned this sweet beauty since your momma and daddy were in grade school, the one inanimate of mine that has ever been worth more than the sum of its parts."
The sunburst, familiar looking broad had stylized f-shaped holes on her sides, one partially covered by a black pickguard with white trim.

"Do you recognize this machine Rupert?"

"I'm not sure. I've seen pictures of B.B. King playing a similar lookin' one, but his was made by Lucille I think.".

"Well, your slightly misguided understanding allows for a better discussion. It's the same brand and type of pistol B.B fires, but he was so in love with these guitars that they became like women to 'im and Gibson customized several as per his request with 'Lucille' fashioned in a more elaborate lettering than stock editions like this one. I purchased this masterpiece in 1958 Rupert, the Gibson Electric-Spanish three-hunnid 'n' therty-fie, the most perfect instrument ever constructed, maybe tied with the Stradivarius for that distinction. My boy this peach hasn't once lost her exquisite action, you could leave her to dust over for ten years and she'd remain perfectly in tune. You can play whatever style of music you damn well please on her, she can hum every tone and at any intensity. Now my amplifier blew it's top over 25 years ago, and you ain't gonna argue with me now, you take this thousand dollars and have yo daddy drive you down to the Guitar Center, and I want you to buy a Roland Blues Cube BC-60, a few coiled metal cords, a case of strings with 10mm first and wound g strings, a mess of I'd suggest medium picks, and whatever effects you desire with what you have left. Ok?"

"Jesus Elijah, you don't have someone in your family you wanna give it to? You know I never wanted anything from you for helping you out a bit, that I get as much, I get more out of our visits then you do, right?"

"I do my boy, I do. As you know my sweet Ida Jane and I never had any children, and the only blood I suspect I have left is swamped away in the Bayou somewhere; you're all I've got, and how lucky I am to have you. Now I don't want you to just play this guitar, I want you to learn everything about its origins and its history, ok Rupe?"

"Of course Elijah, every printed word. You know if you had called an hour later my dad and I would have been on the way to Sam Ash to buy a Squier Strat and whatever cords and amp fit into the $125 I saved up and he matched for me. Jesus, thank you so much Elijah, I'm overwhelmed."

"You are so very welcome Babe Rupe my boy." Elijah had anointed Rupert with that nickname, tossing him the ball and gigglin' like Muddy Waters years before. Rupert helped Elijah to his feet and kissed his left cheek as they wrapped necks.

"Rupert, I love you ya know."

"I love you too Elijah, we shoulda told each other that a long time ago."

"Well it's on the record now child, and that's all that matters, we just retroactively applied it to every time either of us has thought it."

As they untangled, Rupert asked if there was anything he needed done in the house.

"Rupert you was just here yesterday, I'll be ok 'til Wednesday. What I want is for you to hitch a ride down to Larchmont with yo daddy, you remember what ta buy yourself now?, and when you get back I want you to start addin' finger resin to that sassy little chick's neck, understood?"

"Understood. I'll bring the set-up by on Wednesday and show you, I don't know, something."

"Terrific, I can't wait. Perhaps I'll pick out a little number for ya, if I still got one tockin' around. That is if you don't mind me puttin' my hands on yo lady."

"From now on that'll be your privilege, yours alone."

"I appreciate that Rupert. Now you go get whatcha need and start kickin' some dicks off, ya heard."

"I heard ya Elijah, thank you, well, I can't even say how much, from here to the Heavens."

"My most absolute pleasure Rupert, I'll see you on Wednesday."

"Thank you from the recesses of my soul Elijah, yes I'll see you then."

"Ok my boy."

Prior to that afternoon Rupert had fucked around with Isaac's '63 ocean turquoise and tort Jaguar here and again, itself a beautiful beast, though mostly before his hands had become big enough to stretch beyond two of her frets or finger all of her six strings at once. Isaac was almost jealous but far more so thrilled for his son when Rupert walked in with the '58 Gibson and when they returned from the Guitar Center he patiently showed his son how to configure a starter kit of major and minor chords and scales. His man sized drum kit, a Bar Mitzvah gift from Johnny Slapshaft, remained untouched between Sunday and Wednesday as he learned how to play and sing the melodies at the heart of "Drain You."

When Rupert went to see Elijah on Wednesday he was laid out, arms folded, in the small room at Clark's Funeral Home, the population of which the Sauersteins doubled. Elijah had been anxious to share his interpretation of "Nobody loves Me but my Mama, and She Could be Jivin' Too" with his favorite young man that day. Rupert held his hand for a few moments as he admired the sagely, loveable nuances of his face one last time. He placed the baseball Elijah had taught him to throw a splitter and for which Kayiane had bought him a clear cubic case beside his dear friend and sat with his family to hear the kind words that Minister Isaiah, Elijah's other close and implicitly entrusted friend, spoke to his many admirable years and accomplishments, the most devilish anecdotes never previously relayed to his dear Rupert, whose youthful innocence he'd forever coveted. He hadn't let it show but seeing the cancerous disillusion which stole Rupert's spirit in an eighth note a month earlier pained Elijah so irrevocably that it had torn open his heart and siphoned several months from his lifetime.

As that most miserable freshman year had finally been fucked off and overnighted to Hades, Rupert had navigated second through 9th grade with degraded spirit and without intimacy. His one-way soul was so ardent that there remained only one girl he wanted to kiss, only one who could have prescribed the perfect opiate for his intensifying pain.

Chapter 4

Intercoursing and Alternative Ejaculations

You could get yourself off to your favorite song, I can betcha honey that it won't take long
When the song's over and you've blown your mind, I could call you up and I could get you off

Get you off, get you off. would ya baby baby I could get you off
Get you off, get you off all nite long and I won't get soft

I can rock 'n' rolla, faster than a motor, I could shoot you up and I can get you off
I could smoke-a lightnin' all nite long, all the young girls can come along, yeah

(refrain)

You knock me down, ya step on my face, I could shoot you up and I could get you off
When you wake up got nothin' ta do, I can give it to ya like ya want me to

(refrain)

-Bobby Harlow

On July 17th of 1994 Rupert hopped a flight to Hartsfield-Jackson where Onyx awaited was awaiting, jittering and clutched to Xaviera's elbow a few feet from gate T9, in all-consuming anticipation of his arrival. The Jamaican lovebirds had dedicatedly regenerated themselves for one another by way of photographs upon notable experiences, haircuts and wardrobe upgrades spanning their eight years apart. Reassuring and pleasurable as each obtained photo had been they were unquantifiable with the real, fleshy thing. They'd been missing each other daily at lunch and bed times.

They hadn't allowed even a weekend of disconnect, Onyx had called Rupert the morning after the family put wheels on Georgia. They spoke on the phone enough to pump up each family phone bill hundreds a month, though their parents were happy to budget for it, straight thru since the Grahams' devastating mid-summer, pre-second grade departure.

For the first few years Rupert had sent her original recordings of love songs to reel, his expressive little voice double tracked, Isaac laying bass and guite over Rupert's tiny kit of Pearls and Zildjians. Upon graduation from Brooklyn College Johnny Slapshaft, lead guitarist for The Blue Wails, had opened an independent music store in East New York called *Give it Yur All or Go Sit on Yur Balls*, and had conjointly given Rupert the set as a sixth birthday present after he'd requested one of Isaac and Isaac asked Johnny to place the special order. They met the band's drummer 'Uncle' Elmore Adonica at the store the following two Sundays and after Johnny flipped the sign and lock Elmore gave Rupert two hours of masterful tutelage in the studio while Isaac and Johnny reminisced and picked out a few of their jams in the store.

Rupert then brought the kit home and played it daily inside a family made studio forged simply from thick foam, fashioned with a door, and placed in the far corner of the Sauerstein basement. Rupert was fortunate to have gained this interest when he did, as it had him ready enough to keep close to metronomic timing before sweet Onyx sailed away. Where his timing missed a little Isaac would obscure it thru crafty production and manipulation of the ten strings he used to help his son hold his old lady sentimentally tight.

The weekend following the second lesson grandpa Oscar was up in the northern Westchester woods visiting the fam, killing it for the boys with his unfiltered hilarity. While the boys were young his gramps enjoyed telling Rupert he was 'his favorite oldest gran'son of da nawth', as his other grandchildren were spread throughout the deep south in Staten Island and lower Yorktown, and as if 'favorite oldest grandson' wasn't a distinction that ate out its own meaning like a sarcastic ouroboros. There are many items in grandpa Oscar's bag of wackiness and his quick wittedness is unparalleled, one of many things that bonded Rupert and his grandfather so spectacularly thru the years; in no one else would he ever find such a kindred spirit. He and Elijah had been similarly likeminded, though as it goes whilst Rupert loved Elijah to death there's a Dead Sea sized gap between the power of association and blood.

Rupert's reverentially called him gramps since he was eleven and nowadays he proudly gramp's eleven grandchildren. He's spent three fold more time alone with Rupert than the 10 others as a collective, made possible by Rupert's age and, later on, his professional status. He visited him jocundly every time he did so, not once did he turn down Oscar's invitation to lunch or dinner at one of their favorite joints and if his proposed slot found Rupert busy they'd choose the next best one.

Though there came a time when jokes about Rupe being his favorite ceased, Oscar's such a kooky, honest, Hell of a man, that if he flat out spoke every truth it would be known that Rupert was more specifically his favorite grandchild, something well suspected by Isaac, Kayiane and all other adults on both sides of the family. Il Bambino Primo, unequivocally special to every family in the world blessed with one, Rupert and Oscar are wholly aligned on all matters philosophical, their souls and personalities conjoined by an unfettered genetic leapfrog.

A month after god decreed Rupert's manhood, Oscar did something he'd sworn he'd never do - suburbanize. Rupert had made an impassioned plea to that aim as he lit his gramps' reverential candle during his Bar Mitzvah *simkhe* at Crystal Bay Seafood. That was all it took, it erased every sub-molecule of Oscar's apprehension. He didn't move across the hall from grandma Miriam as Nava would have insisted, the apartment was occupied anyway, (grandma Nava would have used her beauty and graceful charisma to get the current occupant to swap places) settling on a bungalow in another of the many Jefferson Village enclaves.

In the course of four hours of kickin' jerks in the dick with Elmore it had for whatever reason occurred to Rupert that while most of the people the family knew were white he and his dad both had black best friends. He asked Oscar if by chance his best friend was black too.

"Nah Rupe, my best buddy was a Jewish fella, from Cuba. Dark as night though. Ya' grandma Nava's best friend in high school was a black goyl from Brownsville, a Jewish goyl and a black goyl strollin' tha avenoo tugetha' in da '30s wasn't somethin' ya really saw, unless gramma and Anita wuh togetha', which they always wuy, when ya' beau'iful grandma wasn't wit' me anyhow. Neitha' gave a shit what was said about it, the whisperin', people with a problem didn't exist ta' them. Yaw grandmutha' was da only whitey at Anita's wedding, hu maiduv hona', I would have made two had I not been in the soy-vis. She sent me a postcard aftawoyds and asked when I was gonna loin ta dance like da bruddas. I told hu she should jus' be thankful I was hung like one."

One of his trademarks thru the years was to feign anger and/or psychosis to juice up his punchlines. A couple of decades passed and Rupert, Benny and he were at the Colonial Diner for dinner where gramps was on an absolute tear, still, a month shy of his 88th birthday. Rupert spent a third of the time they were together that mid-August early evening in hysterics, one particular riposte Oscar lent to a curiosity of Rupert's has charmed and cheered him every time he's recalled it since. Rupe. was wearing a seasonally inappropriate, thickly knit long-sleeved St. Petersburg t-shirt from one of the thrift stores on 23rd between 2nd and 3rd, as to obscure his open-wounded, caricatured jsbx Theremin tattoo, and it prompted him to ask his adored kindred spirit:

"Gramps, I was thinking, I've never known I don't think, where in Russia was your family from?"

"Right on da kawna dayah!"

A more witless grandpa with parents who hailed from the same spot would have answered Minsk, which Oscar did just the same once Rupert calmed down some. The following week he was on the phone with his Uncle Sele, with whom he's also notably like-minded, Isaac's little bro by 6 days shy of three years, and asked if Oscar ever voiced a distaste or disappointment as concerned his several tats.

"No he never gave a shit, he voiced his unrelentingly honest opinion about why each was kind of stupid of course, but as far as the Jewish cemetery thing he couldn't give a fuck. What the Hell does it matter what happens to my, or your, or anyone's body after we're dead? Feed me to a polar bear before I spoil for all I care. What's the tat you got?" Rupert explained it, and Uncle Sele checked out the cover of Orange on his tabla-pod. "That's pretty cool, I'll check these guys out."

"You definitely should, they're fuckin' awesome. I changed the color scheme a bit…. I feel the same way. If we in fact have a soul it's not inside us by then anyway, someone decided for everybody else a long time ago. And what the fuck, the Nazis tattooed dead Jews and now live ones are supposed to let that dictate whether or not they get 'em. Seems a bit counterintuitive. My grandma

Miriam was cremated when she passed in March, and she's more like a God, more a source of inspiration to me than anyone else ever could be. The second my mom told me she was being cremated I decided I knew I wanted that too.

"Ah Rupe, your grandmother truly did have a wondrous, extraordinary spirit. She was a saint, more than worthy of the distinction I'd say. I'll probably be cremated too. Far less morbid that way, why not see people for the last time while they're all nice and warm and organic."

"Yeah. She was the best. I blow her picture a kiss like every day, cry for her probably once a week. I'll show gramps the tat next time I see him and tell him it's a device used during World War I to determine which herds of Australian cows were real and which were German engineered imitation cattle designed to be puzzled together to form an Ostend Carrier Pigeon Detachment. I'll let you know what he's got to say about it when we meet on Wednesday, that Mexican place on Avenue A I was telling you about, ok?, midway between 9th and 10th on the west side of the street."

"Sounds good kiddo. I love you."

"I love you too. See you then."

"Yessir. have a good night."

"You too Uncle Sele."

That conversation rather well sums up the perspective common to the folks on both sides of the family as concerns arbitrary convention, every one of 'em kind, loving and spiritual, in a way uniquely their own. Oscar for instance grew up Orthodox and spoke mostly

Yiddish in his childhood home, but in the 35 years previous to this parlay had only been to temple to see his grandkids Bar and Bat Mitzvah'd. In Rupert's mind they're all gonna make it into heaven and he's gonna be the one asshole in Hell but I see it differently, biased though I may be.

The first affectionate composition he wrote for his sweetheart was a tuneful little number he named "*Onyx (that girl's a roamin')*," and she reciprocated with what was once a plain sheet of printer paper, now centered with a smack of lipstick, blockaded by flowing string and a curvature of block letters in oil pastel comprising a necklace that read "I LOVE YOU RUPERT LOVE ONYX."

Each was moved and more in love with the other upon arrival of these first gifts, which rank highly in sentiment and excellence within the catalogue of their creative correspondences, every one a tortured process as neither would send a less than superlative representation of their abilities, obsessing more tirelessly than artists with ambitions of getting every eyebag or earball world over on their work; no eyes were put on any of Onyx's work other than Rupert's and no ears got at Rupert's recordings besides Isaac's, his collaboration a touch that Onyx loved because she could feel it connect her a bit with all of the Sauersteins. Kayiane once offered to harmonize with her son but he tactfully explained that thanks but it was ok.

Thru the years the collective of Onyx's masterpieces floated between the outer limits of abstraction and reality. While her gifts were always in the form of two-dimensional, unaffected water or oil paintings, Rupert hit a songwriting lull between the late springs of '92 and '94 and chose instead to send forged, kilned and painted sculpturizations of animals from ancient and modern ages until primed and inspired to revisit the production of original recordings, made on his own to cassette from then on, using the trusty Tascam PORTASTUDIO 414mkII purchased with the $250 of his (and Isaac's) that he had in addition to the g Elijah gave him, prompted by a restored sonic impulse and Onyx's mention that she missed popping in fresh tunes and bathing them in.

They'd spent all of Isaac's reel-to-reel, and while he'd offered to buy more for his son, even though it had become quite expensive as availability thinned, Rupert said he wanted to switch to cassette, his real reason for turning down his dad's generous offer because he'd begun fashioning songs that were so revealing and blatantly intimate that he didn't even want Isaac to hear them. Plus he'd become capable enough on the three core instruments to lay down and engineer his own tracks, which he expected would further impress the only girl he'd ever aspired to.

Rupert knew before his visit that Zane had accepted an executive position with his former company in Treasure Beach and as such the Grahams were headed back to Jamaica five weeks after their reunification. Onyx and he believed themselves reconciled to this, really it was irrelevant they thought, the only thing of current consequence being that one week of time together, two months beyond Onyx's 15th birthday and two other ones before Rupert's.

From the moment plans had begun to be made for the trip Xaviera with Zane and Kayiane with Isaac began discussing exactly how to play the long-awaited reunion, as Onyx and Rupert hadn't seen each other for 8 years and were now, Onyx notably more than Rupert, through the out door of puberty. Xaviera and Kayiane would then get on the line and share each set of perspectives. They all well recognized that the two ached with love for each other and that their dedication while separated by 900 miles for so long was a beautiful thing. I don't need to tell you what terrific, nurturing parents all four had been to their children every day of their now not so little lives. The day before Rupert smashed clouds Xaviera and Kayiane concluded their depositions.

When Rupert and Onyx caught each other by the retinae at the airport both time-travelled back to the Mahopac A&P, August 20th, 1984, 2:17 p.m. She ran to him faster than a speeding baby Benny and jumped into his arms, wrapping her legs around his waist, kissing him passionately, lips ready to burst, pulling her head back momentarily so they could examine each other anew; they then started sucking on each other's lips and tongues with such urgency and barbarism that an ill-informed onlooker may have feared doomsday had just entered the atmosphere. Standing 20 feet away, where a moment before Onyx had held her in anticipation, Xaviera waited until she could no longer and yelled "Ok Onyx time to get down baby!"

Down she came, just as obedient to her mother's wishes as she was as a little girl, grabbing Rupert's hand as she let out a lustful 'oooh', pulling him towards momma Graham, still as striking, perhaps with a few new pounds for Zane to leverage.

"Oh lord Rupert you're a man!" she was delighted to witness and express this inevitability. "Come here baby I've missed you too," she confessed, planting a cherry red impression on his cheek and grabbing him up, licking her thumb and removing the bold impression she'd made on his fair skin after letting him go. "What's this now?" she giggled, pulling a 13 pronged tortoise shell afro pick from his curls, which ran wilder than they ever before had.

Onyx grabbed the pick from her mother, tossing Rupert's curls like an orange bean sprout salad for twelve and as she replaced it she kissed him, soft and sweet. They sat holding hands and commiserating in the backseat as Xaviera navigated towards the Graham residence in Castleberry Square, parts Tudor, Colonial, and Medieval estate, separated from the boulevard by a serpent of cobblestones.

Zane and Amoya sat enjoying leftover brisket and hush puppies as the three came through the inner garage door, Zane quickly napkinning his lips and fingertips and hustling over to welcome Rupert with a warm handshake and hug. Amoya was still the apprehensive little girl Rupe remembered her to be, only now a beautiful 12 year old instead of a precious tadpole cheeked toddler. Recognizing he should initiate their reunion Rupert stepped up to her, took hold of and kissed her still soft left hand.

"Amoya, look at you, if only I was a couple of years younger," he aped from he couldn't quite remember who. Amoya blushed and swung her right leg over her left as Onyx smacked Rupert's right shoulder with the back of her left hand.

Onyx no longer wore an afro, rather her hair was dead straight and threatened to undercut her bellybutton, all her own, all Rupert's. She was spiced with cocoa butter from toes to nose and wore the homemade Blues Explosion Theremin t-shirt he'd made two of with a pair of jeans Xaviera bought in Kingston in 1973 and had recently bequeathed to her. As this isn't *Lolita*, I'll simply relay Rupert's interior opinion that she had not a single cell in place he'd endeavor to rearrange; he wouldn't have traded this long awaited reunion for an eternity of menaging Ms. Goodridge and Rihanna.

"Ok, well, the fridge is stocked, there are important numbers and some cash on the table, we're gonna get going ok you two." Onyx's face grew astutely rhapsodic as Xaviera offered this partial and entirely unexpected info.

"Get going where, momma?

"We didn't tell you?," Zane interjected, "we're taking Amoya to Disney for the week, you're welcome to come."

Onyx flashed a wry, devilish smile at her father as Rupert commanded his erection to grow up into the waistband of his boxers rather than directly towards the Grahams.

"I guess not," Xaviera confirmed what she needn't. "We'll be back in time to take you to the airport ok Rupert?"

"Um, yes, fly, thanks Xaviera, fly time."

Amoya hugged her big sister goodbye and gave Rupert an unexpected kiss on the cheek. Xaviera momma-bear'd them 'round their reconstituted shoulders and kissed their closest dimples. The roamin' female Grahams headed through the inner garage door as Zane walked up and pecked his cherished baby girl on the forehead. He shook Rupert's hand and said "It's wonderful to see you Rupert, I suppose we'll catch up when we return."

"Yes Zane, yes, return it twice," Rupert failed to up the quality of his hormone demented syntax.

Halfway across the kitchen he opened the oven mitt drawer and pulled out a 25 pack of lubricated Trojans, lofting them into Rupert's hands. "What are you gonna do if these run out?"

"Buy more daddy," answered Onyx, too zealous to be embarrassed.

Stupefied Rupert was about to offer a reply of 'pull out?' but luckily Onyx buzzed in first.

"Good girl, baby. You two understand that your parents adore you and collectively decided that this was deserved, you're not getting away with anything, your devotion to each other needed be rewarded."

"Ok thanks Zane, buy more," Onyx smacked Rupert's shoulder once again.

"My man. Bye sweetie."

"Goodbye daddy. Thank you."

"Thank you baby," Zane echoed, venerating the fifteen years of sweetness and love his daughter had drenched him with, further thankful that somehow there existed a boy who he wanted to take her virginity. As he moved through the doorway Onyx ran to the bay window and waited to watch her daddy's vintage Mustang cobra backwards down the driveway and redirect out of sight. As she did so, Rupert stared at her curvaceous figure, mesmerized by the shape it made as she put both knees on the cushioned bench of the bay, her back arched towards the glass, her perfect waist and hips pushed out and at him and her canary yellow toenails wiggling just below the ledge. 'I hope she knows what to do.'

Not thru experience, rather ancient instinct, she did.

During their first hours alone they rested upon each other in front of the television, chatting intermittently, sharing an ingrained comfort that kept the silences from being all too unhinging. If they didn't know that soon enough something momentous would happen there'd have been no unease a'tall.

Onyx wanted her man to make the first move, Rupert knew it. He seared his brainstem, begging it for some sound advice. Gingerly grabbing her by the waist, his pinkies resting on her hipbones, he began kissing and gently sucking on her neck. A moment later they were face to face, straddling each other, Onyx's legs upon Rupert's and bent at the knees. What they did all week was certainly not fuck. Four days in they went out to re-up on the Trojans.

When they woke up beside each other that final morning they got moving immediately, quickly toasting some frozen blueberry waffles and retreating to Onyx's private bathroom to make love in the shower for the 5th time out of 48 rapturous entanglements. They dressed with scrambled emotions and composed themselves with enough time to make out a little as 'Dynamite Lover' blasted before Zane, Xaviera and Amoya came through the door rockin' Mr. Toad's Wild Ride t-shirts.

Rupert shared tender and authentic hugs and words of farewell with Xaviera and Amoya as Zane retreated to restart the car, taking Rupert's luggage with him in patriarchal fashion. Onyx and he followed, dragging their feet on approach to the death chambre, by which of course I mean the airport. It took but a speck of Zane's tact and intellect to pre-assess the melancholy he was to chauffeur, rattling off a thousand notions of affected cheer to Rupert who sat at the back right and his beloved Onyx who'd seated herself in the middle, her head on his shoulder, their hands interlocked upon his lap.

Zane issued his handshake, hug and warm wishes to Rupert as they entered the vacuum of Terminal B and then remained planted where he stood, opportuning his sad little daughter a last hand held walk alone with their favorite young man. When they reached security they shared what they both sensed was their final embrace and she kissed his forehead as softly as a mother would her baby, washed, bundled, and returned, their hearts way down in their knees. Rupert dumped his bag on the conveyor belt and ached his way undetected through the plastic precipice, angling slightly to his right and crossing the hallway to gate B17. The stream of tears widened upon Onyx's creamy skin with his every step. His boarding pass and heart conjointly ripped in two he put one salty eyeball on her as the jet bridge angled him out of view.

Rupert telephoned right after he and Isaac arrived at home though not again until Onyx's return to Hartsfield-Jackson en route to Treasure Beach. They continued to correspond, and Onyx stayed true, though the virtuous puppy love that'd overheated their hearts for a decade now felt as remote as were Treasure Beach and Yorktown.

Sophomore and junior year expired sexlessly as Rupert sought out alternative stimuli but by the start of his final year of high school incarceration he couldn't help but try sticking it somewhere.

Prior to his senior year he'd only made music on his own, with Isaac, and on occasion as a member of various unreformed Blue Wails incarnations. A chance encounter behind the weed-smoking shed out back behind the Lakeland High annex led to the formation of a band of zingaros he'd give the name The Dirty Doses whilst their third slopped up jam session reached its atonal conclusion. Stoning himself there as Rupert arrived to do the same on the second Tuesday of the school year was Sweet Nicky, a dopey freshman who Rupert suspected to be a selective mute until he revealed his name in response to the sixth question Rupert blew in his direction.

As it were, Nicky was and undoubtedly still is the most fleet fingered and inventive six-stringer to ever redeye his way through a Lakeland corridor, Rupert got lucky to have as the catalyst and provider of the very vast majority of real quality that zoeticized his oeuvre. Together they enlisted Maxwell, a junior and transplanted Brit who could perform the tri-state's best Billy Corgan impression on the drums and Scrimmo , a 7'2" sophomore who tripped himself to the ground several times a song, on the bass. Perhaps their greatest fortune was that Scrimmo's always warm and inviting parents freed their souls to raze Hates in his bedroom after school and all the way up to suppertime.

Within a month they'd developed enough tone and chemistry that they were comfortable enough to enlist an audience, and the room was amply sized so that 3 or 4 petite females could hug their knees against the spare wall spaces unoccupied by the four anarchic burnouts, their equipment and thrashing. The cute little rock chicks in their school knew how nasty Sweet Nicky's playing was and were most commonly psyched to go watch them practice because of it. The girls bonobo monkied Rupert's libido and he began fearlessly inviting those amongst their audiences who most enticed him to walk his natural wood and smoke his skunky weed.

Though a qualified loser and psychopath in the capuchin do opinion of the majority of chicks and fellas at his school he was no exception to the rules of teenage intercoursing, established in the '50s, which ensures high school seniors who are capable of screaming, strumming a guitar and driving a car, no matter how well or whatever else rounded them out as a dude, can entice ripe rock 'n' roll 'n' cock crazed darlings to join them for a roll in the moss. As much as he enjoyed handling their supple, freshly formed bodies while making them cream and moan it amounted to nothing more than stoned carnality, the fleeting good times he shared with 11 white girls that year failed in amounting to a sense of authentic conquest, seldom did he look up or down at those girls while inside them without wishing they were Onyx instead. Only twice in fact has he truly been enamored with a white girl, one of whom's older than his mom and whose name he doesn't even know, the sweet-smiling and mesmerizingly groovy chick dancing with Noddy in the video for 'Take Me Bak 'Ome.'

A week and a Sunday before senior year was to begin Rupert was by his lonesome in the family room, watching the intense final moments of Se7en and the phone rang as Morgan Freeman readied to blade the box open. He paused the DVD and slid head first down the hallway just for fun to answer it in the kitchen.

"Hello?"

"Hey it's me."

"Hey, is everything alright."

"Yes, I'm ok Rupert but listen.....I've met somebody."

"Is he nice?"

"Yes silly, he's nice."

"Well then I'm glad. We knew one of us would someday."

"Promise me you'll find somebody too."

"You know that's not something I can promise, but for you I'll try. Give me another 17 years, ok?"

"You know I still love you deeply don't you?"

"I guess in asking me that you well know how in love with you I am and I imagine will always be?"

"Oh Rupert, if only we'd have stayed up there. You are the kindest, most wonderful boy ever."

"Well my beautiful Onyx, you're the sweetest Georgia peach ever picked."

"I love you, ok."

"I love you too. Bye Onyx."

"Goodbye Rupert."

They blew each other sad smooches and with delicate remorse replaced their handsets, ending transmission. Each would have begun to wail feverishly had they extended this colloquy. Though the Jamaican love-birds ached in that moment, theirs was a closure befitting their relationship, no regrets, no animosity, their fondness for each other petrified and placed in an impenetrable vault. A week and a day later a thin 22'x14' manila posting arrived with the mail, inside a Rockwellesque painting of them as precious little ones, all alone in the cereal aisle, bending at their waists, a milli-moment away from their first kiss.

The following Saturday morning Rupert and D'Shaundrius made a quick stop at JV Bagels and jumped south on the Taconic destined for a visit with D'Shaun's cousin Gates, whose great-grandparents had chosen against a move to New York with the majority of the extended Biddable family in the mid 1870s. 33 at the time of the visit, Gates had lived his entire life in downtown Charlotte until five years earlier a calamitous break from his Onyx hurt enough for him to leave his home behind forevermore, baring down in an unincorporated, unknown to the outside haven north of Cherryville, first settled by a faction of exiled Baptists. Utilitarian wooden homes, a sky scraping, steepled church, preciously archaic shops filled with every home grown, slaughtered and woven essential, surrounded by natural hillsides from which they harvested some of the finest ginseng in all of Appalachia. Rupert was sure it was a place where he could enjoy killing a few decades.

He was met with handshakes and hugs as Gates took them along their first country bird passage through town. Metered wind gusts produced euphoric melodies, percussing the leaves and newly sprouted branchlets which outlined the Utopia. As quiet and unassuming as the town remained between Monday morning and Sunday afternoon, the sweet quietude mutated into balls-out church-pine stomping and inebriated barbeque gnashing beginning with Reverend Mookie's first invocation and ending whenever it was that the last man's legs gave out and his cheek flattened against the trampled grasses out back of the church. The preacher, bigger than Otis and more debonair than Sam, a pitch perfect growl more powerful than Pickett's, commanded the stage more hypnotically than any of them. The backup band could best be described as Stax meets The Sonics.

Two prerequisites for residency had been set at the time of incorporation. Newcomers had to be invited to join the community by someone who had lived there harmoniously for 3 years or more and must hold atheistic and naturalistic beliefs coupled with a reverence for their ancestry and empathy towards the struggles of any and all of the world's downtrodden peoples. As had Gates, the other 279 residents of the commune had chosen to leave the suffocating capitalism and overt racism of the lower 48 behind for the recondite backwood, anti-christened Mount Dope by the Cracklin brothers and Shiny Arbuckle, mashed up and cannabis maddened as the sun rose over July 25th, 1937.

Reverend Mookie had fathered eleven children since his arrival in July of 1983, ten boys and his youngest a girl, who would you believe it just so happened to come online sexually the morning the boys arrived. She had stayed in bed making ovular orbits with her middle and pointer fingers inside her pussy and as to distract her daddy as little as possible with her late entry to the temple she tiptoed into the nave, sitting at the far back right, grazing Rupert's curls with the crown of her feathered, sky blue wide-brimmed Sunday best hat as her electric ass met with the pine pew.

Rupert had never talked to a Southern girl before, in fact of all places in the world the only one Isaac had ever cautioned him against visiting was the Deep South. But he'd always been smitten with the accent, adorably, painfully sexy if it came out of the right mouth, and had massive curiosity beyond what he'd learned from Elijah about what must surely be the most polarizing, creatively lush and tragic place and time in human history, that of the American Southeast in the 20th century. Jim Crow and the Ku Klux Klan proliferating alongside some or most of the best rock 'n' roll and R&B ever made. MLK and James Earl Ray, Muscle Shoals and the segregated lunch counter across the street. But he couldn't do much about that now and her pheromones had landed him with a gigantic, up-tempo throbbing erection, which he angled up into the waist of his pants (surprise surprise) and tried not to betray the downplay of his drunken stone as he walked over to her once the congregation had moved outside, India Willoughby, the ¼ white ⅛ Apache, otherwise All-African American slamming hot 15 year old virgin daughter of the town's spiritual leader and de facto monarch.

"Whatchu doin' here? Who you wit?"

"I'm here with my brother, my friend, D'Shaundrius, visiting his cousin Gates."

"You from New York? You've never been down here before?

"No, the furthest south I'd been before this trip was Washington. But it's laid back, down here, beautiful, nothin' but brown and green and beautiful girls."

"The beauty loses its charm a little after a while, the guys, the people are a bore, got nothing good to say."

"Well let me know what you've been lookin' ta hear."

"You'll be here a few days right? I'll tell ya some shit, I promise. And anyhow, I think it's my responsibility to you as our honored guest to make sure you have a pleasant and memorable time. Would you like that?"

"Yeah, of course, thank you."

"Good, my pleasure. Which do you like better, goats or pigs?"

"Um, uh, goats."

They went into the barn, from which all of the day's offerings had already been hand-picked and therefore where there was minimal likelihood of their being interrupted. And they, you know, fucked Jesus out of North Carolina for a couple of hours.

"Aren't they gonna snort at us, or try to fuck us or something?

"Nah, they're all my friends, I told them this morning that this might be happening."

Some clucking hens had begun murmuring and speculating about their being the only two unaccounted for folks at the barbeque, and it didn't take very long for Reverend Mookie to deduce that Rupert was off as he put it 'stealing my baby girl's sugar sheet.' He planned no interjection or retaliation, however, the man is no hypocrite and he had taken his first 15 year old white girl to the hen house when he was right on about Rupert's age. Very fortunately for Rupe he was already headed back up New York way before any of her 10 older brothers caught word one about it. He stored away Mount Dope as a place well worth knowing should the country be given to fascism.

On Isaac's insistence, as he had no interest whatsoever in going, Rupert went to college at SUNY Geneseo, way the fuck north and west from Yorktown out in why bother country, a town of 4,800 hicks, 200 career academics and 5,000 university students, approximately. His time there was far more full of mis-remembrance and disciplinary hearings than it was intercourse. He's correct but not entirely sure that while in town he had sex 5 times with 4 sorority girls, each of whom's name and face has long since faded from his memory. Each one of them was slammin', there weren't many Geneseo nights on which he wasn't mashed on either whiskey or LSD, so when those nights came his brain and dick maximized and made 'em count.

It was simply the wrong place for him to study, if study he must. Few of the professors piqued his interest and the place stunk whenever the wind wafted the aroma of the alfalfa which gated the community from every direction, twice mistaken by RAs as marijuana being smoked specifically in Rupert's dorm room, towards campus. The student population was so crackery that upon arrival every black person quickly came to know all the other blacks, Jewish people every other Jew, Hispanics all other Hispanics, etc., and so forth. Several students discovered they'd become totalistic cultural anomalies and quickly came to pining suicidally for their outer-island borough homesteads.

Fortunately for his intellect, penis and psyche, as fucking only sorority girls and rarely at that had done him no real good, during his senior year Rupert was upgraded from alternate to bonafide cloud-smasher days before the Israeli Birthright trip, putting wheels upon a Ben Gurion runway on Christian New Year's Day, 2001. He probably felt least religiously like a Jew out of all the Geneseo students he accompanied on that flight; though his religious devotion to the tribe had long ago disappeared he's always maintained an appreciation for his heritage, and will still in talking to most people identify as a Jew out of reverence for his dad and gramps. His heart bleeds for the millennia of deathly plight his ancestors have endured and he has a violent contempt towards Americans, Europeans, anyone who doesn't know any blacks or Jews and thus proliferates a cousin fucking lineage of hatred for them, the most apt example of the human tendencies to kick people while they're down and comfortably allow ignorance and mob mentality to fuel their rationale.

Based on his less than tenuous faith and the mission statement of the fine philanthropists who devised Birthright to reinvigorate individual devotion to Judaism he should have been the first Jew-ish person selected, I hate to have to be the one to tell you this but life can occasionally be unfair. Of course it's moot in this case, as there he was ready to get hip to the Palm Treed city of Tel Aviv, where the grass is green and some of the dopest girls in the world dance on nightclub tables caged in by an outfacing perimeter of their militantly protective brothers and cousins, legally provisioned to pulp you with up to 1 and ½ Uzi clips should you gaze at their vagina'd kin for upwards of five contiguous seconds.

During the two week trip the Geneseo folk shared a bus throughout the Jersey size and shaped Holy Land with a group of college going Chosen Ones from the state of Texas. After four nights in Tel Aviv they ventured north for an overnight stay in Haifa, back southeast about 30 miles for three days on a kibbutz, continuing in that direction for a dip in the Dead Sea, filling out their tour in

Jerusalem after a short ride west with a pinch of back north.

The sun was glazing Gaza as the bus pulled within view of Hephzibah, at which moment Rupert's breath left his body and his brainstem sequestered itself inside an epiphany. The miraculous, rolling city sprayed sparkles from each of its hand painted lines of contour, it's tear duct besieging architecture merged in his mind like specimen plates sandwiched amoebae with the topside view of Rome he'd begotten years before when airplaning earthward at high noon in sub-apperception: though he didn't personally choose to de-fictionalize storybooks, that so many others had done so bestowed upon the world some absolutely godly localities. That the breathtaking construction in such places can be heavily attributed to slave labor didn't enter his mind in that moment. Nor was his awe disturbed by the invisible description of Jerusalem, a beautiful dream turning true as the tides into a nightmare, wherein animosity presents itself with no mislead as Edification encourages you around the corner but she's been eaten by ethnocentrism before you can catch up to him.

Amongst the Texans was Ayana, a grey eyed girl from the Gulf Coast border town of Brownsville. Of the 54 who shared hotels and buses during the tour only she and Rupert had arrived with holes in their clothes and without combs in their luggage (Rupert's hair was at the time sub-afrotic and hued pink and green).

He aggressively claimed the far back right window seat as they boarded their tour bus at the airport. It might be obvious that his choice of the farthest back seat stemmed from his distaste for authoritative blabbermouths, while his proclivity towards the right can be attributed to it being his chosen position in a fully loaded Sauerstein motor carriage. Benny never took issue with this, he always thought that his brother took the right side because he in fact preferred the left.

He initially shared the seat with Alex, amongst the 32% of residential Jews who then populated the county of Rockland, across the Hudson from Yorktown and the rest of the Bestchester, with whom he'd become acquainted on campus and had, in the 24 hour span of waiting around, being overkill screened for death threatliness at Newark Airport, and the flight to Tel Aviv become a qualified friend to Rupert. For reasons only known to Cookie Monster, Armaros and herself, Ayana spent the initial few bus rides directly in front of Rupe, a few strands of her hair breaching and thereby sharing his seat.

Somehow he'd forgotten to pack his black nylon rounded rectangle 32 slotted zip-up cassette case and was left to feed his grey and yellow waterproof Walkman only with the small but quality collection of tapes that happened to be in his black North Face, Dyslexicon, Black Sabbath, and two meticulously playlisted Nirvana mixes. Not in any way as an insult to Alex, simply because the DNA had made him that way, whenever he boarded the bus he twisted in his earbuds and began singing aloud, fully unconcerned with any annoyance this behavior might elicit.

Ayana found the three broken up hours of Rupert Sauerstein sings Kurt Cobain A Capella that first day adorable and enjoyed his unabashedly, though without direct intention Kurt-like, throaty, uninhibited, impassioned timbre, a take shared by exactly no one else on the bus, whose collective admonishment wouldn't have stopped Rupe had he heard them taking it up with him. He didn't sing along when he next slid in Black Sabbath, seven minutes into the tape reverby old Mr. Harmonica invited the other instruments to join him with a winking grin in queuing "The Wizard" and a moment later Ayana's blue-eyed face and the entirety of her slightly greasy, middle-parted shoulder length hair emerged over her seat back as she gave Rupert the universal sign for 'take off your headphones.'

"What is that?"

"Black Sabbath's first record."

"Do you mind if I listen with you?"

Rupert flashed Alex the globalized expression for "you gotta get the fuck up now please' and he and Ayana switched seats, initiating two weeks of symbiosis and affairing.

Ayana was a freshman on academic scholarship at UT Austin and shared Rupert's birthday. At the time of their trip she had already paced herself well beyond normality towards a medical degree. She'd grown up so hopelessly impoverished that to hear her story any dreadful redneck would say it was impossible for it to be that of a Jew.

She had two goals: to become a pediatrician and to provide stability for her mother, two little sisters and little brother for the rest of their lives. She was so brilliant and full of driven promise that the dean of admissions had amended her scholarship to include an off campus house well comfortable enough for a family of five and a $500 per month stipend. From the moment her emaciated jeans hit the back seat until their farewell at the airport they spent less than an accumulated day out of 15 apart.

Both disliked the idea of following the itinerary, like an assigned reading list or a syllabus it would have sucked the mystery and pleasure out of their experience. They had each thoroughly researched the places they'd be visiting, knew what they wanted to see and just as importantly what disinterested them.

While head count was taken upon each boarding and re-boarding of the bus, they found it was rather easy to slink off shortly after a destination was reached should that be their wish, which it wasn't more than two-thirds of the time, the oppressive nature of an itinerary embittered them but this particular one wasn't forged to be unbendingly academic, the most fascinating sights in each city were on it, and it's division ensured to alleviate certain panic, as most people, especially whilst transplanted, feel fuzziest when consistently told what to do. But in every city there are uncommercialized, unpublicized, offbeat treasures to be found, and as such a third of the time they dove to the bottom to see what delights they might discover.

For starters, playing soccer with a bunch of silly Palestinian kids wasn't on there. They were forbidden from entering the Arab Quarter when the IDF chaperoned group was allowed to roam Jerusalem freely for an afternoon though they chose to fuck that directive off, otherwise they wouldn't have seen the most customarily ancient and true locale either ever has, truly medieval, admirably so, occupied by people of every age only visible in their wide eyes, the suspicious, hostile glares they drew from many of these new moons raced their heartbeats, precipitated by the thrill of danger. Men pounded away at weaponry and four-dimensional Islamic symbols, the flying sparks conjuring memories of the youthful Fourth of July bliss a child feels running aimlessly around in equal parts dark and bright warmth with sparklers combusting in both hands. Women worked feverishly to create mythic tapestries from hand dyed thread.

It did not insist that the students pair up with their favorite companion and roam the outskirts of the Old City, with direct orders to eat the most delicious sesame seed bagels the world had ever boiled and baked, dressed with cream cheese and lox that fell from the Heavens whenever a customer approached the humble little open-aired shop.

Nor were the students told to meet a man named Amram and accept a warmly insistent invitation into his impossibly aromatic home to dine alongside his brother, their wives, each of their precious young son and daughter and his host-of-hosts of a father upon his *mame-loshen's* exquisite incarnations of bourekas, shakshuka, shishlik and halloumi kebabs, kibbeh with open-flame broiled baba ghanoush, and four varieties of rugelach to complete the feast that seemingly couldn't get any sweeter.

For three hours they were part of the family and neither had ever enjoyed a finer meal. They left with the remnants of kisses all over their cheeks and a ten pound bag of leftovers, handing much of it out to the downtrodden as they buoyed each other's footsteps into an unnamed park, both weak and delirious from so much eating, nestling themselves into the summoning embrace of a Syrian Juniper's hammocked belly for a deep, digestive, wistful nap upon one another.

As stunning as she was, green eyed, glimmering little cubic zirconia nose ring, slim, tight, blue collar body, she'd been openly desired by nary a boy until Rupert put eyes on her in Tel Aviv. The boys in Brownsville were undignified, the oil monied UT students couldn't see her beauty but only her lower class attire. Our Rupert was enamored with her from the moment she stepped onto the bus and began walking the aisle, disappearing inches away from him, spare locks of her slightly greasy yet splendidly scented hair draping the top of her seat.

Though it goes against an unscientific fact, the founders of Birthright have spared no expense in providing a lush and classy retreat for the strangers they've opportuned to experience their homeland every winter since the one preceding Ayala and Rupert's. They stayed at four star hotels in each city and while of course the lodgings on the kibbutz were constructed to service function over form Rupert found there to be a profound nobility abounding the entirety of structures and cropped fields that comprised it.

All but two of the excursion's amenities were more than what either expected. They sat together in the dining room the morning after their arrival and pushed the buffet style breakfast that was oddly identical at each hotel around on their plates like finicky three year olds; over salted skin on fish and equally briny cheese along with sub-par and nearly stale sweets didn't summon appetite within either of their bellies.

And so Rupert grabbed Ayana by the hand and they exited through the door-manned hotel-face, turned left and sauntered until they happened upon a bakery, sharing goat cheese and blueberry blintzes, a tall, ornate glass of puréed yogurt, banana, pineapple, mango, strawberry and dates, and a bottle of Prigat apple juice. They made a charming tradition out of hunting down blintzes and indescribably scrumptious blended fruit drinks on every Tel Aviv and Jerusalem morning that followed.

Their final morning in Tel Aviv they sat enjoying each other and their delectable breakfast when Ayana stirred Rupert's insides all around by posing a captivatingly bold and vulnerable question.

"You can tell I'm a virgin, right?"

Rupert employed the totality of his masticatory expertise so as not to choke on the forkful of blintz he was working on and once finished chewing he replied, "I'm positive that you irradiate a singular beauty that overtook me at first glance. I've wondered a thousand things about you since but no I haven't considered whether or not you were. I've been entranced by your devilish lips and seductive dimensions, truth be told."

"I don't think I wanna be one when we leave Tel Aviv. Actually I couldn't bare leaving here one. Do you think I can find someone to take it from me?"

“There’s gotta be someone willing to accept responsibility.”

“No one in particular comes to mind though?”

“I’m pretty sure there’s this one dude with us who’d be delighted to do so.”

“Do you happen to know if he has a gentle way with girls.”

“I’ve heard rumblings that he’s uncommonly skilled and that the satisfaction of the girls he makes love to is the cynosure of his desire.”

“How many colors are in his hair.”

“Two I think? Well three I guess as his roots start to grow in.”

“Will you point him out to me when we get back to the hotel.”

“I mean I guess, if it means that much to you. Are you positive it’s what you want?”

She stood up from her seat and seductively made her way around the small square of a table, sat down on his lap and gave him a kiss so sweet it rivaled Onyx’s most erotic oscillations.

'Mmm-hmmm' and a corner to corner lick of the lips was her adorable, post-kiss reply. She stood up, turned away from him and extended her slender arms backwards so he could take her by her hands, aspiring to hold him as well as to obscure other diners’ visage of the full-blown erection she’d generated, having avariciously claimed it for her own, demonstrating that she no longer felt any less entitled to obtain that which she desired than the shamefully bred rich kids with whom she’d crossed the irrelevant ocean.

That night they walked the most splendorous streets of downtown Tel Aviv hand in hand, Allenby, Kikar Hamedina, Rothschild Boulevard. Rupert bought Ayana a bracelet of her choosing at Hagar Sadat. All the while she was moist with anticipation; he couldn't wait to undress and make delicate love with her, though all the while a perplexing question pleaded with him for a resolution: where?

The hotel had a swimming pool, a carpark, linen closets, washrooms in the lobby, but these were not places wherein this fair, admirable girl should fuck for the first time. Nor did he want to embarrass her by asking one of their roommates to take a walk. As they neared their hotel they came upon the Fire and Water Fountain and it's radiance froze Ayala's momentum, halting Rupert along with her. They silently extolled it's kaleidoscopic dance for a few moments, and at the precise moment when Ayala drew Rupert close Moses radioed him a solution to his conundrum.

Back inside the aureate, 17 story hotel, they took the lift one level at a time, walking the entirety of each until Rupert suggested they continue to RISE. It was near 3 a.m., and though Ayana, thirsty and anxious as she was, persistently asked him what they were doing he remained vague and coy. Once they were 13th floor elevated, exited the lift and took a few spare steps beyond its corridor, Rupert glanced down the hallway to their left to find that their search was complete. Anxious to know if his plan would come to fruition, they briskly approached a housekeeper who was restocking her supply cart, having just finished tidying an empty room. He peeled a hundred dollar bill from the wad in his pocket and asked her if they could use the room for the night. Tickled by the libidinous way of their faces, she accepted their bribe and raspily asserted "you must be to go by ten or manager vill shit a fit on me."

"We hafta be on a bus to Haifa exactly by ten so there's nothing to worry about," Rupert assured her.

As he took her hand and began through the threshold she eked out a bashful "thanks," to which the woman replied with an encouraging wink.

After parting ways, back in Ben Gurion, Ayana went bounding forthward aboard a crowded uptown express, sparking the tracks, expeditiously bound for the salvation of her family and thousands of precious little ones. Rupert hunched over as the single occupant in a stalled downtown local, clambering on saving himself, regretful he hadn't honored his instincts and exiled at the Wailing Wall to sob his bones dry, suicide by catharsis.

Beyond college, unable to envision any fulfillment or success were he to explore a career in Subcontinental Textile Design, as he'd been bestowed accreditation in the discipline yet left Geneseo with little retention and piss-poor skill in the discipline he'd so apathetically chosen as a major, he shot the moon and wrote an essay which earned him acceptance into the world class Getty Square Brainery for Zoological Intrigue and he determined to begin looking into rental of an apartment in Yonkers.

Before he had the chance first to procrastinate in his search for a roommate he could be found THC'd to the gills at The International Cheddar Cheese and Salad Dressing Bazaar and Museum up in Dutchess County, striking up a kooky conversation with a short, handsy and rather green individual whom Rupe expeditiously deduced was a creature of kindness.

Chip Bearius immediately endeared himself to Rupert and their circumstances couldn't have been more suited to each other as Chip had recently enrolled in a program at Manhattan College for those who were specially physical and desired to teach special education. They found a dope place on St. James Terrace which put each a crude missile launch away from their campus.

Rupert found Chip to be the most naturally hilarious and unique fellow he'd ever known. Had they not found themselves in the same circular video room watching an enthralling documentary about the pride and joy of Somerset Village they'd never have known the other existed though not long after that day Chip had solidified himself on Rupert's cautiously composed short list of friends he felt he could trust implicitly.

Chip was extraordinarily well rounded in interest and personality, thin and stick like in his physicality, a metabolism so hyperactive that not all of the cheddar cheese in the solar system, marinated in every manufactured ounce of semeny Ranch dressing, could have plumped him up.

He was parts gay, subversive, athletic, intellectual, compassionate, artistic, absurd, and loyal. One thing he certainly wasn't nor attempted to be was cool, to Rupert this made him uniquely awesome. His sexual past could be described as checkered. His self-confidence and social skills fell well below those of Rupert; along with many others a time came when he surpassed Rupe in both capacities.

If ever Rupert knew someone who shouldn't finagle with the use of illicit substances that someone was Chip: his abstracted brain chemistry held him perpetually higher than the Burj Khalifa. Every evening, the timing unpredictable, he reached a point past which it became an impossibility for him to evoke a semblance of productive interactivity, overcome by a rave of absurdity until guffawing himself to sleep. During these late night hours Rupert came to expect Chip's shockingly large and off-colored penis to end up in his eye or hairline with no prior notice. Often he'd re-enter their shared living room where Rupert was a stoned, flow-blooded still life on the couch by silently mantising the edges of the room beyond his periphery with the intention of getting to his buddy sans detection and either draping his Dominican hued dingus on ol' Rupe's shoulder or poking it into his ear.

Unborn with the crutch of self-consciousness, Chip was paramountly comfortable with Rupert and let his peach fuzzy hair down to the maximum when the pair were alone. From the onset of his nightly delirium onward, Rupert understood that anytime he used the bathroom Chip could be standing with his damned dick dangling from the waistband of his athletic stretch pants as he exited the latrine, lunging or skying in an attempt to poke-violate Rupert's leg or asshole with it.

Chip's favorite game, above even fallacing him, was to snatch Rupert's Ball jar, the inner walls of which were caked with a foggy decade's worth of hair and crystals, and stash it covertly within their spacious second story apartment. It would never be long before Rupert would want for it and discover Chip had performed a transplant, at which point, to their mutual bemusement, Rupert would inquire "Oh Chipper? Where-are-my MARIES?!"

Neither had any sexual prospects when they moved in together and both were financially flush, Chip having won a rather fruitful settlement resulting from discriminatory hiring practices at a mega-conglomerate 17 months before they met. Sitting around one night watching The Office with lonesome boners, Chip suggested they go online for prostitutes, something that hadn't occurred to Rupert as an option until Chip suggested it whilst Michael Scott break-danced above a frigid Lake Wallenpaupack.

That first time Rupert chose a stunning eighteen year old Haitian girl who wasn't accustomed to the capabilities of a magical cock such as his and came four times during their hour together, the fourth simultaneous with the Babe's mighty orgasm. Chip selected a 350 pound Puerto Rican girl with a bodily mole for every liter of her aqueous personage. When she left he finished himself off with his left hand; she'd shattered his right ulna while beast-riding his little body, she smelling as does a rhinoceros fresh from a dirt bath and sounding off like a howler monkey whilst she destroyed green ol' Chip. Sickened and wanting for his beautiful little Haitian and he not to endure the presence of the beast Rupert lit half a box of nag and turned the dulcet tones of Solomon Burke to full blast as to drown out the wall of smelly sound produced by the jungle in apocalypse that cascaded thru the apartment.

Two nights later, ready for more action despite the mutilation of forearm and soul he'd just endured at the hands of the most hideous female Rupert had ever seen, Chip's vitiated mind shot an idea around the sharp curves of his brain town and thru his face hole.

"Hey Roo-bags?"

"Yes Chip?"

"You wanna try something?"

"Something odd?"

"Nah-bags, conventional-ragged."

"Well I guess so," Rupert bemused, a halcyon awareness that Chip was about to propose some Satanic anathema. He'd become allegiant to the nuances of his diminutive new pal's preciously nefarious psyche; he knew he was likely bound to honor whatever suggestion was about to slip from his buddy's Gomorrahan mouth.

"Let's call a hooker-face, tell her there are two of us and that we will present her with a special request-bag when she gets here."

"Go on."

"We'll sit on opposite sides of the wall beside the entrance to the kitchen and have her sit straddling the door frame so she can jerk-bag and suck-rag us simultaneously while we talk-bag."

"Is this a fantasy you've had for a while?" Rupert asked, recognizing the rhetorical quality of his question, as most everything was fantastical to Chip, the bi-curious Care Bear. "Sure dude, go find her."

Chip sprang to his feet and scooted across the apartment to his bedroom in his usual Mandotean manner to grab his cell phone.

"She better be less than a buck forty with smooth skin or I'm out!" Rupert qualified assertively.

"*Sheket b'vakasha*, ya turkey!" Chip's psychopathically delivered reply bounced forth and back towards Rupe's earbags upon the walls of their happy home.

'I shoulda put myself in charge of selecting this poor girl.' he thought, giggling and continuing to roll a joint.

When their invited guest arrived she appeared to be pushing 140 but just the same she was a delightful and beautiful fetish fulfiller of a girl, composed of 5/8ths Angolan and 3/8ths Swedish DNA. She processed and affirmed Chip's request without a flinch.

The three got themselves in position to do the Devilish deed and Sapphire started to get that money. As she worked her magic Chip became more interested in watching Rupert get sucked off than in his own gratification. When she'd shift rupeward, Chip peered his Area 51 honeydew around the doorframe to catch a glimpse.

"Dude I won't be able to cum for a month with you salivating like that, back on your side please!"

"I don't want you to cum, I just wanna watch Saphypants blow you for as long as possible."

"Sapphire, please push his scrawny little body back on his side of the wall and ignore his pleas to the contrary."

Restrained against his mighty will, Chip employed his trademark juvenility and began misbehaving in the only available capacity, which of course was to do his best Rosine impression. "Rupe, I lu dat shit. I'm gonna lickded that shit, then I'm gonna suckded that shit. Saphypants, when my man ejaculizes for you baby gimme that shiny fuckin' shit so's I can slurpded that shit straight thru that shit, ok baby?"

Sapphire looked to Rupert for his approval.

"if he wants to suck my cum out of this condom, let him have at it."

"Oh thank you baby, bowf you babies. I'ma buy yoos bowf lo'stas sos you could lickded that shit and then I slappded that shit right off yo tables."

After some doing, Sapphire gave a tremendous blowjob or they may have been there all night, both fellows came and Rupert slipped Sapphire an extra 200 bucks for her pain and suffering.

The following afternoon they sat in their assigned seats on the couch outside of Rupe's bedroom when Chip got a phone call from his former neighbor Arnie, then 35 to Chip's 21 and Rupe's 24. Arnie had twice been by the apartment since the deprecated duo moved in together, as Rupert had noted to Chip that he found Arnie to be an entertaining dude he put the phone on speaker for his bud's amusement.

"What's up Arn?" Chip answered.

“Fuck man nothin’, I’ve been waiting at this fuckin’ mansion in Chappaqua for these cunts for a half hour.” Arnie’s charge was limo-driving the county’s vast 1% to airports and exclusionary hideaways.

“That blows Ruperts, you have a paper with you or something?”

“I got nothin’. I need to stop doing this fuckin’ job, most of these fucks don’t even tip me.”

“So you’re just sitting there?”

“I am now. I just finished jerking off.”

“Sweet. Where did you shoot it?”

“...right in my unda’pants.”

As the years uprooted each other Rupert continued to find himself without a psychological capacity to meet girls conventionally and Chip’s exhortation led him to further explore the escort scene. He was meticulous about the girls he chose and had a proclivity for 18 and 19 year olds as they were ripe, unstretched, uncynical, didn’t teem with a furious yearning towards insemination, and tended to be maturationally compatible with him. He grew adept in determining the authenticity of a girl’s photos and kindness on Craigslist and later on Backpage.

He paid to fuck some fine young pussy in the weeks to come, often seeing the same girl several times. Doing his due diligence one night in August of his 28th year he came across an ad posted by Daniela, an 18 year old, light skinned Cuban girl of 5’4” and 107 pounds, whose post stated she was a working model looking for a nice guy to spend time with.

Rupert had happened upon several girls on the website claiming to be models in the past, deducing the claims were fallacies derived from self-esteem issues. Daniela had no reason to spin such wool into gold, over time she brought Rupert lingerie catalogues and obscure fashion magazines that featured most every gorgeous inch of her. She showed him YouTube videos of her in body paint fucking the air at openings for bourgeois night clubs in the city designed to draw in the dudes with the shiniest plastic in their wallets and the chicks with the priciest plastic in their faces and tits. Otherwise, the only videos she posted were of her playing with her two little nephews, which he found rather cute.

The first night she came over, having taken a cab from her home in Getty Square, she put the $120 he'd placed on his dresser for her in her purse without checking if it was all there and seemed to be in no rush. They sat on Rupert's bed without removing any clothing for 17 minutes, acquainting themselves with replete honesty. When their pre-foreplay dissertations had run their course they began kissing passionately, eventually stripping and tenderly fucking, Rupert intensifying and softening his thrusts unpredictably to both of their gratification.

Every girl in the universe will tell you that doggy style is their favorite position, Rupert was in no way averse to it but far preferred facing the girls he was with and analyzing their stimulation. He gave Daniela a tutorial and positioned her to perform what's best known to the great sinners of the world as froggy style. For the Mormons, Catholics, Muslims and Hassids reading along this is where the gentleman lays on his back while the gentlewoman stands and straddles him, squats down like a catcher on the gentleman's phallus, bounces and bounces and bounces some more.

She fell into an instantaneous swoon, the exertive, unfamiliar, ultra-stimulation of their positioning led her to roll back her head, whipping her long hair, and she began moaning an ambrosial moan, before very long coming all over Rupert's cock, he in turn inside both she and a Magnum a few pumps later. Rather than rising to her feet to dress and depart, she cuddled up on Rupert and they talked soft and sweet for a few minutes before he delicately readied her ship sinking body for the other most favored page in his personal *Kama Sutra*.

He placed his two pillows at the side edge of his mattress and delicately maneuvered her baby-makin' bottom upon them, establishing what to him is the penultimate penetrative angle. Standing beside her laid out body he tickled her clit with the broad head of his penis before slipping it into her orchid of a pussy, followed gradually by the totality of his shaft, measuredly intensifying and softening the depth and power of his thrusts. She was enraptured in the precise way that most gratifies and turns Rupert on, closing her eyes and biting the right side of her lower lip while most feminine tones of fulfillment hummed through the thin opening on the left side as her teeth provided them pleasurable pain and ridged her lipstick. Fully inserted, Rupert bent over and began sucking on her neck, putting her deeper in it.

They came again and laid down, Daniela sleeping through the night with her arm across Rupert's chest. He woke to the one wakey time surprise superior to the smell of cooked bacon, a smooth and sloppy blowjob. They showered together and walked down the hill to Yonkers Avenue for a greasy spoon breakfast after which Rupert offered her a ride home that she politely rescinded. He demanded to give her some more money but all she'd accept was $10 for a cab.

She lived but a few blocks from the Brainery and while Yonkers allocated hundreds of millions of borrowed dollars for upper-middle class bullshit intent upon drawing parliamentary bloats to the nearby waterfront they seldom put a nickel into the decaying downtown.

The 14th time she visited him she walked into the room, asked to use the bathroom, and shortly thereafter came out ready to pounce on him. As she passed the dresser and the $120 fanned out in its customary spot he pointed at it and said "that's you." She slowed, stopped her approach and locked her fingers against her tush.

"Listen, I don't want you to pay me for coming over anymore."

"Really?"

"Yes really. I enjoy coming here, a lot. You've been nothing but sweet and considerate since the first time I came over. No other guy has ever been either to me."

"Well obviously I like you too, I've been paying you to fuck me three times a week for a month," Rupert responded, making sure that he said this with an unmistakable sarcasm.

"I know, if anything I should be paying you. I love your fucking cock and what you do to me with it, and I love being here with you."

"Since we met, honestly going back a while before that, the only time I'm like truly happy is when you're here or on your way over. Can you at least start letting me pick you up?"

"We'll see."

And if you're ever a little strapped promise you'll let me help you out?"

"I'm not gonna be strapped. How about instead of talkin' all this sappy bullshit you get inside me."

"If I must."

She used every bit of might in her little body to push him onto the bed and extricated his pants with her teeth. They enjoyed the Hell out of each other until the fabled, anomalous Yonkers rooster crowed.

They remained true to each other for two years that would have been but a meaningless bore without her. When Rupert decided it was time to get the fuck out for a spell he told her he thought she should come along, but as did Ayala she had family to support.

Rupert and Chip, the fine buddy boys who'd found each other through their shared passion for cheddar cheese and a simultaneous attention to it, each happening upon the Somerset Village viewing room at a very precise moment in human history had a great run together in that apartment, sharing 71 St. James apt. #2 for eight years in unencumbered, nutty harmony until one day came along a young lady who adored Chip as much as Rupert had and took his hand in a bit of a controversial yet successful and harmonious matrimony.

In the years to come, Rupert summoned few erections and nodded through life with no more than rare and rapidly fleeting shows of libido, leaving me to wonder if he'd ever return to his masterful, pussy-slamming ways.

Chapter 5

Capitalization

I don't want no gold watch
For workin' fifty years from nine to five
While the boss is guzzlin' champagne
And I'm beltin' beer in some dive
Cuz I want to be, happy and free
Livin' and lovin' for me
I want to be, happy and free
Livin' and lovin' for me
Just like a natural man

- *Bobby Hebb*

Rupert's grandparents had given him government bonds in accumulation of an approximate $50,000 face value demarcating every birthday, Christmas and Chanukah since his conception, worth nearly twice that when he began cashing them several years beyond their date of maturity. When redeeming them he made sure to keep the cash they turned into separate from his other monies, wanting only to spend his grandparents' hard-earned bread on savory needs, never on sadistic wants.

Upon Elijah's passing Minister Isaiah was readied to endow upon him a briefcase widened by one-hundred and fifty k in 20 dollar bills, untouchable, as Elijah had made painstakingly sure, by the government, super-conglomerates, any and all deviant shadow megalos worldwide in fact. Also inside the parcel were instructions, a suggestion really, to tell his parents that he'd been bequeathed 10% that amount, which he did.

When Rupe was 25 Franky, 'the gentleman drug dealer,' his punctual, amiable and generous cocaine dealer asked him to hold onto 200k for him for a few days. Three hours later poor Franky found himself the rather dead owner of 9 new bullet holes in his face and throat. Hearing about this gruesome and somber quietus Rupert dressed himself in black and drove his pinched nerves to Harlem, purchasing $1000 worth of crack and a Raging Bull Hand Cannon from some compatriots down there.

The sun wasn't quite all the way gone when he returned to Yonkers, parking a few blocks from the house, slinking, rolling and laying beneath his car until all that could be heard were a mid-night snacking raccoon and an existentially unsettled warbler. Certain that someone would be coming for the money, he spent the subsequent six days sleeplessly toking on the base, the pistol otherwise held high and lineated with one or another of the front door's kill shots.

Once convinced he was alone in knowledge of the big bag of change's whereabouts he chewed up a baby's hand full of Xanax to ease the crackiness away and drove down Tuckahoe Road to turn the weapon over to the YPD. All of that and with the value of the '58 es-335 being about 80k, he'd amassed quite a stockpile of capital by doing nothing other than living his stupid little life.

Before deciding he wouldn't have one anymore he did get one job, worked admirably for six summers starting the July after the 0.44's worth of GPA he'd earned in his first at Geneseo, as an assistant counselor at a nursery school camp for the children of Jewish 1%ers. Not fucking around, if not for his affinity for kids and dogs Rupert would've blasted his head open by tenth or eleventh grade. He fell for a freckly little one named Lily that first summer, with her wistful attitude and psychotomimetic imagination.

Headed one morn by bus to the Greenburgh Nature Center, Lily plopped herself in the far back window seat and by decree Rupert took the aisle beside her. Driving through Thornwood, Rupert remarked to Lily that a pizzeria they were passing served especially delicious food. True to the dimethyltryptamine in those sweet brainwaves of hers, she replied with "why don't we go in there and put some ham on our faces?"

"Ronny," Rupert called to the driver, "is it cool if we turn around real quick?, Lily and I wanna stop at Napoli's and put a bunch of ham on our faces."

"We're a little rushed for time Lily sweetheart, maybe on the way back if we can squeeze it in."

"Ok thank you Ronny." Lily was well bright enough to recognize that there would be no stopping on the way back, and Rupert's convincing show of disappointment assured her of his being more bummed than she.

"Don't worry Rupert, there'll be plenty of time to put ham on our faces."

"Well Lily, I hope you're right, I really do."

Beyond that, he graduated second in his class at the Brainery, having already published several groundbreaking essays on big cat psychodynamics, and he was sought by zoos and private collectors from every collective and continent. Having always felt that southeast Asian cats had the most humility, (this was based in no part on any research or education, rather on an insurmountable inkling) Rupe quickly narrowed into negotiations with Anada Nguyen, chief advocate for and confidant to felines throughout Thailand and Malaysia and highest ranking trustee to the Chiang Mai Zoo.

There is, unfortunately for Rupert, great disconnect and fragmentation amongst zoological types, and while folks like the great Dr. Nguyen had been tracking his progress since his first weeks at the Brainery those in for example the jungle reptilian world would never have heard his name, and so once Anada, along with the hand drawn contract he had readied for Rupert, went overboard south of the African horn en route to personally greet him and hammer out the formalities of their relationship, the opportunity ceased to exist just the same. He took it as some sort of cosmic hint that he wasn't meant to work with those animals, or in that part of the world, or anywhere. Otherwise put, someone like Rupert, that is to say someone who has assured their self that the fates had long ago been concretely maligned against her or him, and whose every action is prejudiced by obsessive compulsion and fear of failure, may in a case like this see no merit, no self-pride, no peace in anything other than what has become imbedded in their brain as the greatest and thereby only option.

He has since been sustaining himself on the unusual acquisitions mentioned above, though my concern, as well as that of those more conventionally invested in his vitality, has been that all these years he's had nothing to work towards, to occupy the most malevolent corpuscles in his brain at times of despair and existential bankruptcy.

To ignore the fleeting joy gotten from material possessions over the course of a lifetime is beneficial to the wallet and the soul, useless though if one spends every day getting dead on drugs. In the end it's far more prudent to stay sober, do worthless work for big dividends and buy the fuckin' Communist Manifesto television set and the super-performance Nazi motor carriage. Finding he had developed a crippling unease on the East Coast and wanting to give himself a chance to run out of drugs and then get soberish Rupert got his affairs in order, evacuated the apartment and spent a week hugging and kissing his family, stuffed his car until the back window was 98% obscured and got the fuck outta there, chasing an antiquated destiny to the Pacific, maybe to accelerate straight into it if the feeling wasn't quite right when he arrived.

He powered through all the way to the northwest suburbs of Chicago the first day and was at his first destination in Woodbury, Minnesota by two o'clock the following afternoon, planning for four or five nights with his aunt and grandma Miriams.

It came as no secret that Grandma Miriam was the smartest person he'd ever known as well as his favorite, her name's come up in most every conversation on intellect he's ever had and he's spent more time sitting and thinking about her than he has anyone else. Shortly after her 90th birthday it was decided that she would go live in Minnesota with her first born daughter and namesake, 7 years older than her baby sister Kayiane. Rupert never protested anything so vehemently in his life, but once he accepted that she needed more assistance than he'd realized and recognized that Aunt Miriam wanted to spend time with her mother while she was still her vibrant self, Rupert eased up on his revolt.

35 years earlier, Aunt Miriam had met her kind and easy-going husband Markus, who is no longer with us, while both were in Washington D.C. taking inventory, as it were. Markus was as authentically Minnesota German as is grandpa Oscar real deal Brooklyn Jew.

Theirs was an assiduous courtship and not a year after their chance unification they shared a marital home in the Minneapolis suburb of Roseville, very much like Yorktown, just a bit cleaner and more so devoid of dope and hooligans. As she's now spent half her lifetime in Kings County and half in the Twin Cities, aunt Miriam has the most fascinating hybrid Brooklyn-Minnesota accent. I'm demonstrating it for you now but there's little likelihood that you can hear me.

Rupert stayed with them for five nights, piling up losses to his grandma in Scrabble and backgammon as she played to about half of her ability, cooking frittatas and grits for his beloved Miriams in the mornings and sarma and beef pie with his grandma in the afternoons, taking barefooted walks through the wood between the condo and the nearby lake when in need of a joint or a moment's introspection.

As he was departing, he came back in from the garage twice to give his grandma extra kisses, wanting never to leave her side, only able to because he planned to come back through town on his New York way back.

From Minnesota to Montana the terrain and the sub-zero blizzardous conditions were really depressing to Rupert. Bleak, flat nothingness. He did though enjoy a bonafide few moments of fun in absorbing the jolt and maneuvering to control the car whence passing 16-wheelers at silly speeds.

When he'd pull into a gas station to fill up and the attendant saw his New York plates a conversation was inevitable, about where he was headed and why, about a great aunt who'd performed on Broadway in the '60s, about a cousin who'd long ago played guitar for Willie Nelson and was, down to the nuance, Rupert's precise look-alike. He was cordial, comical, as while these conversations meant nothing to him and held him from his destination, he recognized that they were exciting and tale-able highlights in some wretchedly mundane existences. Which made him even sadder, as you can imagine.

He zipped along, absolutely disinterested in nominal detours towards Deadwood, Mount Rushmore; towards a mind boggling in its mere existence and from what he gathered a county sized tchotchke market called Wall Drug that was heavily advertised for several hundred miles on approach of it, often topping 100 on the speedometer when the road was empty and straight; though there was a Duke and Gonzoesque briefcase amongst the items stuffed into his trunk (he'd tincture down on and off of the goodies within and not replace them once they were gone, he told himself) he had little reason to fear the police, the spaces so open that a cop car would have been as remotely visible to him as the Statue of Liberty to an empty gutted mass-migrant, hungry just as animalistically for gold as he was flesh.

So sad and bad were the feelings he got when passing the half-horse towns which dominate that expanse, many adorned with an 'M' or 'W' on the facsimile hillside 'cross the byway from the habitat laid out by its earliest settlers, ('really they couldn't spring for the entire fuckin' name?') who'd loped their way upon the soil once our noble army ants'd eviscerated and thus freed them from any cooperation or coexistence with the last of those pesky Natives at Wounded Knee.

Had there not been one or more of his favorite people waiting for him at each destination he may not have made it all the way. When he pulled into his cousin Henry's Big Sky driveway there he stood, encircled by his collective of feral cats and disowned dogs, lighting a great fat joint as Rupert turned his key counterclockwise and offered his engine a well-deserved respite. The aroma of Henry's locally grown kush was overwhelmed by that of schnitzel, spätzle and mushroom gravy as Rupert shed his jacket and backpack upon the sofa.

He had begun his journey on the morning after Thanksgiving and as the southwestern Montana December temperature hardly fluctuated outside of the -20 to -30 range he did little more during his three week stay there than discreetly snort and eat his drugs, collaborate in multi-ethnic feast making, Google and YouTube search things aimlessly, read Bobby Dylan's autobiography, watch bighorns jump into and out of trees through a side window and bald eagles size up baby moose out the back of the log cabin home which Henry had designed, built and located himself at the foot of his own personal Rocky mountain. More hugs, some more sentimentality and back at it.

The next little leg was a slow grind from Big Sky into Reno for a restless, paranoid motel stopover, the highways along the way blanketed by compacted snow and ice thicker than the concrete below. Less than an hour into the drive the following morning he began to feel reborn, having crossed into the rust, blue and green of the California Republic, in his best on-road state of mind yet; once he hit Mendocino his rush to get everywhere dissipated, the landscape grew greater with every foregone mile north on the meandering Redwood canopied roadways, two hundred miles of paved River Raisin.

A few seconds after he pebble-crunched the car curbside directly in front of his dear old friend since Hebrew School Ben Steinway's house in Arcata a cute blonde girl, who Rupe correctly presumed was Ben's new lady friend, rolled up and parked behind, Ben loungin' in the passenger seat with his hearty, mellow and melodic self.

By the time but two or three moments of congregation had passed they'd settled in the bedroom to get high and Rupe and Ben's girlfriend Viktorya were already buds. Being that she liked Rupert and that he was a long-reliable friend to Ben she had no apprehension in chronicling for him the gypsy's life she'd begun leading as a four year old girl until at fifteen finding her rightful fit in the giganteum-ocean-farmland hybrid radiance of Humboldt County. She had been through so much quantifiably tough shit yet her cheer and perspective assured that through all of it she'd remained tougher than the times.

Ben was a fine host, waking Rupert most late mornings for a scramble or buckwheat pancakes, always accompanied by stiff French press. The Sunday after he arrived he decided to give Ben and Viktorya some time alone and headed on foot northwest towards a recommended wood a few miles away, visible from Ben's porch beyond the tallest proprietary structures of the university at its southeast edge.

Of the irrational and situationally automatic terrors Rupert suffers through daily, the fiercest panic seems always to erupt should he get himself lost. He's never able to control his reaction to this, screaming and punching his steering wheel, screaming and kicking trees or trash cans... But as he entered the forest that day, one goal in mind, he didn't give a piece of a dead hyena testicle where he walked or how lost he got, a week of concentrated coordination confusion wouldn't that day have bothered him a lick.

He ignored all trailway and instead trekked alongside a thin, bathed stream, 6 inches wide or fewer most of her way. Where the stream broadened a bit red-legged frogs were there, floating and croaking. As it still is and forever will be throughout the hundreds of thousands of blessed acres which comprise that wood, the ground was foamy 'neath his toes, moist in the permanence of a perfect climate.

Rupert ended up spending nearly a third of his waking moments over 7 months in Arcata walking that wood, which for the time being rendered every other inferior, superfluous even, though whence he embarked upon his next approach to Morla he was reassured to find his wood had retained its significance, upholding a mirrored polarity with the Redwoods and the coasts that sprang them.

Where the stream brushed up against one of the nation's eldest magical namesake residents and should there be an accumulation of bark and clumped mud where they met, Rupert would gently burrow in his gunked up, cigarette smoky phalanges, an academically versed student of the environ previous to this saunter. Euphorically as a doped up hedgehog with a big dick he dug that day with patience that eclipsed his showing of that misappropriated virtue throughout his previous 31 spins.

Just shy of four hours after he'd entered the wood he was performing this delicate surgery and fingered the certain stickiness he'd set out and so hoped to, having internetted and researched the cutie-pies native to Mendocino and Humboldt while in the Montana freeze. Gingerly plucking each soggy fragment from atop of her she was soon unearthed and wiped clean. 5 and 11/16 inches long, 7 months old, stripes of Cuban orchid and pony brown mimicking the contours of the stream bed which had nurtured her incubation. She has the eyeballs and sockets of a crocodile, sixteen white tipped toes and gesticulative little arms which mobilized her zaftig body. As he took her into his hands a tear trickled from his left eye, her right. He kissed her on the lips and choked out "well Lucy, I guess you're mine now. I love you. Please try not to hate me."

Without trepidation she accepted Rupert's cradle and they studied each other intently as they walked the 7 miles back to Ben's. While staying with his friend of 20 years Rupert squatted in an empty upstairs room. He'd set up his floor tom as a terrarium late the previous night, unsure how Ben would feel about giant salamanders in the house and thus not having asked permission as he knew having to return her to the forest would devastate him. But don't worry, deducing a couple of weeks later that he was off in this assessment he presented Lucy to Ben over breakfast and they too became fine friends.

In mid-July Ben and Viktorya decided they'd together move into a cute little mother-in-law house beginning in August, giving Rupert a very clear departure date for Southern California. The half-brothers by last name would next see each other on Rupert's 34th birthday.

This timing proved metronomic in that it allowed him a quick visit with his cousin William in Los Angeles on his way to San Diego to stay indefinitely with his friend Reyansh. William is Henry's older brother and was born precisely four years before Rupert, a charming little footnote to the nonpareil sisterhood of Kayiane and

Miriam, so unlikely in Miriam's mind that it took a second phone call from Kayiane to convince Miriam it was so after the reputationally Lincoln-like Isaac had failed in his endeavor to do so.

Rupert had been hyper-conscious and fearful of overstaying his welcome as he traveled and though he never quite did he often felt as though he had. Being that William arrived in L.A. less than a day ahead of him and would soon begin the astro-physistries that had beckoned him there, coupled with Rupe's fervency at that point to get to San Diego, he spent only two nights on his childhood idol's couch, helping big cuz unpack, smoking purple pot and catching Joey Diaz at The Comedy Store, so psyched to have seen both Minnesota cousins as he roamed.

As boys, there was such a thrill attached to each family's annual flight to see the other, the Fischers heading east at Christmastime and the Sauersteins west during the summer. Only coming together twice a year made for heightened thrills whence those congregations forth came. Fond photographs from these visits abound; Rupert most recalls playing King of the Mountain on a turtle shaped rock outside and uphill from Miriam and Giuseppe's front door. The three elder cousins would let Benny beat Hell from them, overpowering each advance with his tiny body and tossing them to the grassy mat like the cutest little Ultimate Warrior impersonator you've ever seen. Today that sacred stone graces a plaque in recognition of the noble, humanitarian displays that fueled the life of their dear Grandpa Giuseppe Lepore, in Sheepshead Bay and Jefferson Village alike.

Reyansh had graduated from Thomas Jefferson Elementary and on through Lakeland high alongside Rupert and Ben though he and Rupert were never much more than fond acquaintances and playground compatriots in their youth. Had technology ceased to expand from the time they were children to the time they were addicts they would have followed the archetypical path of graduating from high school and never seeing each other again.

Their generation, though and of course, is that of the social media age, and while Rupert never felt comfortable or compelled enough to open a Facebook account a fevered attempt by Reyansh to reconnect with those long since forgotten had prompted him to locate Rupert a few days before he was to set sail for the Pacific. The conversations they shared as they reconnected provided each with more interest in befriending the other than they ever had as children, this though pretty much just as quickly lost again when the time of their physical reunion arrived.

He had been living in San Diego for four years at the time of their reunion, describing the city to Rupert as one would expect a loyal resident to, the beaches and hot, clear skies, the Socialist mentality of the eclectic folks who reside there. Rupert grew intrigued as he elaborated, though wasn't fully sold until without any ulterior motive or insight Reyansh mentioned the world class tamale shop that could be seen across the street and diagonal from his porch, tamales happening to be Rupert's all-time favorite food.

San Diego commonly suffers but a few rainy days in the course of a year, most or all of them during the winter, though it had begun pouring as L.A. faded from Rupert's rear view and showed no signs of dissipating as his visit reached day two, day three…Though it was dark, starless nighttime when he pulled up to Reyansh's Oak Park home it was quite clear they were in a ghetto the likes of which Rupert had only previously witnessed in Poughkeepsie, Baltimore and the South Bronx, all places he'd never slept. He notified Reyansh of his arrival by cell phone and as he tenderly removed Lucy's terrarium tom from the passenger seat his still diminutive brown friend approached with the same radiant smile and goofy gait that were about all Rupert had remembered him by. Electing to save their cheerful reminiscence for after they'd gotten out of the downpour they began scurrying toward the house.

"This way," Reyansh redirected Rupert's rush for the entrance.

"That's not the front door?"

"Yes, it is," he confirmed, leading Rupert around and behind the house to what he deduced was once an auto body garage.

Entering the abode, which he then learned Reyansh shared with five others, their rooms segregated by an elaborate system of tattered blankets and shelving units, Rupert was greeted by, and this is not hyperbole, a pile of dead and dying dogs, wincing and rotting underneath an overflowing sink of dishes and silverware, caked with a seeming century's worth of moldy instant mac 'n' cheese globules and bent black spoons.

Amongst Reyansh's roomies were an undead Sinead O'Connor lookalike who had a standing offer of $5 to any guy in the house who would fuck her, an offer, Rupe was told, yet to be accepted. Across the hall I guess you'd say from Reyansh was Jimmy, an amiable, handsome, wavy shoulder-length haired 24 year old fellow esquire whose presence there saddened Rupert deeply, and with whom he shot dope while Reyansh was out telemarketing for 10 hours each day. This was a really awesome dude, one Rupert wished he could have met in a different life. He was one of 7 or 8 people Rupert ever met who had passable taste in music and one night he cooked ghetto Beef fuckin' Wellington with curried potatoes and cauliflower for the whole household.

When Reyansh peeled forward the door to his bedroom Rupert was astounded in discovering that somehow it was no less repugnantly filthy than the sink and dogpile by the entry, and though he's always been rather a slob himself he insisted on spending the next few hours cleaning it. Reyansh didn't outwardly object, nor did he assist. Perhaps a clean room was a bit nose in the air in these parts, Rupert surmised.

He felt notably more comfortable once it was tidied, though he suspected that sleeping on its floor atop what he imagined was decades of calcified depravity was not going to suit him. Fortunately, he was given clearance to sleep on the couch of the main house. Equally unfortunate was that this clearance was issued by the most frightening person Rupert had ever met, the patriarch of this nonfunctional family, a towering, malevolent warlock with waist length grey, purple streaked hair who smelled like a perfume alchemically concocted from the essence of disease and who along with his equally terrifying and militant girlfriend was the only inhabitant of the property's only humanely inhabitable sector. Unable to summon the courage to say no, and of appreciation for his hospitality, Rupert drove him about town to score black tar and methadone every morning of his stay.

Upon the couch while he was being shown to it was his newest best friend, a breathtakingly gorgeous brindle boxer, born of a great dane. Nameless, the enormous puppy was owned by the Salvadoran family who lived upstairs, though by decree of their patriarch he wasn't allowed inside. Sweetness incarnated, he ached for the affection only sparingly provided him by the children of his owner and particular members of Reyansh's household; he and Rupert fell instantly in love.

During his stay Rupe was uninterrupted by a hollowing concern, however substantially dulled by the heroin, that he was gonna be robbed or killed. Upon finishing the only shower of his visit he drew open the curtain to find that someone had ganked his crocodile boxer shorts and self-designed, hand silkscreened Jim Jones Revue t-shirt. The dog protected him and his essentials and cuddled him up real good on the couch every night, repelling any further harm and assuaging the boy's concern. He decided to shorten his stay from indefinite down to four nights, and at 3:59 of the morning he'd chosen for a mum departure he tiptoed out of the house and into the garage, giving a tender record-scratching to Jimmy's comatose shoulder until he awoke.

Handing him a rubber-banded stack of 33 hundred dollar bills he whispered simply "please man, get yourself the fuck out of here. I'll see ya around."
Returning to the couch, he got nose to infinitely moist nose with the beautiful puppy dog and wrapped his fingers around his ears.

"You're not nameless anymore sweet boy, nor will you spend another milli-moment unloved. You are now Noddy Rambo Sauerstein, and that will forever be your name. I love you and I'm not leaving you to this Hell, we're leaving together right fucking now ahead of the sun and we're never coming back."

Rupert kissed Noddy's flocculent cheek and the majestic 9 month old put his paws upon Rupe's shoulders so they could share a passionate embrace whilst the soon to be liberated angel-pup catharted muffled tones of sweet relief. Together they tiptoed to the car and as quietly as he could Rupe removed the remaining components of his drum kit from the backseat to the curb. Noddy bounded inside, Lucy perked up in her tom drum, Rupe hit the gas, the rains ceased and the clouds parted, lending credibility to Reyansh's description of the city to which Rupe had accumulated a rather singular association as he drove eastwardly out of it .

A little cocaine and 14 Red Bulls enabled him to angle ferociously through worthless red states for 25 ½ hours without breaking until he re-reached the isolated blue of Minnesota and on arrival he let himself inside with the key that Aunt Miriam's mystic motherly instinct had prompted her to give him on his way out the first time through. Neither Miriam nor the sun were up yet and Rupert settled in for a few hours of recuperation.

He stayed just one day and night, wanting to get home in time to be a playoff exemption on the softball team organized by Chip which he had played on for 5 seasons, 3 of them having culminated in championships and requisitely subsequent Irish Car Bomb blackouts. Aunt Miriam had a pickleball tournament in St. Paul that afternoon, leaving him blissfully alone with his grandma. When Rupert woke she delighted in making the acquaintance of Lucy and Noddy.

"What should we do?" Rupert asked as they finished their final game of post-breakfast Scrabble.

"It's a beautiful day, why not take a walk to the pond."

"Yeah, of course, I'd love to, are you sure you can?"

"Yes dear, I'm as agile as the day you were born. I'm ready when you are."

They meandered down to the lake and Rupert helped his grandmother to a seat on one of two benches directly opposite each other at the broadest point in the pond. He stepped to the bank to see what might be streaming past for a moment before having a seat beside her. As he did so a young family of ducks glided in and began to swim.

"Do you remember how excited your little brother would get when a paddling of ducks would land in the pond behind grandpa and my house?"

"Yeah, he was the cutest."

"You were the cutest too dear. You still are."

"Thanks grandma, you're pretty cute too."

"Thank you dear."

"You're welcome grandma. I just wish I knew what I was doing."

"Sweetheart, you know your grandma, I wouldn't say it if I didn't believe it, I have more faith in you than in anyone or anything else in the world. You take your time dear, you'll find your path. Never worry about what other people have, or have done, focus yourself on what you want, and what you're going to do about gettin' it. The only things of any value in this world are love and peace of mind. When you're ready though dear, grandma's not trying to rush you."

They sat hand in hand talking for a few minutes more and after a stray raindrop bounced off of Rupert's nose they collected themselves to leave, turning back towards the condo not a second too quickly to notice the Siberian crane swooping by.

As they ate pot roast and mutually roasted green beans for dinner grandma Miriam got up for a moment and returned with a home bound book, an anthology of her poetry that she and Aunt Miriam had just finished compiling. Rupert opened randomly and began reading 'Lost Hopes, Shattered Dreams':

Somewhere amid these ruins, lies my dream

A monumental spire to good intent.

Procrastination nibbled at its face

And lassitude wore the marble down.
The wasted years rushed swiftly round its base
Toppled it over - I watched it fall
And break into a thousand shattered hopes.
You, stranger, with the lantern in your hand
Come, search with me among these mounds of clay
And help me find a piece of yesterday.

Chapter 6

Psychopathology

Manic depression is touchin' my soul
I know what I want but I just don't know how ta, go 'bout gettin' it
Feeling sweet feeling, drops from my fingers, fingers
Manic depression has captured my soul

Woman so weary, the sweet cause in vain
You make love you break love but it's all the same, when it's, when it's over
Music sweet music, I wish I could caress, caress, caress
Manic depression is a frustrating mess

Well I think I'll go turn myself off
And go on down, all the way down
Really ain't no use in me hangin' around, in your kinda scene

- Jimi Hendrix

Colony collapse disorder and neonicotinoids. Group A streptococcus. North Korean bombs aimed directly at his cock and other complexly industrial, militant potencies. These were the types of curios Rupert most optimistically studied as he existed through the meat and potatoes of the information age. Spend enough time thinking about suicide and it can be rather liberating to hear about these mostly invisible things that could theoretically save you from it any day now.

Rupert began showing neurotic tendencies a couple of days after the passing of his Grandpa Giuseppe. It was that moment of total clarity, the one where for the first time you accept and envision the death and rot of every face you've ever seen. His adjustment to it was violently chemical, for many months he'd stand screaming and hyperventilating at his bedroom window, a clear view of the Curry and Timberlane corner, watching cars commuting home, and starting at 6:29, because Isaac's E.T.A. was 6:28, with an arbitrary number of cars in mind, thinking to himself perhaps 'O.K., if dad's car is one of the next 9 to drive by, everything will be fine.' He never realized, and this behavior type more than any other has led to his social marginalization, what a stress and strain his institutionalizable psychosis placed on his mom and baby bro on those nights.

But now that I'm thinking about it, and I don't know how I forgot, it goes way back before then. On the entire opposite end of the spectrum from his triceratops-topped adventures was a dream he had equally often which, each time it surfaced, jarred him as much as would the other delight him. Through a slotted chestnut door with a cabin lock adjoined to the Sauerstein basement is what's always been known as the storage room. Not quite a death knell, it housed Isaac's tools, the snowblower and lawnmower when they were off season, file cabinets for keepsake-able schoolwork, a big ol' decadently framed and adorable portrait of Kayiane at 5...The amount of real danger it posed irrelevant, always the cautious and protective father Isaac insisted that young Rupert and Benny never go in there, which they never did.

In Rupert's dream he is playing with He-Men on the family room floor while Kayiane is in the kitchen stuffing artichokes and gabbing with her best friend Giovanna on the telephone.

"Oh no!" screams Isaac from the basement.

Down the stairs Rupert runs to see a two or three year old Benny, beheaded, shuffling his feet, no blood, no bones, no head on the floor even, just a body that has had the skin where a head could be smoothed out like clay by history's most gifted plastic surgeon.

"I told you never to go in there!" came the rest of Isaac's excruciated exaltation as Rupert's sweaty self jolted into woken reality.

And it just grew from there. He puts the most pessimistic spins on things, and speaks obnoxiously in conversations with those whose views he most offends. Like with music. He has for a long time felt that his musical tastes were impeccable, unimpeachable, better than those of anyone he's ever met with respectful deference to Jon Spencer and B.B. King, and as much and the same as he stood by the bands, dudes and chicks he revered under particular circumstances he would antagonize and often irrevocably offend someone behind the angry adrenaline he would pump out over how inexplicable it was that such terrible music was pleasing to any set of ears.

His rationale for this behavior was that he had a very basic and precedented right as a patron of the arts to voice unabashed and hyper-critical reviews of anything he saw or heard. He'd use the example of a wealthy old married couple of Upper East Side whatever-the-fucks enjoying an afternoon promenade through the Guggenheim.

"This is a dreadful and sloppy composition Dotty," would comment Bernard.

"I disagree dear," she'd reply.

"Ok. How about a quick romp in the little girl's after this room my dear?" Confrontation averted.

And it could be that simple, civil and quick, but it never is, the Phish fan or whomever always insists upon having a debate of opinion and walks away, every time, in shame or in fury. Should his opponent voice their utter distaste for the Blues Explosion, or Fats Domino, he knew what he dug was all certified killer so he wasn't gonna bother arguing over veritable fact with some Dave Matthews Band fan or what have you. It was all stupid, a waste of energy, but part of his life and insanity just the same.

Things made him crazier all the time, he'd never conclude his battles with anything, they'd pile up, overlap, interact, and it's just been breakdowns and drugs and insomnia all the time since. It's strange, I could try to describe how this feels, but it's not close to replicating the experience of deep down depression, probably a minute or two of feeling it inside and you'd never complain about inane bullshit again.

He thought about suicide obsessively and concluded he couldn't and wouldn't really do it, it was just too selfish. It was a smooth and desired way out, a lifetime of ache and second-guesses for those who love him, who just so happen to be some of the most wonderful people alive. He pushed the thought out of his head as defiantly as he could.

Looking at it objectively the things that got to Rupert were your very typical teenage angsty types of shit. Religion and hypocrisy let's say. All he wanted was people to make the most excruciatingly obvious and peace-loving choice of following the Golden Rule. No matter how hard you might try, there is just no wiggle room for justifying any other philosophy on the treatment of others as more fair and sound. In any case I'll note that he only practiced it most of the time. He tried his best but at weakened moments it's hard to do what's so glaringly right when it rather seems that those who most heartlessly and by design ignore it are pulling way out in front.

It's not a religion, so it has no ulterior motive, right? At the core of his philosophy was a quote he came across in high school by a fella named Stephen Roberts, who asserted that 'when you understand why you dismiss all the other possible gods, you will understand why I dismiss yours.' For sure as indefatigable as the Golden Rule, it goes because of bitter stubbornness, and one would have to presume intentionally so at times, over the sanctified heads of far too many.

He would recite this quotation as his third expostulation of four in his attempt to squash a conversation with a religious person, taking on the role of the atheist against the zealot, rather similar to the role of rock 'n' roller against cock rocker.

This conversation was commonly more of a drag than any sonic one, bad music is generally more palatable than even the best religion. The first thing he'd say was matter-of-fact and certainly as maturely devised as Rupert's capable of. Verbatim, he'd throw out that 'I'm sorry, I don't care to discuss religion, politics, music or eating pussy.' If this wasn't enough to give the impression of a conversation that would get as ugly and long, step two was to ask the lady or fellow across the aisle if they'd mind submitting to a polygraph test to prove their devotions. If none of the first three did the job step four was to wish them a Happy Hanukkah and briskly amble away, praying to the ladybugs they weren't afollowin'.

He simply felt a bit hollowed out and let down that the majority of his countrymen and women held to ideals that were so foreign and contrary to his own. Ideals as divisive as can be, these arbitrary all or nothing ideas that split people apart for absolutely no imperative purpose. The one time Rupert's felt truly proud of his American nationality and brethren was the night that Obama got elected. 'Maybe they're not as wicked as I thought' imagined millions of folks, as world peace evolved inside of a week's worth of imagination. But no, I mean of course not, he was an insurgent, a homo, a Muslim, a Socialist. He was able to make good on his dreams same as a $3 nigger at a Mississippi slave auction. That voice is always gonna be heard, he knew, because it was a voice that got louder the less it knew, the more it drank, and the more self-hateful it got. If only he looked a little more like Adam Clayton Powell and less like Malcolm X he might have gotten a fair shot at it.

Economic totalitarianism was a worry that seeped in later in life, he having filled his head over time with an overabundance of Noam Chomsky and web-surfed skepticism. He was worried about this long before he knew it or had taken to study of it, having had a dream in Israel that I'll always remember. An interesting enough side note is that, as you may or may not know, an authenticated and peculiar side effect of chronic marijuana smoking happens to be that an individual may lose up to the entirety of his ability to dream during the night. As Rupert fits this bill he's scarcely had a dream to remember since he was 15 or so, the one exception coming during his two weeks in Israel, blamable upon the actions of an ex-commando, one of eight charged with guarding his group, who on the first night in Jerusalem and in less than an hour had hunted down a state enemy who'd sold one of the Texas kids some weed, setting out with no intelligence other than a basic description of his face and a point in a vague direction to direct him.

In the dream he sat alone in an enormous hotel dining room and I sort of wisped over and sat on the table that fronted his.

"Rupe, should I jack up the bad guys?"

"I think you gotta."

"You were given the codes. May I have them please."

"Banana. Umbrella. Parakeet pie."

Reasonable or not, he developed a sense that maybe 500, or 1,000, some unknown but not very large number of particularly ruthless and megalomaniacal people co-conspire unopposed to control all the billions of others, thwarted and opposed by no suspicion or public animosity. On a particularly insular day he might hate and love, cry and laugh over and about 50 different things. More often than not, he's a big fuckin' mess.

So you should not be surprised to learn that Rupert has been on and off of antipsychotics and requisitely so in and out of psychiatrist's offices for a couple of decades. But the pharmaceutical industry, the prison industrial complex, the NSA, (relax dear Rupert, relax). He can't quite find a route towards full-on cooperation with psychiatry or its many potions. It doesn't make any sense to him how a textbook understanding of the human brain could possibly translate into any sort of insight into the workings of his uniquely afflicted wiring and existential discomfort. And if they got to interview him, the doctors that is, shouldn't he be afforded a brief interrogation just the same? Really quickly, are you a Republican? Anti-Semitic? Pro-life? Certainly Rupert wouldn't be the only sicko who'd opt out of paying to rely and confide in a doctor who answered 'yes' to any of those inquiries.

They can't be blamed though. If they allowed themselves a full show of empathy for every excruciating sadness spewed at them they'd be the ones crying atop interlocking plastic suicide bags.

If you asked me for a stone solid list of two entities that definitely don't kill people I'd probably go with Satanism and marijuana. What's so funny and endearing about the Satanists is that they are so far off in their embodiment of Him. Unless you are silly enough to interpret literally, the typical Satanist notion of Satan is a fun-loving guy who just wants to fuck and get fucked up and grab a piece of the pie before it's all over. But he's not even that unwholesome.

He's a big, hot, translucent to the human eyeball lug, 40 feet tall, insomniatic sleepwalker, unintentionally razing the ground, dragging a stuffed Easter bunny and wearing footed pjs, suckin' on his big fuckin' thumb.

So like I said, just unresolved angst, nothing you could call unusual. But all of it just distractions, an elaborate circuit of excuses. What was he really worried about? Same as you, same as me. Loneliness. Being disliked. The more he pushed people away from him, the more he feared that soon enough there would be no-one left to alienate. There couldn't be a woman in the world capable of tolerating his volcanic ups and downs over the course of a whole fucking lifetime. Absolutely no chance. So he was gonna end up decrepit, broke and alone, no matter how many times he got high, no matter how many pussies he slipped his cock inside, no matter how many jobs he worked, no matter how many 'pleases' and 'thank yous' he enthused.

All of it has only amounted to one legitimate suicide attempt. While living with D'Shaundrius he came up with the idea to duct tape together an impenetrable blanket of garbage bags and lay, tape and drape them all over his little room. He called the police, propped the main gate to their colonial mew, left the apartment door halfway open and sat Indian style right in the center of the black and silver pit he was ready to die in. It was 3:42 in the morning when D'Shaun walked through the door, his game in Boston having been snowed out, and by not quite 3:43 he was calmly coaxing Rupert's favorite serrated knife away from his throat and out of his grasp. If you're wondering, or wanting to ask 'Hadi, do you know if he really was gonna slice his throat that night,' my answer would be 'yes, I believe I do.'

Chapter 7

Heroin

Use just once and destroy, invasion of our piracy
Afterbirth of a nation, starve without your skeleton key
I love you for what I am not, I did not want what I have got
Blanket acne'd with cigarette burns, speak at once while taking turns

-Kurdt Cobain

It was in late February of his sophomore year, on the recommendation of his caricature of a health teacher, that Rupert began his tour through the capacious realm of drug abuse.

Her approach in addressing the dangers of marijuana that late winter afternoon was through a series of ham-boned theatrics, setting scenes and performing horrifying scenarios one might face should they ever go down that dark and predictably conclusive path.

First she was stopped at a traffic light in a drizzly dusk, wobble headed and lethargic with her fingers loosely laced to the steering wheel, her head angled and sunken into her sedan such so she could spend a few brain damaged moments tinkering with the pre-programmed radio stations, dramatically interrupted away from this activity when someone honked her from behind, in fact she became more surprised at that moment than it is possible for a person ever to be. She wiped her eyes, red and glazy from suspended disbelief, in an effort to relinquish her imaginary stone, and began driving through the intersection, slowly and with supreme concern for the people, places and things which she had lent psychotropical actuality all over the place.

She then performed in monologue a two-way dialogue in which the student played by her from the windowside of the classroom, which may as well been the Belasco Theatre the way she went for it, said something that wasn't conventionally humorous, but the student she darted to play by the door laughed at it uncontrollably because she'd succumbed to the drugs and the insuppressible dybbuk laughter they provoke.

Most horrifying was her depiction of a handful of healthy teenaged friends, down in one of their basements, so ripped outta their muthafuckin' minds on whip-its, weed and whiskey that all they could get themselves to do on a Saturday evening was eat snacks, giggle, watch some of their favorite films, cunnilinguify and fellate each other.

Rupert sat in the far back corner of the classroom and most typically stayed attentive to Mrs. Hammers' absurd though caustically cultivated and very well intentioned depictions, tutorials and philosophies. Where the chalk tray and blackboard met behind him rested an aesthetically handsome visualization of LSD-25's chemical components, which he had little control or compass against stealing one day whilst she was pre-occupationally in the throes of a meningitis aside, and which still hangs on the wall of his Timberlane bedroom as you read this, or at least as I wrote it.

He had gotten a 99 on the earth science Regents the year before but beginning with the open of his sophomore year science was without contention his poorest subject, though he found history to be even more boring and inapplicable. He was struggling his way through chemistry that year, and was thrilled when he passed the Regents with a 72, a full 16 points lower than he graded on any other state examination he took and the only score he ever gave a goddamn about, cuz he knew he was gonna be close to a ghastly sub-65 that would have meant summer school, and could very well have been reason enough to say fuck it real quick and jump off a building; he was certainly the most outwardly apathetic towards education of the 20 odd scholars alongside whom he cut-cornered through the Lakeland honors program, had he been required to sit in with the stupid kids for a summer long redo it would have crippled and ashamed his secreted intellectual elitism.

Anyhow, though he's never followed the directions on the LSD poster and concocted his own he has benefitted hundreds of times from the work of the adroit, anonymous chemists who devise that wonderful stuff. His use of it ceased entirely for more than a decade, it's worth mentioning, after an incident in Buffalo during senior year #1 of college, involving a large dose of liquid, a makeshift barbecue grill, some deceitful, self-aggrandizing flames, much vaguery to the pace of passing time and a gnaw into some pussy-pink chicken that led Rupert and Casimir to double over and remain seated in icy folding chairs, clenching their salmonella flooded stomachs long after the moon began making judgmental, antagonistic faces at them from above.

He's got ultra-precise memories of his first experience with a laundry list of narcotics, through the years he's taken 22 bonafide ones for a spin. Of all of them, I'd say there are four with which he has had an enduring love affair.

Let me preface a quick detailing of his first time smoking weed by noting that in fact his summer camp job was the third job he ever held. The second, during his senior year of high school, was as a pizza delivery boy, best job he ever had he would tell you. He began his loyal servitude to god and country as a bagger of groceries, retriever of shopping carts and thief of cigarettes at the D'Agostino's supermarket in Jefferson Valley. As far as he was concerned, two of his co-workers there were two of the coolest people he'd ever met. Kali, with rings all over her face, neck tattoos and prismatic hazel irises and Jake with the pink and green hair and locally revered punk-blues band, both a sagacious 19 years old at the time.

Warmly accepting Rupert's request, viewing it as a reasonably entertaining way to spend part of their lunch break, though to her credit Kali spent the first two hours of work that June Sunday morning grabbing $10 from Rupert, going up the street to buy a bag and rolling three joints, somehow all the while fulfilling the manager's expectations of her as a cashier.

When 12:00 came the three clocked out for their break and quickly ate a lunch ('if you eat right after you smoke it makes you less high' they explained to him). Rupert was all excitement and nerves as he accompanied the two of them to the dumpster behind the store. Predictably, Rupert got not the slightest sensation from the two joints they smoked. When work ended at 6:30 Kali gave Rupe a ride home and they smoked the third joint in her car, parallel with the 145 Timberlane mailbox, shaded by the tallest evergreen on the Sauerstein estate.

As they smoked she taught him the ins and outs of elusive pot use, Visine for your eyes, Ozium for your car. I'm sure Rupert would have loved for this tale to have ended up in the intercourse section of his story, as he had a searing crush on Kali, but rather once the joint had been smoked to the fingertips he over-thanked her for all of her efforts and kindnesses throughout the day and went inside to disappointedly play his guitar. The only way to explain highness to someone is to tell them 'you'll know it when you feel it' and alas Rupert wasn't gonna feel it that day.

A couple of weekends later, upon his sixth smoking, he came to understand what she had meant, as the handful of Caucasian friends and acquaintances he sat with, smoking and drinking around a deck-top table, became, one by one, Chinese-faced. He just had to know, and upon locating the first floor bathroom of the adjoining funhouse he discovered that he too had become a very Chinese boy, silky black hair and all.

Marijuana is a bit of an anomaly in this way, every other drug he's consumed got him high on the first try. In the case of LSD, the first time he ate it remains the most profound trip he's ever taken.

As he recalls, inaccurately I should note, his primary high school weed dealer, an inhalant junkie in his mid-twenties named Andy whose home was less than a mile away from the Lakeland campus and as such quite convenient to visit during a free period (that is until two seniors in the grade ahead of Rupert got way toasty on coke in the janitor's office one morning and left school so they could die in a high speed wrong way wreck, prompting the campus's closing and a short-lived drug war throughout the district so well devised that it accomplished as much as many drug wars proliferated by entire nations).

Andy, like Kali and Jake, was such a cool motherfucker in Rupert's estimation. Of course, just like their facsimiles in every American municipality they're quantifiably deplorable to society and shameful to their families. But as Rupert's burgeoning objectives were only to stay high and die painlessly, he saw a nobility in their anarchic ways. He should perhaps be given less acclaim than warranted by the couple of sentences above, as much as he admired those folks because they looked cool and didn't give a fuck he could envision no reality within which he'd have anything less than above-average success in the decades of endeavoring to come, for he'd been of decisively high order academic and economic standing since his conception and fully expected that there was nothing he could do to uncourse himself from effortless linearity towards that precise mold, vague though a notional certainty as it navigated white matter tracts and a handful of cortexes over and over again for a whole bunch of years.

There was to his knowledge no acid in his filthy bedroom when Rupert asked him about it, but Andy was selfless enough to throw a couple of cans of Glade into a plastic A&P bag and shotgun a Thursday afternoon rupeside drive in Kayiane's old Civic up into the rural, almost West Virginian recesses of Putnam Valley to score two paperized hits of 'super heady Jerry Garcia acid.'

Though Rupert has always been terrible at and frightened of athletic activities that take him off of his own two feet, he had most gladly accepted participation in a skiing trip to Vermont that weekend, as the generous parents of his wonderful, uncircumcised compatriot Otis had rented out a little lodge for he and a hand selected few to bask in a weekend of teenage speed and optimism.

Armed with the knowledge that an acid trip lasts 8 hours and supreme confidence in his resolve not to give a shit about anything he ate one tab in his car on the way to school and, in proliferation of probably the most overused cliché in all of lame-o drug culture, impatiently and with a freshly procured (quite coincidentally they were circulated that day) D.A.R.E. sticker on his forehead ate the second whilst his just narrow enough to eschew a description of 'Hitlery' mustache wearing European History teacher led the rest of his first period class in The Pledge of Allegiance.

As the bell rang and he stood up to embark for 2nd period tapestry weaving goddesses began levitating off of the term papers stapled to the caulkboard by the classroom entrance, swooping towards him whilst his classmates' mobilized bodies began to swirl like a barber's pole first from and through their torso and then growing rapid as they spun through their legs, finally sloshing about their glowing heads, each of which now sat atop a neck that was of at least double the length it had been an hour before and textured now like narwhal horns.

At one point during the day he was pulled aside by Otis and his ski trip consigliere Parker who matter-of-factly told him that they didn't know what the fuck he might do or be capable of in his current state, and thereby they were dis-inviting him from the trip. As if this wasn't an ample enough show of policemanship they made the bold dictation that he could be trusted precisely nowhere, and by way of threatening him with exposure of his having eaten a concoction made by the motherfucking United States government to his mom and dad they got him to relinquish his car keys. It took Rupert well into his thirties to gain the ability to accept as opposed to deflect responsibility for his indiscretions, and it was well more than two years ahead before he again spoke with anyone involved in the foray.

When the school day ended, having made a disgraceful (though rather hilarious to the right person) pasquinade of 8th period chorus, he was approaching the peak of what would by its conclusion be a 27 hour trip. He headed for the wood nearest school and was fortunate to come across an active colony of formica ants, whom he helped with a nudge back or forth wherever he saw a need until the sun went down, at which point he rolled his hoodie into a pillow, located and removed his headlamp from his bookbag and finding also his copy of it read 'Haroun and the Sea of Stories' all the way through. When he finished, realizing that he was perhaps risking death by remaining in the December freeze for all those hours, he gathered his things and made his way to the nearby house of his bandmate Scrimmo, plucking a ladder from the detached garage and climbing up and into his attic bedroom. When he woke up he called home for a ride and Isaac answered. He and Kayiane had already heard through the ol' winevine that he hadn't made the trip to Vermont.

In ten minutes of driving home together that afternoon father and son shared less of a bond and with their silence told each other more lies than they had throughout the 17 plus years which preceded it. The whole ordeal may have been forgotten or at least more easily repressed had Breaky not heard of Rupert's little adventure. She made sure to catch him as he goofballed his way past her office towards European History on Monday morn.

"Hey, Rupert, come see me today when you've got a minute ok kiddo."

"Yeah of course, I'm free third period, I'll come then."

"Ok terrific."

He had such an overactive invincibility complex that he didn't for a second think about the possibility of a transgression being the impetus for her request as he hadn't broken any laws or school policies yet that morning and thus in his mind he was working with a squeaky clean slate.

"So dear, you took two hits of Jerry Garcia blotter acid at the beginning of the day on Friday?"

"Who fuckin' told you?" was his brilliant, succinct reply.

Kayiane left work and drove to the school, she and Breaky having determined that his punishment would be an extra trip to his shrink that week. The whole damn thing marked the first occasion on which effectively his entire community of friends apart from D'Shaun and Caz considered distancing themselves from him and his parents had a real evidentiary catalyst for being dreadfully concerned about their son as a person quite capable of getting dead on drugs.

Cocaine ingested singularly, at least when it goes singularly up and into Rupert's nose by and large produces tense and unnerving feelings, but mixed with lots of booze, heroin or both it can be a Hell of a scream. They had been doing as they do on a Geneseo evening, Rupert, Casimir and Ignatius that is, when on their wayward walk to the bar out from a heated mist appeared their fine little funny friend Eric Zhang, who asked if they wanted to help him get rid of a gram. They ended up buying 3 more grams throughout the night and into the morning, all gone by 3:15, Rupert having killed more than half of it himself. Fortunately they were pounding whiskey and beers all night, at least in that Rupert's understanding of how miserable that shit can be on its own would wait for another time.

At the first sign of the sun the four went out for a predominantly bacon and biscuit breakfast and Rupe grabbed a six of Natty Ice as he stumbled all of 50 feet to his shitty ass Main Street apartment. As was his bedtime tradition when neurosis or depression had set in or seemed possible, which they always did when his blood got cocainey, he sat Indian style and slammed all six in shy of ten minutes and slept for the next 53 hours.

Rupert had been eating and snorting codeine, and morphine, Vicodin, Percocet, OxyContin for nigh on ten years by then, culminating in one of the most delightful days of his life, when he was 27, almost 28, on a sunny Brooklyn Saturday.

After college Casimir had found an apartment in the Ditmas Park neighborhood of the borough which had borne every of Rupert's grandparents, each of whom epitomized that precious place in their own wonderful way. Having been turned onto the notion of snorting some h by a co-worker he had called Rupert the previous night to see if he too was interested. Though he had years earlier committed himself to drawing the line on his narcotics pyramid below heroin and methamphetamine, the latter of which he's still yet to taste in non-pharmaceutical form, in that moment he thought it was the greatest idea he'd ever heard.

He woke up at 8:30, more alive and hopeful than he'd been about a Saturday since the days of YAC baseball and SOAC basketball games, ate a bagel, drank some apple juice, washed his face and hopped in his car. He made every light, there was not a stitch of construction on the BQE and he found a parking spot straddling the front door of Caz's row house on East 16th.

He let himself in and as Caz heard the front door open he activated the record player, which he had set to precisely perfect three person hangout volume. One of their mutual very favorites the Kinks' Arthur began and dear Casimir was at his bedroom doorway to hug his friend, fresh from a climbing in the stairwell as Ray reminisced on when "sex was bad and obscene, 'n' the rich were so mean."

Taking a seat in the super comfy chair that his folks had bought him before the fellas headed off to Geneseo he encouraged Rupert and Dion, his partner on the line at Tom's, where they most pridefully cook up the best and craziest breakfast for fuckin' macrocosms around, to interlock and shake their hands up and down and then say nice things at each others' faces. They surely did just that, after which they made a near precisely fair market trade of 5 bags of really beautiful dope for 50 bucks.

He loved every little thing about it, starting even with the seaweed Greenhornes type good times stamp on the plasticine pouches it came in and the color of it as its speed seemed to soften whilst being poured onto Caz's scuffy ol' mahogany desk. He emptied two of them, chopping and running his Hart library card over the little mound and slowly pushed it back together, let it spread out and cut it into two cigarette sized lines.

The flavor was of something bolder than caramel and rose petals, Rupe's nose had only the slightest certainty that it had snorted something. It took but fragmented moments for his insides to redefine euphoria, at which moment he went dead on the bed and played husband and wife cuddle time with Marzo, Casimir's giant ass grizzly bear who'd been born the same year as Teddy and Freddy.

They meandered ecstatically through to the early afternoon until Pakistani food was mentioned and it became the entire focus for all three. Rupert consumed his third little baggy, saving the fourth for after their meal and on an accredited suggestion the last one for the morning after. Outside they went, floating down the boulevard. Every other high comes with some sort of unease, but not this one. The simple spirited passersby were givers of life, the smoke of a cigarette the lick of a teenage pussy. The walk to the restaurant was about 15 minutes but it seemed that the elapse had instead been why the fuck would anyone ever care how many minutes something took. About halfway there Rupert felt like smoking a joint and lit it up as if incarceration for such an act were a concept still centuries unfounded.

They each grabbed an armful of IPAs from the bodega next door and became the insides of the pompless restaurant. Though Rupert sort of forgot to keep his memory plugged in while they ate come the morning he'd remark on how fuckin' good those vegetarian goops had been. Though it was but 6:30 when they finished eating they three each had already the feel of having spent either an untimed or an eternal day, and Dion broke off for home somewheres along their retreat.

Rupe and Caz arrived on a viewing of the thickly nostalgic A Clockwork Orange which they watched lying together on the latter's big ol' king bed. Rupert fell asleep before anyone had been killed by even one gigantic, ruby red or porcelain cock and slept without micro-interruption, which in a pre-dope calendar year he might have done twice. He woke around 11:30 to an unfamiliar sense of peace, noting that he had finally found a useful cure for insomnia. Caz was still in deep slumber, and Rupe went into the kitchen to make breakfast in bed for his cherished wife-buddy.

He would tell you that despite all the black thoughts and experiences drugs have been a marginal positive in his life, and that they've scarcely predicated any lasting consequences, but he'd be mistaken. From the moment he first decided to use and began openly glorifying and recommending drugs to others he was seen and treated much differently, falling entirely off of the list of people who are to be taken seriously, though he couldn't see it and so never lobbied for reintegration.

Truly though his decision to get high had been made for him many years before Mrs. Hammers and her Healthcapades, like when he would listen to Weird Al polka medleys with his friend Richie from across the street and spin around in super-fast circles so that once all of the oxygen in their heads had whistled out their ears the world would begin spinning as they came to a stop, the music would lose its time signature and become mega reverberated, they'd finish stumbling around and smash into the ground slewin' all types of guffaws. Or, when at extended family gatherings in Connecticut he'd drink something like an accumulated 3 ½ liters of high octane soda-pop, bounce around the basement for half an hour and spend the rest of the afternoon assed out on his back in the bed of an unfamiliar room. This was all just Rupe getting fucked up on what was available at the time, and a reliable predictor of his willingness as a teenager and adult to keep trying all new things as they too became attainable.

His constant intoxication put him a step behind the truly unjudgeable many who decided not to be fools. Maybe, rather definitely worse than this is that as his abuses multiplied and he lived his life with increasing secrecy, he spent depleted amounts of time with the people who had filled his youth with holistic pleasure, his mother, his father, his baby bro, grandma Miriam and Grandpa Oscar, D'Shaun and Casimir.

A suitable exemplar of his mutation into absurdity is the trip to London, Rome and Florence that he took the week after we met. Undoubtedly one of the most harmonious moments of his life occurred during his first night there, in London, after checking into his room with Casimir and having covertly, as Caz was still among the innocents, though a sweet little meniscus toppling drop away from overflowing with curiosity, rolled a great fat joint with about half of what was in his sock and got high in a lounge chair all alone at nightfall in a mist, an ocean away from home, providing him a real moment of pure peace, of strict, exclusive positivity. And who could take much offense to this, or grow fearful that it could destroy the fabric of a young man, a solitary joint smoked at a precisely perfect moment.

That same night however he discovered that his English teacher's son and his friends had traveled the Atlantic expanse with ounces of assorted marijuanas sitting in the pockets of the very pants they wore through customs and then the sky, and he and Casimir spend the entirety of the London leg of their expedition getting mashed on weed and vodka cokes with those fellows and the more sinful young ladies who had made the journey along with them. This was his first experience with true round the clock intoxication, and he embraced it with a carnal lust.

In Rome he became a lone wolf, sneaking off as early each day as he could to mix with the filthiest, most drugged out townspeople and wayward wanderers he could find. There were very strict behavioral guidelines, laid out at a parents, students and chaperones meeting two nights before the trip, he could hardly have broken them more often or thoroughly and for his disavowal of them he should have been sent home when, mashed and entering their hotel at 3:58 in the morning he was ambushed by the English teacher's husband to discuss the procedures they would follow to fly him away, alone, that afternoon. Rupert began by explaining that he was on a new antidepressant that had become largely effective for him though it had a high probability of wanderlust as a side-effect. He told the man one Hell of a sob story that morning and got himself out of a pickle. He had no glaring preference about whether or not he stayed, he just didn't want to have to justify, then, now or in any way, his drug and alcohol addictions to anyone but his own damn self.

So that same year, back in Yorktown, when he was caught off campus by Lorraine the omniscient Lakeland minivan cop and subsequently found himself high on LSD in an office with two deans and a bookbag full of weed and mostly homemade paraphernalia (fortunately one of the deans was Ms. Breaky, who allowed him to leave after removing and replacing the few things in the bag that were school appropriate), or when, having put precisely no time into preparing for it, he went to the AP European History exam, three drops of liquid in the Altoid he sucked away on the drive over, drunk on vodka, and spent the 45 minutes he was told he must stay in the exam room showing his dick to Maureen Benedeen in the underlit back right corner, (who, incidentally, also attended Geneseo and though she had a gigantic rugbyman boyfriend was kind enough to blow Rupert a few times as he adapted to life as a campusface), in general and otherwise he could consistently be found playing out far from exemplary or fruitfully trajected scenarios fueled and inspired by intoxication.

It might be a surprise to you that, set up by the injury of multiple teammates and vain attention paid to his plumpy physical form since the previous season, Rupert began the tennis season his senior year as the #1 singles player on the Lakeland team. He withheld that distinction until the moment that his first match was slated to begin, as he was nowhere to be found and his coach was left with no delegation other than forfeiture of the match.

It was but spare moments after he had done so that Rupert awoke on the back porch of the Sauerstein home, having deserted school after 2nd period behind a whimsical decision to drink the remaining peach schnapps from a bottle which his folks had cracked years before and had never since poured from. Awakening from his afternoon blackout, in tattered and paint splattered jeans below a white t-shirt with 'vagina' calligraphied on it in hot pink and purple paint marker he drove down and around thru town to Downing Park, where his coach notified him he could and should play an exhibition match against the fellow who had come all that way to entangle skill sets with him, a sober and more skillful player regardlessly, that day's friendly a most glaring testament to these truths.

In the course of the 18 minute long, 6-0, 6-0 exhibition, Rupert made contact with 9 balls during his return of service games. He fell down attempting to pick up a ball 16 times and said 'fuckface' spiritedly 87 (it's simply a fantastic word to stim around with). Having squandered the rather tentative and undeserved ranking the next day he decided to withdraw conclusively from his most inauspicious acquaintance with scholastic athletics.

Let's leave the whole story though, drugs and alcohol were sometimes good for Rupert, just as they are often good for society at large. Getting fucked up allows people to lose their woes for a bit, create distinctive narratives, invent futuristic toys, there's just a tradeoff, a check and a balance of potential violence and early death that needs to be acknowledged and ratified.

Had it not been for marijuana there surely never would have been a 'Marriage of Friendship and Fun,' a sacred union formed between Casimir, Rupert and D'Shaundrius one silly summer evening between their freshman and sophomore years of college. They were solemnized by Super Grover, whom Rupert had found unblemished, lying comatose across the yellow lines of East Main Street, near the Hart library. This happens to be the same Super Grover with whom Rupert went on upwards of 100 completely underlapped, often psychedelically enhanced night journeys during his absolutely in-illustrious tenure at Geneseo. They hastened to gather anything borrowed, blue or the like for the wedding though Casimir wore lipstick and eye-liner and was a beautiful, most coveted bride-fellow.

I apologize but I find it difficult to refrain entirely from making fatherly excuses for Rupert, Geneseo was a dreadfully boring place to live and most of the other kids were getting fucked up too. Genesee and neighboring Livingston counties are rife with beautiful waterfalls and gentle rural landscapes that were only made more breathtaking when consumed with a good psychotropic base.

LSD was as easy for Rupe and friends to acquire as a bag of Doritos in those days as they had an upper class pal named Perry who through an undisclosed source was up inexhaustibly to his eyelashes in sheets of the stuff and would gladly dispense them to particular copacetic folks for somewhere between 50 cents and a buck a tab, depending on his mood, which ranged from stoned and happy to stoned and sleepy, and the current health of the purchaser's portfolio.

And in case that didn't quite sweeten his college experience adequately enough around the same time he came to know Perry he made the acquaintance of Mick, a fellow of equal goodwill and viable commodity, a dashing, bespectacled long-haired frat boy with a sort of

Jesus everyman charisma, the legatee of an institutionalized childhood friend and as such controller of the most mouth-wateringly fragrant, peace offering, size of a disfigured softball, muted charcoal colored smokable putty, he'd pluck a big toe off of the thing, slip it into a Parliament cellophane and ask Rupert for 'three or four bucks or a nugget or whatever.'

By their junior year the three buddies in bigamy and their equally fine friend Ignatius, who'd gotten cold tootsies on the night of the wedding and decided to remain a bachelor, spent most evenings eating acid, smoking weed and drinking cheap, filthy beer in Casimir's apartment, a garbage can lid's throw from the Main Street bars and the village's only convenience store. Iggy had a meatheaded friend whom he'd adventitiously walked in on at the epicenter of a frat house laundry room circle jerk, and who worked at the least cheeseball drinking hole in town, from behind the bar of which, in return for not divulging that the school's most elite fraternity was awash with closet homosexuals, he would ready up for each of the fellas a complimentary pint of Jack on the rocks anytime they stumble-hooted into the bar.

Then there's this, one of the greatest nights ever, any and all dementia and wasted time over the course of four and a half years Shanghaied in the gloomy doom of Western New York were eradicated in one evening of IPAs, macro-dosed lysergic acid and a feverish, clockface lapping shower of meteors as witnessed from the dock behind Perry's out of the way lake house late and into the early morning days before Rupert's departure from Geneseo forever.

But with time these sorts of thrills became prosaic, or maybe he told himself they had as justification for moving up and into more lethal, body-high type drugs. His route was precisely the one Mrs. Hammers had begged the children not to follow by the way, from alcohol to weed to psychedelics to pills to coke to crack to heroin to coke and heroin wrapped around each other like Lam's *Satan* in the barrel of a syringe.

He got more than three years into his affair with heroin before finally he shot it. Armed with all the death statistics Google could avail for him, snorting and smoking it was enough for him until one day it became just barely not enough. The idea that having never shot it would more than likely in the end save his life was until that moment all the justification for abstinence he required.

He once woke needing to take a piss and hovered his compromised dick over the toilet, standing as sturdily and for as long as he could, opportuning his bladder to awake from its opioid induced coma, falling asleep right in that spot before anything at all had dribbled out. He woke planted in that same coordinate 3 hours later, his pants and underwear Isaac Newton'd to his ankles (both had become increasingly loose in their fit as he'd advanced into intravenous use), pissing on his hands, which as he vivified were on display, submerged dorsa down in the toilet water, resting on the shit residued porcelain, providing stability for his half-dead body, he having passed out and folded at the waist moments after attempting the now onerous task which he'd first accomplished once abluted, swathed in a hospital binky and returned to mommy a lifetime beforehand.

He has this really nifty Persian rug that he'd obsessively sought out and selected, a 30th birthday gift from Isaac and Kayiane. One night he got the impetus to masturbate out of the faintest glimmer of a credibly sexual thought, and not having ejaculated in months he slathered moisturizing cream on his long lost pal and worked up and on half an erection for upwards of an hour until a colossal load of defective jism lackadaisically seeped and sputtered out, the most pathetic denouement in the history of narrative. He wiped the majority of it off himself with a cigarette acne'd t-shirt turned cumrag and got up to assess in the mirror precisely how disgusting he was in that moment, though he didn't make it as he tripped his enervated ankles over each other and fell down, kitty-cornering the rug, shriveled and opiate-babied dick still out, nodding off and becoming supersemen-glued to it from his peehole for a day and a half.

But heroin is just so motherfuckin' fantastic. Pure, dark, nag champa ash tinted New York City diesel tastes and smells so delicious, and the moment it gets to work inside of you every problem or sadness you've ever had disappears, euphoria settles in and eradicates your every neurose in a milli-moment. Having popped his diacetylmorphine cherry Rupert had not the fortitude to repel this opportunity to abolish his perpetuated fear and loathing in a mere sniff, dragon chase or plunge. For years the first two delivery methods sufficed, but the point of no return did indeed arrive and he asked his dealer to prep him for a shot of straight heroin, chased the following day with several speedballs, in the aftermath of the 34th birthday party.

There are few places in the world with better heroin than New York and there are a hundred countries that could have birthed him where he may have gone his entire life without anyone offering him that uppermost gratification. Say what you will about the decay facing a society where drugs are plethoric and glorified. One must not look much farther than the disparity between the artistic outputs of the west and east in the past century to see that a doped up society executes some rather dope endeavors. If you don't believe me, go listen to some Chinese music for an hour and let me know how that grabs ya.

At times Rupert has gotten home in a speedy blackout, most typically motored by the combo of dope, coke, drizzy and booze, compelled to write an anecdote or short story. As he'd write he'd feel his prose eclipsing the likes of Kafka and Hemingway but every time he woke up with the moonrise the following day he'd find his newest opus to be nonsensical and unsharable. He had a similar opinion of the woodworking, painting and sculptures that he spent large plots of time creating and with which he overfilled his various spaces. As he wrote he actively and shamefully denounced Hemingway's proclamation that 'all first drafts are shit'.

On no more than one of these occasions he produced a work of (debatable) merit and sense, which I'd care to share with you here:

While generally afraid of slipping into discourse of any reasonable syntactical legitimacy, there were certain things that they synergistically found to be of purpose and productivity. One commonality amongst them was a duly painful aversional nervousness to lapsing into absent-minded defining the idea of 'importance', an imperative avoidable one of Hell's nasty tricks.

Just as only the most talented balloons can be rectangles, resisting the impulse towards dark gloomy death by pop-rock and ether filled carnival dunk tank is only achievable to the boys in a paltry few ways, they having spent a chunk of their harrowing spans trying and clawing and performing their third favorite celebratory routine, the 679th street subway platform squat thrust boogie which quite likely (accelerated) catapulted into notoriety by the Easter Bunny's cleverly hidden gift (it was tucked under the knife and fork) of 38 Chick Willis,

Fats Domino and Thurston Harris beauties as performed by the Jon Spencer Blues Explosion, under the influence of the Vatican's top secret, less common than the vomitously paltry number of wild Bengal tigers euphoria tincture, earns the fellows a cool quarter mil a year, which as quickly as it comes in they use to compensate homeless men for midtown french kissing and tushy slapping the upper echelon of far-right closet cases.

Section of the otherwise useful as a human voice cord nullifying device drawer of cereal eating and cauldron stirring spawns of beings not majorly different than humans though brain capable in a ratio something like us: them: sweetened vanilla almond milk. Into the Satanic dungeon of unconventional thought by years and I own all ten of the commodities that Robin Leach lists as the most important in the world. I just completed this dream collection last week when my taxidermied Iraqi toddler finally arrived in the mail. I got him up there on the wall right next to the baby giraffe head I Talibanned off when I lost a bet and had to go to Africa while my buddy got to go to the Tri-Annual Cheesesteak Crawl in Camden.

Once, for a bit more than two days, he sat on the couch of his and Chip's humble home in nothing but koala bear boxer shorts, snacking on the 25 Vicodin and 35 xani-bars he had just purchased, as domestically and casually as can possibly be. Chip kept an alternating watchful eye on him from above and below as Rupert nodded and drooled, told passersby out his bathroom window that he had a knife, laughed maniacally at a slightly overstuffed peanut butter and jelly sandwich. Since the day he started abusing drugs he's waterlogged or clumsily let smash 4 computers beyond repair, mangled up two cars and burned 3 mattresses as well as a wardrobe's worth of awesome t-shirts. He'd changed from an astute, clever and sought-out companion to a socially withdrawn and unlikeable miscreant.

So what's the last thing I should say here about Rupert and drugs? I'm not sure, but what I want to say is this. Because he used drugs, he lived a more colorful life. He laughed and cried far more than he would have without them. Sometimes they completely connected him with the world, having gotten to work on detaching him from it already. He's got a case of anhedonia that'll never go away. At his worst, shooting speedballs more often than sharing conversations, Otis Redding could have showed up to work out a new tune on their matching J-45s, or Pablo Picasso could have dropped by to collaborative in adorning a canvas with sacred abstractions, he would have been apathetic to the whole thing if there weren't enough drugs to last the session through (and at least a little left to soften the morning excruciation).

What it really comes down to, which I've concluded upon having thought quite a lot about Rupert's experiences is this: once you've made the decision to shoot cocaine and heroin, because that's really all we're talking about, you've opened yourself up to a bit of an inevitably.

Forget for a minute the physical highs and lows, when you decide to really get down with that shit you're accepting the maybe everyday task of meeting with grimy folks in places where cops are looking to make arrests. And Lou Reed was absolutely right, you will wait and wait for those folks, cuz they know you're gonna, even if and when to any and all other responsibilities you'd allot no patience at all.

Rupert and his red afro were saved from incarceration a thousand times, loitering on the corner of Frederick Douglas and 116th, waiting longer and longer every time for skimpier and less potent bags, unaware that they (the boy and the afro) were being protected from inside the department. Had he not been he'd have become a regular face in the world famous New York tombs as years of mid-meal naps and self-compromise went by.

Freeing yourself from coke and heroin is a most physically painful process and demands the highest order of courage and conquest, though it's done every day, and worth every agony. Just the same, some day, perhaps 10, 15 years since your last injection, you so easily could be visited by a mundanity that was once a trigger or run into the wrong guy at the supermarket, a slippery thought or a deja vu flavor in your mouth will have you disemboweling couch cushions and ransacking closets, sniffing, licking, upturning, clawing away in search of a fragment of an Adderall or a morsel of Percocet that you once dropped in some other place where it was stepped on and vacuumed up years ago.

Chapter 8

New York City

Once I lived the life of a millionaire, spent all my money, I just did not seem to care.
Took all my friends out for a good time, bought bootleg whiskey, champagne and wine.
Then I began to fall so low, lost all my good friends, I did not have nowhere to go.
If I ever get my hands on a dollar again, I'm gonna hold on to it 'til that eagle grins, yeah

'Cause no, no, nobody knows you
When you're down and out.
In your pocket not one penny
And as for friends, you don't have any...

When you finally get back up on your feet again
Everybody wants to be your good old long-lost friend.
Said it's mighty strange, without a doubt
Nobody knows you, when you're down and out.

- Jimmie Cox

It's the place one goes when they want to experience the best there is. As a child Rupert saw the finest collections of internationally assembled troubadours perform Miss Saigon, Fiddler on the Roof, Les Miserables. It was at the Museum of Natural History where a set of T-Rex bones befell him in love with every animal in the island universe, within the MoMa that he came to understand the beauty that can be created behind a singular interpretation of experience. It's where as a scraggly little redheaded idiot some insane woman approached with an offer for fame and fortune.

It's where the goddamn Yankees play for Christ's sake. And though you'd be hard pressed to pinpoint a moment along Rupert's way during which the Knicks could be considered an even ersatz best it was on the hardwood of Madison Square Garden where on a ternium of early adolescent nights he got to watch Magic, Michael and Larry do the damn thing.

It was in Isaac's office when as a four year old he was introduced to the kinesthetic anomaly of video games. Years later, when Benny was readied to join them for take-your-little-ones-to-work-day they would feast on paella and leche frita, drinking virgin pina coladas, intermittancing the saunter back to his company in the sky with a stop at the local memorabilia emporium wherein he'd purchase each of his favorite fellas their choice of a 24-pack box of baseball cards. There isn't a city in the whole fucked world more magnificent.

He was there when The Jesus Lizard opened for Rage Against the Machine at Roseland, for The Go at the Knitting Factory. He's seen The Blues Explosion 48 times, he's seen Fats Domino, Little Richard, B.B. King, Albert King, Willie Nelson, Dan Bern, Bob Dylan, Beck, The Beastie Boys, The Beatnuts, A Tribe Called Quest, M.O.P., Wilco, The Flaming Lips, Dandelion, The Greenhornes, The White Stripes, The Black Crowes, The Black Keys, The Black Angels, The Black Lips, The

Black Hollies, The Singles, The Hollies, The Who, The Rolling Stones, Soundgarden, Alice in Chains, Black Sabbath, Neurosis, Pantera, Green Day, The Clash, The Detroit Cobras, The Blue Van, so many fuckin' people, the Cato Salsa Experience, the Flaming Sideburns, Black Joe Lewis and the Honeybears, The Buffalo Killers, The Jim Jones Revue and on and on and before even all of that joined his dad and Johnny Slapshaft for one of three global, invite only conjoinings of Ginger Baker, Ringo Starr, Keith Richard, Duane Allman, Bootsy Collins, Geezer Butler, Bobby Keyes, Maurice Davis, Wilson Pickett, Eric Burdon, Etta James and ¾ of the fuckin' Shangri-Las, who over two uninterrupted hours kicked the cock off of 43 killers spanning the late '50s and early '60s, calling themselves The Big Bananas, onstage at the World Famous Apollo Theatre on a sub-zero February Monday night in 1984, the 18th I think. All in that one little island town.

And what a joy it is for him to nowadays be able to revisit the wonderment of that night several times every week by turning his neck 68 or 70% to the left while he stands there at Freddy Doug and 116th, smoking, blasting his Walkman, pumping his knees and despairing for his man to come slap the next couple of days into his palm.

Outside of eating, shitting and other sorts of bare bones maintenance I can't really come up with any habitual therapeutic, let alone somehow authentic New York experiences had by modern day Rupert, throughout the 59 months since he's been an all the way junky which mirror those of his youth. He doesn't even really like baseball anymore, and probably only stays up on basketball because his best friend plays it professionally. Certainly he pays no mind to the boundless cultural and educational opportunities that are always a hotfoot or a subway ride away. If he is to be found on a subway car it's guaranteed to be headed either to Harlem or back down from there to Union Square, and if ever he nourishes his intellect there's little retention as he's commonly half dead on the couch with a Netflix documentary pixelating the television screen and a cigarette burning through his t-shirt.

On *The Night of Three Fights* for example Rupert had shot most of a bundle of beautiful, smoky brown, clean and potent dope along with just shy of a half gram of good not great cocaine, chewing on six xani-bars as afternoon tended towards evening until eventually he determined to hit the streets, grabbing D'Shaundrius' frayed, dehydrated copy of The Canterbury Tales from the bookshelf on his way out. D'Shaun was off on a west coast clip and when Rupe was left to his lonesome in the apartment he behaved no less, no more than as a rambunctious and senseless psychopath under induction of perhaps a second grade intellect and concern for or understanding of his environment, his propensity for activities leaning towards anarchic, suicide-by-cop dum-dum type envelope pushing.

He felt like a big ol' fraud living in that beautiful part of town, amongst the placid faces of people who had developed the social skills and ambition mandatory for procuring work fertile enough in some capacity to afford them a sustinent life in such an idyllic place. But he had less than 10 grand left when he got back from California, and he couldn't pass up D'Shaun's offer to move in with him 'cuz I need you to feed my turtles when I'm on the road.'

They decided to take a chance on moving Lucy into the terrarium with his two handsome red-eared sliders and were delighted as they quickly became a darling little family. Noddy presented a different predicament, he's way too big to have lived comfortably in that space, but there's a happy ending there too as Kayiane had just retired a couple of weeks earlier and was delighted to have him around to go on hikes and keep her good company while Isaac was off at work. That puppy fell in love with her as absolutely as had her sons and as someday would her grandchildren.

So that night he decided to venture out and show everybody how high he was, turning right out of the Lilliputian apartment complex and left to head south on 2nd Avenue. Incapable at the time of swift propulsion he counterbalanced this, though there was literally nothing hurrying him, by disavowing the Socialist safety of commandeering red hands and bright white men and crossed each intersection without looking around or slowing down, almost dying thrice as infuriated cabbies jammed their over-worked brakes to spare him a languidly demise. The raucous full blast of '*Whatcha Doin*' screamed into his ears which paired with an intracellular state teetering not very far from overdose nullified any awareness of the blaring horns he antagonized into gettin' slammed.

As his Cro-Magnon meander proceeded down 2nd Avenue he noticed two dread-headed street urchins aways up ahead amusing themselves by terrorizing groups of three and four northbound touring or nerdly innocents by schizophrening their tongues and convulsing their arms millimeters from their victims' faces and saying "boo" and "yoop" and those kinds of things.

As fucked up beyond marginally inappropriate for public as Rupert was a prurience for justice overcame him and he sped himself in close on the situation at 15th street. He wriggled between them and pushed each with the full force of his once athletic arms, one of them smashing into a federal mailbox and the other smashing through a large windowpane at the exterior of one of many fancy-panted restaurants on 2nd between 19th and Houston. As each slunk to the floor Rupert's gaze remained inside a southbound tunnel. Apathetically he reverted to his original pace and continued onward, not to look back.

When he reached 2nd Street he turned west and from there began hanging random lefts and rights, zig-zagging northwesterly. He reached Broadway at 7th street, which is double wide between there and 10th. It was 10:05 on a Friday evening and as such the vicinity was dense with souls headed every which way. As he sees it, right up there on an unacceptable par with being late and thus wasting someone else's time, to navigate the city without paying close attention to those around oneself is a less dangerous yet equally deplorable show of discourtesy than perhaps jerking off and playing Gameboy whilst driving on the Sprain Brook Parkway during evening rush hour.

A slick haired imp in pink shorts with a powder blue button down tucked tightly all the way into them was doing exactly this as he came through the horde Rupert's way, his head turned to the right in mirthy conversation with a conventionally attractive, whitebread girlfriend. With his left hand he propelled a wheeled article of luggage and it was headed directly towards poor Rupert, who hadn't the spatial freedom to move to either side of it. Realizing that the dude was not gonna give up any space he was left to evoke his grade school kickball dominance, winding up his lethal left leg and putting a mighty swing on the obstructive carryall.

As he made square contact it began soaring immediately, long, loftily and confident in the sky, surely it would have converted the point after touchdown were Rupert on field at the time with his underrated squad of local footballing dredges known as The Gramercy Smackbags. It somehow came to land half in and half out of a city trash can, and as he had in the immediate aftermath of his first squabble, 7 and change minutes earlier, he powered onward as if nothing had either happened or mattered to anyone anywhere, and of course as he was in the city where more so than in any other minding your own fuckin' business is sacrosanct, there was no resistance to his doing so.

He'd already that night upped his lifetime number of recorded fights by impossible percentages, from 0 to 2, and unconventional in being classified as such as these incidents certainly were, a quick bit of math or a look back to the top of this anecdote will tell you that he wasn't quite yet finished.

He continued heading west, occasionally angling south, stopping at the corner of 14th and 4th to tie off and shoot the speedball that he'd wrapped in a t-shirt scrap and was saving in his pants pocket for the right moment. He checked his wrist for a watch that hadn't been there for twenty years and his phone which was out of juice, a futile effort to learn that it was by then 1:57 in the morning, though he remembered nigh on nothing of the past few hours. The product of his night, even with all the warfare, amounted to nothing more than a sparse strew of sun bleached Polaroids. He scraped inside 7-11 for a bottle of lemon-lime Gatorade, chewed up a couple of Xani-bars as he paid for it and slammed it back, dribbling it all over his chin, wondering if the innocent injection of a night-shifting dentist's novocaine needle and not intoxication covering a smattering of narco-scheduling parameters would be the likeliest presumption as to his inability to get it in his mouth.

At 2:34 he happened upon Washington Square Park and laid down on the first unoccupied bench he came across for a snooze. Hardly a milli-moment later a sizeable fellow with no regard for the importance of recuperative sleep gave him a forceful three-fingered nudge on the forehead.

"Gimme all yo' shit white boy," he initiated.

Rupert slow-motion opened his eyes to size up the man who he already well expected was gonna be as big and scary as was his voice compassionless and maniacal. "Ok man, it's all yours, I'm gonna get up real slowly so I can go in my pockets, please don't hurt me."

"Hurry up nigga, I'm gonna fuck you up in a minute."

Languidly he swung his feet off of the bench and rose to his feet as steadily and appeasingly as he could, sticking his right hand in his pocket. "I got like a buck fifty in here bro, just take it, I got kids at home."

"I don't give a fuck 'boutcho' kids, just gimme dat shit."

"Yes sir, here you go."

He looked utterly defeated, as much of a straight mix of apathy and hate towards living this life inside him as at any other moment, though only he knew it to be an Academy Award worthy feign, cuz he cocked back that lethal left leg of his and smashed it into the motherfucker's ribs. As the dude hunched over and hugged up his crackled row of bones Rupert rose up with his right foot and drove through the guy's face with it, knocking him down and flat out on his back.

The gush of pride and adrenaline that followed this combative triumph was tempered almost immediately by the awareness that this guy must certainly be in business or some other cahoots with one or more of the other crooks and drug dealers who colonize that park at night, and though it's a metropolitan pitch black there after the sun rotates away someone must have seen him jack this guy up.

In that moment he came to know what it must be like to be Barry Sanders, pointer-fingering The Canterbury Tales by their spine and zip-dodging his way out of there, all the way back up to 16th and 3rd before running completely out of steam and once again collapsing on a bench, this time much more safely and with intentions of only a few minute hiatus, as he was indubitably ready to get back to his little room and sleep until D'Shaundrius got home late the following evening.

Instead he woke up at 10:45 feeling truly great, like he'd gotten over on somebody by not letting the sun sneak past yet again without getting a good look at it, legitimately wanting to interact with the city by the light of the day. He took a long, scalding shower to wash off about three weeks of filth, dressed in clothes which he privately believed made him look handsome, chugged a tall glass of ice cold water, wedged a suboxone underneath his tongue, hot-footed down the stairs and on outside to see what was what. He does get like that sometimes, the chemicals in his brain intermingle in such a way where optimism overtakes fear. It may last five minutes, or maybe even 5 hours, but either way when it happens he's keen on playing it out and seeing where it leads.

Though he saw them with graduated infrequency as years melted away, there were still a handful of high school cronies with whom Rupert kept contact, gathering and re-engaging with them most July 4ths and New Year's Days, perhaps otherwise and in addition for an evening of low grade debauchery twice or three times during the playout of a calendar year.
Despite his eternal wariness about her, one of several on sort of the fringes of this collective was Apollonia Stracciatelli, who, at least publicly, had dialed back on perversion as her brain had become an adult, I mean, sixth

grade was like 25 years ago, hardly recognizable as the everyday in-school orgiastic insurrectionist of her youth. For example, her body no longer retained the adaptation it had developed once she'd stuck 50 or so uncoiled clothes hangers in there to do it herself, to self-abort the little ones, thousands of them, which had tried and failed to evolve inside her salty womb over that span.

He had seen her on but scant occasion since high school and when those moments appeared he was hyper-steadfast and mindful of a conversation he'd had with a credible fellow a few years his senior when he was 18, who speculated, based on his experience and that of the 5 or 6 other locals who had fully resisted her advances, that there comes some time, or that there's some number of refusals perhaps at which she employs her wicked mysticism to either end a man's life or make it unendurable. Nevertheless this knowledge never helped him soften the excruciation of their dialogues, he seemed always to find a way to anger her, or perhaps she always decided it would be good fun to debase and humiliate him, even when he succeeded in keeping their interaction to a mere passing pleasantry upon finding themselves standing in each other's eye and earshot.

Imagine how deflated and regretful of his decision to go outside he was as he saw her face that early October noon, trillions of spatial permutations on that island, gridded and coiled beyond its own horizon, and yet there she stood. But as the occasion unfolded his mood changed from terrified to apprehensively charmed, mostly so because of the gorgeous, cooing baby girl she pushed along in a stroller, and notice made that her breasts and vagina were completely unexposed by conservative, matronly clothing.

"Oh wow, Rupert, I just thought of you the other day, you look great, how have you been?

"I'm fine, who is this precious little darling?"

"This is Olivia. She's kinda cute huh. Her first birthday's coming up in December."

"She's an angel Apollonia, congratulations, really."

'Thanks so much. Her dad didn't stick around, but whatever, I'm just so happy to have her."

"I know you'll be a great mom, you're a strong-willed, smart young lady."

"Rupert you're still the same sweetheart you always were, aren't you? Thank you," she said as she gave him what from anyone other than a world class manipulator and sexual psychopath would unsuspiciously be a platonic hug. "You wanna hold her?"

"Of course, I'd love to," he replied, and as she handed her to him each of his eyes welled up with a tear, for two reasons. First, he recalled back to several times in the past when he suspected that contemporaries of his hadn't extended the same offer for fear that he might nod off and lose the grip that his junkied arms had on their darling little one. Second, but certainly first if ranking them by their existential value, because there he stood with the person in his life who he feared and disliked above all others, holding her child and speaking in a wonderfully sincere and amiable way, and this empowered him upon the notion that other impossibilities must have had their statuses altered in that moment also. "So what made you think of me?"

"Well it's that time of year, your birthday, mine, Donald's, Orckie's and Casimir's are all in the next couple of weeks. How about we try to get a bunch of people together for a party, maybe rent a warehouse or something."

"Yeah, I mean absolutely, if you can find us a place I'll definitely throw down on it with you."

"I will, for sure, tonight or tomorrow, let's do it two Saturdays from now, on the 18th, so after midnight it'll be your birthday."

"Sounds good to me."

"Cool. I'm so happy right now Rupert, and I gotta say, I am so sorry for all the shit I put you through all those years, and I'm not stupid, I know you think I'm a giant fucking whore, but I really want to show you that I'm a different person than I was then."

"Listen Apollonia, there can't be too many people out there who are more emotionally juvenile than me, and I'm not stupid either, I know what people think of me. So I hate being judged, and I try my best not to judge other people, and I also wanna try being different than I was. I'm really happy right now too, let's just forget all of it, let's just start completely over."

"Thank you Rupert," she said, wrapping an arm around his neck. "Seriously Rupert, you feel so thin," she noticed, having slid her hand down past his bare ribs to his jutting pelvic bone, "have you been using a lot recently?"

"Uh, yeah a little bit."

"I know, it's ok. I swear to you Rupert, I wanna be a positive in your life, a real friend to you. But honestly kid, you're gonna hafta get sober at some point, for certain people to take you seriously anyway. Forget about that for now. Promise me, if you're ever in a fucked up situation and you don't know what to do just call me, ok?"

"I will, really. Thank you."

"Promise?"

"Promise."

Ever so gently he replaced and strapped Olivia into her stroller, tenderly squeezing her top ten thing in the world baby belly for a moment or two before standing up straight to once again hug Apollonia and say farewell.

"Bye sweetie, I'll send you the deets soon as I figure it all out."

"Alright thanks, should be pretty rad."

"It's definitely gonna be."

By the end of his galavant and during his homebound stairclimb she'd already secured a suitable venue for their hootenanny and called him with the address and sorted particulars about the place she'd found. "Let's just tell people to bring whatever drinks and shit as they want, if we're already paying for the place I think that's fair, right?" she reasoned.

"Yeah that sounds good to me. So I can call like my bro, Casimir and D'Shaun, my friend Chip, and Steinway's brother just had a baby so he's coming into town, he'll be here then I think. Is it ok if you call everybody else?

"Yeah yeah of course that's fine. I'll put something up about it on Facebook like a normal person. I'll call ya in a few days to see what's up."

"A'right cool. Enjoy the rest of your day Apollonia. Really great to see you."

"Thanks Rupert, you too. Bye bye." She blew him a kiss farewell.

"Bye bye," he echoed and quickly hung up.

The pleasantries they shared that day created within Rupert's soul the greatest upgrade in his opinion of another and resultantly himself that he's ever experienced. His self-esteem and valuation of humanity skyrocketed towards Mars and he began looking ahead to strengthening and reinvigorating other relationships and, to put it as simply as possible, living well. He even stopped slouching as he walked in a subconscious effort to diminish his visibility (everything about him, really), hitting the street upright and proud from that moment onward.

Rather than head uptown for dope the following morning he went out for about 40 minutes of briskly walking up and down avenues and running the streets, this got a little lengthier, speedier and more run-centric by the day. When he got home, he banged through three 15 rep sets of push-ups and 20 of these really fantastic and exertive leg lifts, taught to him by Ben's squeeze Viktorya when he was out in Humboldt, taught to her by her world renowned ballet dancing grandma, who so the story goes did absolutely no daily exercise other than the very same number of said lifts and 8-14 hours of dancing up on her tiny, formidable Belarusian toes.

He threw away the stone's worth of sugary junk strewn about the cabinets and surfaces of the apartment and headed over to Morton Williams, buying nothing other than flounder, a chicken, yogurt and a mess of leafy green herbs and vegetables. I must say I was proud of the boy as he did no drugs in the nine days between chance encountering Apollonia and the party, only smoking three joints and putting on three pounds of muscle.

Also, he fucked for the first time in 5 ½ years. A little bored and lonely one night he took a walk down to the Double Down Saloon, which along with Lucy's are the two honky tonks he prefers on the rare occasion he goes out drinking. He went inside and beyond the bar to his left en route to the bathrooms, out from which came two girls from Detroit who as it happened had hitchhiked their sultry selves into New York that very afternoon.

They were both absolutely gorgeous, 22 Rupert thought, one maybe 4 inches taller than the other, decked out in matching 10 gallon hats, crocodile boots, thinly strapped hippie dresses and cocaine moustaches.

"What's your name?" the taller one asked and giggled as their paths met and she corkscrewed a finger through one of his curls.

"I'm Rupert."

"I really like the curls in your hair."

"Thanks. I really gotta take a piss."

"Ok quickly let's go!"

The girls twirled back around towards the bathrooms and Rupert followed them into the men's room. They ever so gently took hold of his dick from opposite sides of him as he pissed, shook him off and the shorter girl bend down to close his fly with her teeth.

He passionately kissed the coke off of their faces and out of the bathroom they went, elbowing their way to the bar where Rupert ordered 6 shots of well whiskey and three PBRs. They threw 'em all back and decided it was time to grab a taxi up to D'Shaundrius', wherein they embarked upon a bi-sexual bacchanal which outlived the moon and even saw Rupert's asshole accept and appreciate a rare bit of satisfaction.

He felt so fuckin' alive in the morning and asked if they wanted to tramp about The Freedom Tunnel with him, which he'd wanted to do for years yet'd never made any effort towards it.

To be on a subway to Harlem without the intention of buying drugs felt strange, certainly quite nice as well. And with two fun and attractive ladies no less. He knew basically what they were to look for once they got there but double checked it real quick on his cell as they got off at 125th street and looked for a little hill opposite the tracks; once they spotted it it was simple as up it and thru a fence, a couple hundred yards of open track and you're in the tunnel, definitely one of the very dopest places on or in Manhattan.

There's many a book written on it so I guess just read one if it sounds interesting, or far better yet I'd say go take a walk thru it, just know that unmanned Amtrak ghost trains come thru every half hour or so, and if you don't want them to stop and abduct you you must run, and run fast, as soon as you hear them coming, for the nearest, widest concrete pillar, and you must then lay there, silent and still, atop the artifacts of a short lived era, one of needles and bones and bottles and cotton, until the last of that train's light is beyond where your eyes can see.

And if you're with two bonkers girls from Detroit once that train's gone down the track you gotta fuck the fallopian tubes out of them atop that compaction of filthy broken dreams until you haven't an ounce of anything left to give 'em.

On the phone the following day his pal Ben relayed a tale that added empathy to the genuine sense of common ground he'd so surprisingly found when he and Apollonia had run into each other.

"Hey man, you're comin' into town soon, right?

"Yessir."

"When?"

"I'll be in next Wednesday and I'm gonna stay like a week."

"Ok cool, you wanna come to a party in Brooklyn next Saturday?"

"You're throwing a party? Are you like a different guy, some kinda cool guy now?"

"Yeah I'm so fuckin' cool now you're not even gonna believe it. No I ran into Apollonia and her birthday's coming up and mine's coming up and a few other people, so she had the idea of throwing a party."

"Stracciatelli? I thought you fuckin' hate her."

"I never hated her, she just always used to fuck with me and yeah I guess she paralyzed me with humiliation or whatever like I don't know many many times or some shit but it was weird we ran into each other and we had this really normal and nice conversation, and she's got an adorable little daughter now, I don't know I really think she's just like a normal non-whore person now."

"Whatever you say there Rupe, I hope you're right about it. I know you don't go on Facebook and shit but have you heard the story or seen the video that popped up of her from years and years ago?"

"Nah I didn't see shit, what kinda video?"

"It's a security video from like 1998 of Mr. Toad's Wild Ride in Disney, I guess she went down there with her sister right before we all went away to college. Obviously the video doesn't give her name but it's definitely her, she stands up in the little cart or whatever while the ride is going and like reaches over to cup a big statue of Mr. Toad's dick and balls with her hand, and I guess her feet slipped and she toppled over the cart and fell down into the mechanism of the ride. Anyway, you can't see her anymore at that point and the video ends but one dude wrote in the comments that he got down with her sometime after that and one of her tits is all shredded and like half missing. Obviously no one is stupid or crazy enough to ask her about it but that's the story."

What a mother of abomination that fuckin' tit must be, Rupert thought. "Who the fuck knows man, I don't even want to see the video and I definitely don't wanna talk about it. I'm turning over a new leaf my friend, a new Babe fuckin' Rupe, only looking toward the future and doing the right thing from today on."

"Seriously bro, it's a great thing to hear you say that. I got like 14 rugelach orders I gotta bake and box up by morning, lemme go alright, we'll talk again before I get into town."

"Go ahead go ahead, if there's time while you're home we'll do some cooking, I wanna make that bomb fuckin' fresh ricotta gnocchi again witchuz."

"Cool cool, later homey."

"Later bud, be good. You still got a bass at your mom's house?"

"Yeah I got a shitty old Squier there still. Why?"

"Bring it to the party, we can fuck around and jam a little."

"I'm rusty as Hell these days but yeah sure."

"Me too, we can just fuck around on some Johnny Cash and Fats and stuff, easy fun shit."

"Alright, hopefully people won't mind listening to us too terribly. I really gotta go before my cream cheese gets too soft and the whole thing's fuckin' ruined. You know how it goes."

"Of course I do, see you soon brotha', lemme know when you get into town if I don't talk to you before."

"Yup. Laters."

With that Rupert walked to the corner of D'Shaun's living room and wrapped his fingers below Onyx's peghead. He'd caressed her more recently than he had a woman previous to the night before but still there had passed a woeful amount of time since he'd aroused as much as a solitary E chord out of her. He recognized immediately that he was no longer any good, but he sat there picking and strumming all afternoon, until a hunger pang forced him to go get a couple of slices, though to his credit he got right back to it once he'd devoured a sausage and onions and a white with spinach slice, the crusts of each ripped off and eaten first, as always. Recalling and re-fingering the structure and his personal touch on a number of tunes that fit the rare classification of being both loved by him and recognizable to a mainstream audience, he formulated a little setlist and practiced it daily until the party, separated from his most recent desire to do so by a seeming lifetime as a social leper.

Apollonia had indeed found a perfect space for the affair, a converted Baptist church in Green Point with a fuckload of room to get stupid in and a stage blessed with a drum set, P.A. and piano which prompted an encouragement towards certain invitees to bring instruments along with them. Rupert and Benny hitched a ride down with D'Shaun and as they pulled up to the curb Apollonia did the very same in her Ford Neron across the street. Apprehensive though intent on second chances, having heard Rupe's story of their encounter, Benny and D'Shaun each followed Rupert's greeting and embrace with their own and the four went inside together.

Rupert was hoping so tremendously fucking much to make this a night of reintegration and self-acceptance. He couldn't believe that of all people he had Apollonia to thank as the entire impetus for the opportunity, and as friends old and new arrived to see them drinking and laughing side by side it seemed very certain that if theirs were not two souls united in boundless, harmonious friendship such a state of being must be a flat out apparition.

Neither expected anything close to the turnout they'd produced, a couple hundred Lakeland graduates spanning probably a dozen different classes and their sexual appendages showed up, but as I imagine the majority of you already know this sort of get-down doesn't really happen anymore as you get into your thirties, get married, have kids, rip off your dicks and decide on favorite candle scents and window dressing textures, and as such it was the most interesting thing to do for most in attendance going either backwards or forwards a right mess of weeks if not years.

The room was amply stocked in every relevant way, people had showed up with all kinds of beer and booze to be shared and half of the folks who were there had drugs of choice in their pockets. Rupert wanted really badly not to get fucked up, nursing IPAs as moderately as he could and ultra-discreetly taking bumps out of a little baggie of dope that an old bandmate had given him as a birthday present. Word went 'round the party that Apollonia had begun taking all estimates of guys out to her car and fucking them, Rupert allowed himself to believe that surely this was a rumor and put it out of his mind.

Aside from calling the few people who he expected would answer the phone Rupert requested the responsibility of MCing the party and with little complaint or criticism the dense, dick and labia swingin' crowd danced and delighted away to the many hours long playlist he'd devised on his iPad for the occasion. When the mood struck he grabbed his es-335 out of D'Shaun's trunk, Steinway grabbed his bass, Chip his ocarina and Casimir his saxophone while D'Shaun took a seat at the drums. They began with Lithium and from there muddled their way thru what amounted to a very sloppy and raucous 27

½ minute medley of other Nirvana, Fats Domino and Johnny Cash songs. Not very good by most definitions but spirited and fun as fuck, and deserving of the only very slightly sarcastic roaring ovation it received, to which Rupert jumped off the stage feeling like an unforgotten fucking man.

His stomach had gotten just a tiny bit uneasy from the beer, heroin, excitement and limelight of it all so he headed behind the stage, down a hallway to the men's room and into a stall to pee and fart. As he came out of the stall Apollonia surged towards him, pushed him back inside with her middle and pointer fingers and locked the door behind them. He got Russian Dick Juice plump and hard and absolutely wanted to fuck the baby Jesus out of her. She pulled his mouth towards hers and as she did he noticed that a thickness of what could only have been splooge was icing the crease between her nose and chin. He pulled violently away from her, knowing with certainty that this most proficient flirt had been fucking the night away in the backseat of her two-door motel room.

They locked eyes but neither said a word, she harnessed a beastly ferocity and once it had reached her fingertips and the veins in her neck began putting her every ounce of strength into getting her mouth around Rupert's cock, it felt as if 7 of her were trying to prevail over him as one. Before too long, but what relevance does duration have as a definitive moment such as that one is playing out, she realized that she could not overpower him and her strength wilted. Standing herself up she yanked her clothes straight with a deep suspire.

With an entirely terrifying eeriness and in a voice not her own she asserted "Rupert, I am going to give you one more chance. Are you going to fuck me or are you not?"

"One more chance, whaddayou mean, Apollonia, please, I can't explain why but I just can't. Ok?"

"Ok, well yeah ok, of course and probably fine. Bye Rupert."

As his mind frenzied for any sentiment at all which might prevent her from whatever she was about to do she laze beamed him taciturn with a fleeting, demonic glare, releasing his cock and balls for the very last time and slithering beside him out the door of the stall, bounding onto the stage and to the microphone which squealed as she picked it up, slammed it's base down and nearly through the floor and addressed the crowd.

"One moment please everybody, please shut the fuck up. I'm in the girl's room just now, washing my hands. Rupert fucking Sauerstein walks in there, locks the door, punches me in the face, pulls up my dress, rips off my panties and starts fucking me in the ass!"

Rupert could hear her and the reaction of her audience clearly enough from inside the bathroom and as the enormity of the situation struck him his head became swimmy and light, his hearing very muddled, heavily fucking impaired.

'Holy god, that jury out there isn't gonna even take a seat in the box, I'm the wretched little subvert they've all always surmised me to be,' he panicked. He could feel he was a few seconds from passing out, before he did so he stole a little nugget from Apollonia's fable, locking himself in just before blacking out and molting with the ground.

He was out for about three minutes and woke to an uninterrupted sense of misery. Hoisting himself up and out through the bathroom window he got himself a few blocks away from the building before hailing a cab back to Manhattan. He shot Benny and D'Shaun a message letting them know that's where he'd be but they beat him back over there anyhow.

When they got up to the apartment they decided to start playing Dr. Steve Brule YouTube videos on D'Shaundrius' gigantic television set; as the two people in the world who most know the real Rupert they presumed, correctly, that of all things it had the best chance of making him laugh, even a snicker would have been well welcomed. But when he walked in he was dead, a ghost, why couldn't it have been the next sperm in the race or the sperm after it, Isaac and Kayiane could have gotten the first born they deserved instead of this lowliest piece of dickshit.

But finally a snicker, 'Jingus' had gotten him again, and though his best friend and baby bro knew that a solitary chuckle put him exactly no closer to the passing point of this devastating misadventure, they gambled a bit on it being enough to begin a conversation.

"Rupert, that was the worst thing I've ever seen, I can't believe she fuckin' did that, but everyone knows how fuckin' crazy she is, nobody left there believing what she said," Benny hoped.

"Check your fuckin' social media please, Facebook and Tweeters and all that other fuckin' shit, I gotta know what people are saying," he requested, his back against the couch cushions at its small and his legs jutting out and under the coffee table, like a toddler in the aftermath of a temper tantrum suppressed before it could fructify.

Look they did, finding an endless array of debasing memes, recycled one-liners and rape culture tirades. They read a little bit of it to him, leaving out the most incendiary bits.

"Please Rupert" Benny continued, "you haven't done any dope for two weeks you said and I'm so fuckin' proud of you for that, and I know you might really want some right now but please don't do it, that could be the good that comes from all of this. I'll stay right here with you for a month if that's what's gonna help you out but please just don't go up there."

"Me too bro, I'll tell the Nets I got syphilis or some shit, I don't give a fuck. It's not like we're makin' the playoffs."

"I love you guys, man I really got the best two fuckin' guys. Can we just go to sleep though? Benny you're gonna crash here?

"Yeah, I wanna get a big bacony breakfast from the diner in the morning."

"Ok kiddo sounds good. Good night you guys," said Rupert as he hugged D'Shaun and gave his baby bro a peck on the cheek and a squeeze. Benny flopped out on the couch and Rupe and D'Shaun retired to their big and little boy rooms, pushing theirs doors as such that they closed in concert. As they made their way towards sleep each expected the worst but with no idea about how 'worst' would come to define itself.

As the party unfolded, and as the boys were at home and suffered to find the right words to say to each other, Eleazer was unraveling into fury up here with me. Once the fellows had all settled into blankets to rest we drifted northward to our usual overnight resting place above the chirping birds and friendly grazers and inside the fresh pocket of air which gives breath to Rupert's wood.

I quickly shot him the same, indifferent, rote insincerities I'd been shooting him in such moments for coming up on a millennium, maybe you're getting a little old for this, what if you get seen and this sort of thing, but not a word of it was heard. He pressed his weight against the floor of our enclosure and raised up, toeing it's east facing wall and bounding away, en route to Apollonia's apartment complex in Darien, Connecticut.

The complex reminisces of the Taj Mahal, by contrast, how in this one same world there exists this mellifluous, color-morphing palace of sick love chipped into creation from ivory and marble by chisels and hands to agree with sacred equations and just the same exists this and hundreds of thousands of the same sterile, devoid stacks of bedrooms and stairwells made from rusty nails and swamp wood with a crane and staples. It was 3:33 when we arrived, separately. She lived on the fourth, top floor and so Eleazer snaked on up there and past 4B, breathing deeply as he took a smell and a listen through the door to 4D before toothing off the doorknob and nosing it open. Unintentionally he loosened the door frame with his left shoulder blade as he slithered inside but it wasn't very loud and Apollonia was sleeping soundly, she'd made it the 70 miles from Green Point to Darien in under 35 minutes, had shot ketamine into her asshole and passed out more than an hour earlier, it being now almost 3:36.

He stalked up next to her bed, his tail wagging in the doorway, got his gorgeous face right up to hers and kinda fucked with her with his whiskers for a second, tickled them on her face, she then brushing the tickles away and continuing to you know just fuckin' be asleep. Then, to wake her up, I mean I brush my teeth occasionally just cuz I'm bored but I've never seen Eleazer brush his fuckin' teeth, and if he gets right up in your face it fuckin' stinks, so that's what he did, he started breathing really bassily and right up into her nostrils, and what with the combination of the reverb and the stench but also the slug of asshole ketamine it took her maybe 10 seconds to open her eyes, but when they opened they did so more widely than they're supposed to, as did her mouth, such so that her upper lip near kissed her eyebrows as her mind examined the possibility of such a humongous blue and purple head, teeth like a Smilodon's under magnification, and before she could wail her guttural goodbye she was in three parts, her arms and chest entirely severed from her head and torso in one gnash. Four mouthfuls later she was gone.

As he'd entered the apartment he was aghast at the seeming disconnect between the diabolical siren who lived there and the way in which it was decorated. Her comforter and an ovular rug at the foot of the bed were very florally and pastel, on the walls were framed butterflies and theatrical housecats. As he ate he smashed these atrocities as well as every other displayed *tchotchke* by spit-firing bone fragments ‘round the room.

Ultimately that crazy cat did a quick once around, gathered up all of his hair and her bones and curled it up in his tail. With a whip ‘n’ a snap he sent it through an open window and into outer space. She’d left a really striking and lovely blood angel on the bed, and the boys from forensics found the DNA sequence of a Russian Blue mixed in with the blood, along with those of 259 lucky dudes. Wriggling back down the stairs he began destitute kitten purring routine as soon as his cute little face came peeking out of the stairwell, I dove down to grab him up and we headed home.

It was weeks before he even gave thought to Apollonia’s death, longer still before he gave of himself enough interest or investigation to realize Eleazer must have eaten her, and not even immediately then did he begin to speculate as to the specifics of the savagery that the scene must have included. D’Shaundrius, Casimir and Benny talked about trying to get him into a psych ward or rehab, anywhere where it would be a maximal challenge for him to jump off a building or eat a pound of pills. Of the 213 folks who showed up to that most regrettable party only 7 have expressed a subsequent willingness to interact with Rupe. It was rough for a while but he stayed alive, super-secretive about his return to the needle, finally running out of money four months after the party, having cascaded all of his change into a Coinstar machine and devoted the $84 it gave him to subway fare and one final fix.

Chapter 9

Metempsychosis

Moments are so precious
They taste so delicious
Like coffee on a Sunday
Or tea with milk and honey
Perfume on your pillow
Buzzin' black and yellow
Apples in your garden
Or bathin' with your darlin'
Maybe, the times are fatal
Oh maybe, the times are dead on

- Steffen Westmark

"As soon as the last bit of snow melts, I promise."

It was February 27th, 2014 and the winter's amass of ice and snow, an automatic post-autumnal bummer and idiopathic reason for Rupert to make everything new by offing or outing himself to Buenos Aires or Hong Kong, deprived of reduction like the city's inhabitants of sleep, a solid iota thicker still than a conventional brick. When it was no longer he'd next perpend leaving the apartment.

His aforementioned last $84 of high had come and gone two weeks earlier and while nowadays a credit card can bring every conceivable, rubber stamped domestic service right to your doorknob he didn't have a single connect who was ably willing to swipe his Discover card for dope or even experimental use Xanax and so he'd been at home, the beneficiary of Benny and D'Shaundrius' coordinated nurture, playing him all of his favorites and saving him from indenture to creditor in willingly purchasing all the reasonably holistic shit he required. Rupert wasn't really cracked out or even particularly miserable, salivating through scalped racquetballs worth of suboxone, toking obsessively on OG kush and sour diesel and, whence his anhedonia ogres'd fallen deep within a sleepy state, strumming up a little on Onyx, wired as she'd remained to a dusty and temperamental old mini Marshall.

And he slept. We all did. It was cold outside and eclipsing that in provision of foreboding was the circumstance of what precisely he could do should he bother to go there. Compete for a job with folks perpetually locked into the workforce, motherfuckingly unstoppable people, doubly dutiful army ants throughout his 13 year retirement from the camp counseling industry, awaiting roll call on an opportunity for which everyone he'd so much as see that day overmatched him under every credible qualification, children included, a wind segregated speck of a rain droplet from another meniscus lost, from finally doing a thing to get himself full-blown excommunicated, something bloody, dizzy and nauseous from the sub-cellular nuclear Holocaust sparked when every valueless and ugly emotion begins brawling inside of you. He could try to make a new friend. But say to them what? He just couldn't, couldn't do it, though (and so in) comparing its prospects to any and all of the absolute and guaranteed disasters ready to get going down out there for once in his life sleep seemed really takable and he took it as it came.

Benny wasn't looking for a promise, nor should a promise from this incarnation of Rupert be seen as anything more than soft currency, he simply sought a bit of context as to when the guy who once protected him as if that was in fact his purpose on Earth, who'd taught him how to hit from both sides of the plate and field all nine positions, was gonna muster up the fortitude to stand up, change out of his resin and cereal milk douched jammies, go out and soak in the light of the sun, which, as it happened, came on strong the following morning. Another three weeks passed and not the teensiest cake of filthy urbane snow remained in the neighborhood underbelly of a sewer grate or the moat of a nearby jungle gym pipe. D'Shaundrius was in Minnesota, Benny took Rupe out for tacos and tamales, gave him $200 and drove home to Kensico, entrusting that his big brother would take a shower and go outside sometime during the upcoming diurnal or two.

Rupert had gotten barely twenty pages into *The Canterbury Tales* the first time he gave 'em a go but felt he might now be able to allot them at least well-intentioned semi-focus, getting up on a chair and plucking it from atop the 6'9" power forward's likewise oversized bookshelf, stuffed with everything from *Ulysses* to *Green Lantern: Rebirth*, replacing its Strand bookmark to beneath the front cover and bounding down the stairs before he could convince himself to lay back down, embraced affirmatively once he'd reached the sidewalk by the holistic sting of earliest, perfect spring, long-sleeved t-shirt under a short-sleeved one temperature, amply scrubbed and deodorized and rightly dressed for the season, feelings of fine subjugating the negativity with which he took on this brave peregrination, if you'd understand that in his mind he was inferior to even the sewers and jungle gym, because they shared not a Satan particle of cowardice or sloth between them. For the first block and a half with each person he neared on the sidewalk he silently repeated the promise to them that 'if you please don't look at me I'll give you a tiger cub.'

The cigarette he'd lit on his way down the stairs became extra delicious as its smoke swirled and harmonized with the fresh air. He left his headphones draped about his neck, opting for a reintroduction to the sideways sounds of the island's mighty ebbs and returns, pulsations and poetry, a card and a contradiction at every corner. Headed down 2nd Ave towards Stuyvesant Square Park he decided to accept an invitation from its East 16th Street entrance, taking in the perfectly charming little place, well-manicured and pleasantly laid out, focalized by an understated, prominently diametric fountain of fresh stone, directly ahead of him once he was thru the city-stock, spired paint black fence and as he turned back into the northern half of the square he took appreciation of the field of oak trees, through which laces a slightly oblate paved pathway, lined along its outer lip with slotted and stained pine benches. Three minutes away walking from D'Shaundrius' apartment though this was the first time he'd been inside the place.

The path conjoins a couple minutes shy of half past and Rupert walked round to his northwest until taking a seat on the bench marking :47 were instead the 60 benches minutes on the face of a clock. His brain hadn't a horse in this decision, his libidinal super-PAC muscled her out of contention when whilst he approached :45 a girl sitting at :48 gave his heart valves a jolt the intensity of which before that particular milli-moment had been generated by none other than the one and only Onyx. But for him to know her it was not to be with such the easy infancy of togetherness with his first love, kissy-facing as they were before either of their moms had evaded the flailing exuberance of their second borns and carted the next item on their grocery lists.

He wasn't sure if she knew he was there, on approach to the bench he'd narrowed his gaze completely in on gathering a seat on it without humiliating his rusty self. It was out from pure need, obsessive curiosity that he took her in again, cautious and quickly, abling to decide what to talk to her about as he did so, not though how to phrase this most unexpected, vital initiation, or if she'd flash him a dismissive smile, morphed into a snarl, a caterwaul, eating his face and ventricles before she walked seductively away.

Once again re-opening and un-reading *The Canterbury Tales* as he tried to infuse some sort of grammatical form into what he wanted to say; it was definitely not gonna be smooth and his stomach decided it was time for a diarrhea fake-out. As he frantically tore through his mind for anything of use the fuzzy sliver of her body liquefied a little in his periphery and ordered his final, meager ration of self-importance absolute attention to the panicked possibility she could or rather undoubtedly would stand up and walk away come any soon to arrive tick, off into the otherwhere of a city in which it's impossible to see the same face twice. So he had to just out with what he had whilst at the least saying something still provided an alternative to absorbing yet another corpuscle of self-repugnance by saying nothing and watching her meander away until his cheeks were so wet they wrinkled and sagged and she was on her honeymoon with her father's golfing buddy's son the stockbroker.

"That's my dog's name," therefore, became the foundation upon which he accorded her the opportunity to deduce his worth, squeaking pubescently a little on the 'd'. Uplifting her head from a copy of *Crime and Punishment* that appeared the victim of a copycatting of its antagonist's vicious god play, lawful retaliation for Raskolnikov's bludgeonings on the cover portrait of him, locked in listless diffidence. Somehow, some Satan determined to save the book, the first 59 sheets needed be taped 2/5ths of the way down and this made them protrude like a motherfucker. And somehow the ugliest book in New York had made its way into the fingers of the loveliest girl.

She then took very many eternities to bloom her eyelashes and allow him a further look into her ½ Persian and ½ Colombian eyes (as she spoke more to her lineage and other notions of unimpeachable delight at her apartment the following evening he studied her knotted cascades of emerald and viridian greens encased in almond eyelids and thought about how all eyes should be basely manufactured on the Arabian peninsula then shipped into Colombian jungles to be inspected and fine tuned).

She smiled brightly in acknowledgment of Rupert's having had talked at her, it's her default to do so, but had no earthly idea what to make of his statement or the fellow who'd manufactured it. He noticed her double sets of dimples as she spoke. "Pardon me, sweetie?" she asked as she tucked her shoulder blade length side-parted pink and blue hair behind her 11 holed, 23 year old ears.

"Noddy, I have a big brindle boxer named Noddy. Well he has a little leucistic patch shaped like Puerto Rico on his tushy but otherwise he's brindle." She'd eschewed a long-sleeved t-shirt in underlay when she'd dressed that morning, wearing only antediluvian blue jeans and a bleach splotched silver-faded-to-grey tee that must've been older than her if not him too, pocked with a circumnavigation of holes below the collar, adorned with a life size silk screening of Noddy Holder's harmlessly maniacal, top-hatted mug.

"Well that's nice to know, if you wanna believe me I almost put on that one instead this morning," pointing towards his paradiddling maggot of a left ventricle. "What might you have said to get my attention had that been the case?" His, cuz you know I'm gonna tell you though you probably don't care, was a light tan Go shirt, the one printed with a sombrero cropped tiger tinkering on an ayahuasca rainbow radiator.

"I wouldn't have said anything probably, I don't like The Go, and I'm tryin' ta be nicer, even though I don't really want to be."

"Yeah they're shitty. Have you heard Fiesta yet?"

"Yeah. It's so good. I can't believe they aren't touring on it, there aren't even like a couple shows in Detroit. People have no taste. It's like Exile on Main Street, or Layla, ya know just like a flawless double record, and I don't care if this is lame to say, if you made me choose between Exile and Fiesta I'd take Fiesta, for the rest of my life, right now."

"Oh, I see. How would I make you choose?"

"Um, you can let me know your name, please, and I'll never listen to 17 of the 20 songs on Exile again."

"The first two and 'On Down the Line' you still wanna hear?

"Yeah, exactly, wow."

"Alright, that's fair. I'm Marisol, but please just call me Mar, it's like torture to my ears when people try to trill the 'r'" she said with a devilish keening of her eyelids which caused their aura to strengthen.

"Pero estudie Español para nueve años, mis maestras de escuela media y alta fueron fantástico y mis favoritos de todos. Estoy muy bien. Justo necesitas hablar un poco lentamente, por favor, señorita bonita." He realized that Miss Goodridge had absolutely to be added to the best teachers list were an entire truth told, but he wasn't about to allow her the opportunity to sour things again, at least not yet.

"Alright, lemme hear."

"Marrrrrrrrrrrisol" (no pubescent squeaks this time) he rolled that shit like he was fuckin' Quetzalcoatl as she countered with an entrancing puff of her cocoa buttered lips, forehead ripple and nod of her delicate, deep caramel neck, one he certainly wished he had money or the help of his grandma enough left to put something beautiful around.

"Ok, that was actually really good, but call me Mar anyway. What's your name?"

"I'm Rupert."

"Really? I've never met a Rupert before." She thought the name quite cute. "Well you seem nice enough Rupert, I'm glad you chose bench 47."

"Yeah, I hated the name when I was little but I've come around to it. You do too, seem nice that is. But is that all I get, to know your name, for giving up on 85% of one of the best albums ever recorded? I think I made a bad deal."

"But there's nothing else I could give you, I'm just a poor immigrant girl."

"Well I was born like 3 blocks from here but I haven't got anything either. I guess we'll hafta make it all ourselves."

"Ok, we can."

She asked him to arrive at 8 the following evening, allotting herself enough time after work to prepare crab and boudin etouffee with dirty rice and remoulade flatbread. They warmed, loosened and lightened themselves with sweet Chilean wine before and during the scrumptious dinner, what Rupert surmised was her own Muddy Waters mixtape perfectly filling the space. As they got into their third bottle both began betraying the decree they had made upon themselves not to allow the other a glimpse of how silly and immature they were until perhaps the more conventionally sought after elements of an adult human personality had a chance to show. She extended her left foot under and across the table and with her big toe began teasing the head of his nope, I'm sorry, the after dinner details, silly or otherwise, will be withheld out of reverence for Marisol, so instead allow me to go back just a little.

More he imagined than any other domestic kitchen hers was without omission or oversight chocked with fresh, origin harvested, semi and fully preserved herbs and produce. Over time she made him the finest and most gorgeously plated meals from anywhere he could stretch to identify on a pre-atomic map, issuing aromas more seductive than any perfume or potion.

The remark upon her home need also include that the place was absurd, the whole 7th of 14 floors of brick and inciteful alpha town statuary ornamentation, tucked into the upper crust of one of the Gramercy Park cul-de-sacs featured in the FBI anti-communism dossier. The floor was dressed angularly with knotty slats of fallen redwood in a pattern reminiscent of a freshly raked stone garden, a whim she'd received from a dream and had indulged a few months earlier, topped with perfectly jagged randomness in the lay of ancient and in some cases historically annotated rugs. Overwhelmed at what to notice from there he began to cross the expanse towards one of two walls to the half basketball court of a living room, festooned each with 8'x8' maps of the boroughs, printed on fiberglass and plastic paper, compelling and abnormal enough to be noted believably as the former property of Batman or Indiana Jones, enlarged and detailed as to show every enterprise and domicile citywide. They were half marked to some sort of beautiful shit with a clearly purposeful designation of pink, blue and yellow hi-liter.

"Where'd you get these?"

"The mayor. My mom. My mom via her girlfriend via the mayor."

"Did you code and mark 'em all up like this?"

"Yeah, for almost two years I've been um, well when I moved here I did some freelance photography work but I started to dislike it pretty much immediately cuz it took the intimacy and the spontaneity, the fun out of photography for me. I mean it's the Muzak of visual art right, in fact it's not art at all, and you can't have it both ways, or at least I didn't think I could, or wanted to. But so I didn't wanna again take something I loved and make it my work, just so I could end up resenting whatever that might be too, so I just thought about something new and pure and began working towards it. I've literally been circuitously routing through neighborhoods and going up to doors and seeing what if anything can be done to help people out. I got a couple of sweet but smart and really hard-working girls who work with me, a plumber, and an electrician, and we just fix little or buy little things for people that they haven't at that moment got the money for."

"Wow, that's so, you're so amazing Marisol. It's through a grant of some kind? Or you work for the city?" Talking about what people do for work was always something Rupert simply didn't do but for once he could listen without having to fake his face into familiar shapes of interest.

"No, it's through, and this is so asinine that I don't even really feel odd telling you, but it's embarrassing for me and you're now one of very few people who know this Mr. Rupert so keep that talented tongue of yours in your mouth Buster," (how did she know already?) "but it's through who my parents are, or who they used to be, that I'm able to do it."

Bashfully she went into a broadly stroked version of her parents' personal histories, her dad a reformed Columbian drug lord who from what his men could ascertain had gotten out a day or two before the CIA otherwise would've smithereened his face to bits. Her mother, an unimpeachably regal former Saudi Arabian princess, excommunicated as the result of having leaned inexcusably too far and publicly to the left as concern reproductive rights and contraception in her homeland. Each had in their time amassed more capital than the next 100 wealthiest people Rupert ever met. Collectively their affluence was obscene and, in the perception of their only child, a barrier to be broken through in deducing the intentions of everyone she confided in. They owned the building Mar lived in and she was its rent-fixing landlady. Already quite in love by the time he uncorked that third bottle they removed themselves to the sofa where they duskily planned for familial introductions and for Rupert to move Noddy and himself into her apartment. The matter of whether or not Lucy and her baby turtles Sal and Rasheed would join them to be revisited upon a discussion with D'Shaundrius, as he'd come to love Lucy and would never give up guardianship of his Chinese ponds.

Of all the magically colored notions they exhausted while they laughed and sipped, her head on his left forearm and her toes curled up beneath her, the stand alone anxiety inducer was for Mar to join Rupe, Kayiane, Isaac, Benny and his fiancée Louise for Easter-Passover dinner Timberlane Court style in two Sundays' time. When the day arrived Rupert and Mar hit the Hudson Line on an express 10:32 and by noon were sifting through perishables with momma and poppa Sauerstein, momma having picked up the ingredients needed for Rupert and Mar to chop and shape their way through a hyper-rustic rendering of Italian Wedding Matzoh Ball Soup. Kayiane was such a delightful, accommodating dote of a goofball that afternoon into evening, the first time adult Rupert had ever requested to bring a young lady home, the long ago unhooked and freed daydream she'd had of a time and place wherein she sat with both her boys and both their girls in a setting the sort Rupe had excoriated as 'too fuckin' stressful and tacky' some threadbare spool of time foregone.

"Mar dear, how do you like living in that part of the city?" Kayiane entreated to know once everyone was seated and served. Rupert had warned her on the train that morning that his darling, potently maternal mommy had interrogated quite a bit about her out of him since he'd decided to let her know she existed. He made it well known to her that neither she nor his dad would ever be judging her on anything other than the way she treated their first born.

"It's great, really comfortable, you can kinda zip every which way really fast."

"Oh that's wonderful dear, and you're always welcome here if you need a little respite. Isaac lived not too far from you guys before we got married, 13th and 1st. I lived there too basically but this was the 70s so as far as my father knew I just spent a lot of nights at my girlfriend's apartment. And Louise, you lived in Murray Hill, right sweetheart?"

"Yeah, for almost two years before I moved in with Ben. I miss it sometimes."

"Hey," Rupert abruptly and somewhat awkwardly rerouted the conversation "I was thinking can the four of us go out for dinner in the city maybe the Friday before the wedding, is that alright?" Rupert was aware that by way of the openness of her relationship with Benny Louise knew far more than most of the depravity and decay he'd coursed through the preceding decades and figured all he could do was make use of every opportunity to gain her trust, to see how much he adored the young man she was readying to wed, and how much their children would love their Uncle Rupe.

"Yeah of course we can, right?" replied Louise, to the nod of Benny's perpetually cooperative head and triple clapping of Kayiane's overjoyed hands, her pleasure receptors treated to a fleeted flyover of motherly bliss. Plans continued to beget plans, smiles trajected towards out and out laughter, Rupert couldn't deny the fact that none of it was put on or forced, he was simply his own damn self in enjoyment and facilitation of that day, unable though to repress inevitable disappointment through his frantic best ratiocination. He just couldn't imagine how a modicum of this was sustainable, how he could possibly navigate the one and only flawless path of all the many that were laid out ending with him not having fucked everything up.

The thought pervaded straight through to their evening in the city together, the Saturday night before the wedding. Of course it shouldn't have, evidenced by the peace and joy that was becoming his new normal, be his time spent prep-cooking, reading, sleeping, any damn thing as long as it included Mar and Noddy, or even a recent and fond enough memory of either while they were out doing her daily philanthropies (with what for her became newly doubled efficiency and delight, having discovered that Noddy was more than keen on taking her upon his back and zipping around town in the bike lane) was one of pre-biblical, guilt-free joy.

More so than any other undervalued simplicity he adored taking an after dinner stroll around the neighborhood with them. Though his numerous, daily suicidal ideations had steadily and dramatically diminished since that afternoon in the park he had not yet found a way around the one obsession which developed alongside all that affirmation, embedded in the aftermath of what had happened in October, the awareness that all but for the now whittled down handful of friends and family with whom he shared time and confidence, the notion that should anyone else in the world find that he'd crept into their consciousness they would meet him there with disgust, they'd wonder if he he'd gone and died yet, that filthy, sexual sociopath and incurably miserable drug addict. But therein lies the potency of Mar's effect on him.

These thoughts were of a deep, daily hurt, outweighed though, overmatched by the pride and optimism she imbued by taking hold of his hand along a digestive sunset walk, or when occupied by nothing but the puzzle page of The New York Times magazine, animal print pajama'd and sharing a blanket of Noddy's big ol' body. When she'd ask him a question the subtext always divulged hints that she had a unique interest and investment in the safe passage of his soul.

"Rupert?

"Yes gorgeous? How many points did you say we need to be geniuses this week?"

"22. Rupert, look at me please? What do you want to do?"

"Tonight? Some kissing might be rad, did you do something to your lips?"

"There's a new kind of Palmer's infused with collagen and bumble bee venom, that's probably why you wanna suck on them extra much. So fine, we'll have transcendental kissy sex for as long as you can stand it, sleep like doped up lion cubs, their puffy little paws plucked of every thorn, and then we'll wake up, tomorrow, or whenever we want to, and I guess that's really what I'm asking, outside of what we normally do and what you've ever gotten up to before, what do you really want to do? Where do you wanna go? What do you wanna see?"

"There's one thing" he confessed as she leaned in against Noddy's gravitational might for a largely symbolic sharpening of her perspective. "I wanna go in the bathroom one morning and look in the mirror, and on my chin or my nose, it doesn't matter which, actually no on my nose, right here, I wanna see a fully sprouted, virile fuckin' whitehead, ok, the 4d printed fac-fuckin'-simile of the one I've gotten a hundred times before, only this time, when I squeeze it, it's not gonna sputter and squirt a little bit of watery, pussy blood, it's gonna be a freshly strewn strand of capellini, five, six feet long, kinking and curling where it must. I don't know what I'm gonna do with it at that point, maybe flash fry it and pop it in my mouth, I just know I wanna get it, just once, I'm legitimately jealous of people who've had one of those. I'm pretty sure I've watched every single pimple video on YouTube."

"Rupert, Jesus Christ, you really just said that didn't you?" eyes sparkling and lips curling as she inquired most un-rhetorically. "I've never mentioned it to anyone besides my little cousin, and she doesn't even speak English yet, but I've always wanted to do that too. It looks so satisfying. And delicious. I really think if I got one I'd wanna cook it too, but I can't figure out what would be the best way either." Within the revelation of this duality of desire and all its empowering peculiarity they fell in unbreakable love. "Is that it though?"

"Well I want to be with you forever and a day, I hope you know that by now, and I wanna go to the, fuckin', Caño de Cristales, and swim along the side of a blue whale."

"El Caño? Verdad?"

"I had this jumbo-sized hardbound book when I was a kid, I had a million books but one of my favorites was called I think just succinctly The Golden Rule, I'm sure my dad knows precisely where in the garage it is. And it was a book for kids obviously but like I guess as vital a notion as it is it's a little too self-evident to fill a respectable non-fiction volume, so I think as like an author's addendum the dude included the story of his favorite place, where he had taken an expedition of his most cherished friends and family upon having found his own path to The Golden Rule, by way of if I can go back 25 or so years in my memory and read between the vagaries surviving some sort of overdose or other blowout of his humanity. And whales, you know, blue whales especially are just so fuckin' awesome, so big but no one knows where they go, so streamlined and one with the sea that their passage creates less of a wake than that from a little baby gosling lagging half the lake behind his momma and sisters and brothers. Those big ass eyeballs they got, I just wanna get mine right up to one and see if there is a connection."

"Ok, I know, I'm in. After your brother's wedding we'll set out on a bit of a roam."

"Really sweetheart? But what about your work?"

"Oh don't worry about that, or anything else if you could please help it. We'll go to El Caño and then we'll go see some whales. Easy. Can we also go see my parents and grandparents in Dubai, just for a couple of nights, please?"

"Of course darlin', I'd follow you anywhere, for any reason, for reals."

"Ok Poopert" (She didn't nearly lose a ball like the 3rd grade classmate who now had his own little sui generis going on with Silly Miss Marisol in calling him that). "And, hey, you, um, think maybe after a few however manys have passed you might wanna put a baby in me?" Though she so wanted an answer to this question, one assuredly unfiltered of sincerity (and happened to regret asking it immediately) she'd deliberately phrased it in this most casual and goofy way to give him a way out and around a reality-based response. Not that he would've fooled her around, his faith in her having grown inexpugnable.

"Honestly darlin', I've never thought about having a baby with anyone before, but with you I feel this absolute confidence, that was gone since I was a kid, restored by you, truly I'm in disbelief at having the opportunity to make a little baby with the most sunkissed, phosphorescent girl in the universe. Just gimme a little more time, just to make sure my brain isn't gonna go berserk again anytime soon."

"I know hunny, and that's so ok with me, I just want us to be at peace and continue to enjoy being with each other, cuz Rupert I'm so happy when I'm with you, I have the warmest and most positive thoughts about us, I really feel there is no other way our lives could have gone right, could have mattered, in a world of even any humanity, than for us to have met and be together. I love you so much."

Immediately upon offering this sentiment she broke down into a deep sob, of relief, of wanting to create a permanence in the present, and of knowing how much the fella she'd said it to got all empowered and mollified having heard her and in feeling the emotion she'd committed to saying it, how he had feelings of even more deeply painful love and obsessive admiration right back her beautiful way.

They held each other on the couch while a David Attenborough documentary pixilated the movie wall, his paradisiac voice filling the apartment, she crying a quick little more before a shift into sleepy giggles and sighs, she fell asleep and he a few minutes later, after an exhaustive flash through the enormous prospects of the next few months, so many chances to create and destroy vital propulsions that he got a step and a half or so into the initial space-headedness of a panic attack, a bit proud of himself at how quickly and calmly he was able to take it down. He grazed her shoulder with his lips and shut his eyes.

Benny and Louise got married in her childhood church in central Connecticut and the celebration to follow was held at The New Britain Museum of American Art, where at first sight of *Fallen Mias* Rupert became enamored with Walton Ford's delicate mastery of mood and as he'd thereafter discover shared obsession with Animalia.

The preceding Friday night they'd gone out as planned, just the bros and their beloved, left to Rupert's choosing of Indian yumminess inside the psychedelic subway car of Panna II, followed by the bar in the world most precisely aestheticized to his enjoyment, Lucy's, just a jukebox, pool table, stiff well whiskey drinks, and pompless macro-tapped beer, the height, grain, slope of the bar, the look in Lucy's granddaughter Ksenia's inviting eyes, on up and down to finer details than these, careful I shall be not to hastily omit mention of Lucy's having drenched Rupert with affection at the close of his first visit in late summer of 2001. His face, as Ksenia submitted visual evidence of, the doppelgänger to that of her cherished husband, who'd passed away one Indian Summer afternoon the preceding spring. His visits always included a cuddling of their handsome Russian Blue Fyodor, a hug and kiss from and a shot with Lucy and/or in her absence her babushka Ksenia, a game or two 'top the billiards felt and the sweet sound of honky tonk 45s, with some scrupulously selected early rock and roll thrown in for posterity. It was never crowded, never empty, attracting people of soft motion and fine cheer, some evolutionary sidewalk aesthetic providing a safeguard against machismo and hostility at the doorway.

They ate tandoori and paneer and drank vodka lassis for two laugh-laced hours then gingerly made their way through the narrow and near manically vibrant shipping container of a restaurant, beginning to walk zigzaggedly, in the spirit of digestion and in the vague direction of the bar, the ladies in front with their arms interlocked and the fellas in back with their pride beaming. Though the least outwardly emotional of the four Benny was in fact the happiest, so proud of his big brother and the change he saw in him he forgot it was his wedding they were out to celebrate. Forty-five minutes later they arrived at the bar to find it fit to bust, a wall of chatter drowning out and disrespecting the Faron Young record spinning in the juke.

Mar and Louise wriggled through to the left and with an assertive collective of tootsies and tushies took possession of a table that was just opening up whilst Rupert broke right to get drinks and introduce Lucy to Ben, a delight for all though stripped of casual intimacy and detail by the chaos of the crowd. They took a shot with her, Benny handed her a twenty ('for Fyodor' Rupert'd always say as she'd refuse, in fact none of Rupert's money was ever placed in the pre-war bar-top cash register) for the round of whiskey and ginger ales and they maneuvered through the crowd to join their better halves at the table. Each was parched from their long and wayward stroll and needed to refresh their fading buzz. As sucks on their straws began to produce more air then beverage Benny excused himself to the bathroom and Rupert to enjoy a cigarette whilst the girls fought through crosstown traffic to the bar and ordered up their next round. When he finished his smoke and yanked open the door to reenter all that he could see were five bodies and the bar, Mar and Louise backed into it and Benny backed into them, a foreign and deeply troubled look on his face, faced by two meaty men dressed as professional football players.

a palpitation Rupert made it six and was looking for answers. He gathered that the tall one had come up from behind Mar and effectively finger-banged her through her jeans, though everything Benny said was yelled over and contradicted by the two predators. The whites of Rupert's eyes filled with blood as his pupils blackened and expanded.

"Fellas, these are women of grace, of peace, of high regard for everyone. They can't be disrespected like this. Would you care to pacify this situation with an apology?"

He was enraged as he spoke and wanted to kill them both, slowly.

"You know what fuckface," began the tall one, "there was a time when I would've just mashed a fag like you in the face at a moment like this, but I've grown up too. Ladies, with total sincerity, I apologize. We've been drinking all day and that was a rude and disgraceful thing to do."

Not entirely pleased that he chose in apologizing to deflect responsibility over to his alcoholism, Rupert looked over and into his beloved's eyes and decided she had enough toughness and resolve towards a peaceful big picture to approbate the apology and forget that the two of them existed. Deciding not to waste any additional oxygen on such archaized discussion he took Mar by her hand and said "let's go home darling." Turning towards the door he caught a reflection of the quarterback assaulting his beloved Marisol in the very same manner as his friend had.

Witnessing it before his eyes Benny shattered the man's wrist with a strike that needless to say freed Mar from his grasp as Rupert's fingernails taloned and wrapped his neck, crumpling his windpipe and dialing his third and fifth cervical vertebrae way the fuck off of their axes. With a pint glass still in his right hand the burly one unleashed a haymaker towards Rupert's powerful grip, the glass shattering against the knuckle of Rupe's thumb, redirecting, of its utility the equivalent of a fully agape piranha jaw, towards his half gone pal's multiply mangled jugular, gashing through and scooping up his buddy's Adam's apple and windpipe. The body fell back, resting on and drooping over the bar. Benny wrapped one arm around the neck of each of the girls and walked them outside. As if by planned detonation the skin at either side of the quarterback's potted esophagus began to split like spent lengths of duct tape. The ripping stopped and a marvel combination of sinew strength and futile determination kept his head attached to his body by of a width of skin three-quarters of an inch out from the edges of his spine, rested against the inner lip of the bar upside-down, still a big head, now though by fewer definitions. It held to its precarious suspension as the four gathered outside, finally losing its uphill battle with gravity, tearing entirely away and plunking to the ground, bouncing twice, rolling in curvature and getting just enough bounce off its right ear to clip and spin into a perfect Olympic landing in the grit of Fyodor's litter box precisely as Rupert lowered himself to the curb and pulled his phone from his pocket, with one flick of his thumb scrolling down to the letter E's amongst his 63 saved contacts.

"Hey Uncle Elmore, are you in the city now by chance?"

"I am buddy, I'm on my way to you in fact. Just sit tight, don't worry, if anybody with a badge asks you anything just quietly show them the card I gave you. I'll be there in three and a half minutes."

"I'm sorry Unc. Thank you so much. See you soon."

"Yes you will Rupe, it's gonna be fine."

He put his phone back in his pocket, lifting his head to see that the world at large had returned to view. Eight officers were already working the scene, engaging everyone in the vicinity other than the group of four seated on the curb. They confiscated bar security tapes, looked for and erased voyeuristic videos from the phones of other patrons, acting on orders from Chief of Department Adonica, who'd been detailing officers to extra-special service and protection of waywardly Rupert since his ascension to that post in the winter of '09. When he arrived he pulled one of the officers aside and after a brief chat he thanked and dismissed each of them individually. Taking a seat beside Rupert he began telling Benny how much he and his wife have been anticipating his wedding, introducing himself to Louise and Mar. Without saying so they came to the collective decision not ever to speak of the scene that was still spilling out behind them. They got to their feet, climbed into Elmore's car and he dropped them off in front of Mar's building. When they got upstairs they split into the two bedrooms and collapsed with nervous exhaustion, sleeping deep into the afternoon.

Rupert was once the extrovert, the 5 year old with the witty syntax and imagination of a much older, urban soul. The 10 year old who could talk baseball with a 40 year fan of the game. He was ringleader for The Kindergarten Circus, scripting the thing right off his fancy little cuff. On a week-long nature-retreat with his eighth-grade class he raised his hand during evening assembly and volunteered to come front and center to share a riddle his grandpa Oscar had told him. But less than a year later he was not the same kid anymore. Time spent on thoughts of Yankees, Dinosaurs, Disney World, reallocated to drugs, suicide, existential pessimism. When he woke that afternoon his first thought was of how in less than a week he'd be standing in front of 150 folks and several camera lenses, speaking on reminiscences of love and optimism as his baby brother's best man. He knew that in attendance would be several people who'd been there for his accused rape of Apollonia and dozens more who'd heard about it. He was terrified by the approach of that moment, but he knew that the fear would not stop him from honoring his brother, for whom he would do any conceivable thing.

Perhaps sensing his anxiety Mar awoke partially at 4:17 and cuddled up on him, whispering that Ben and Louise had gone home an hour or two earlier. He issued nearly no reply and she sat up, stroking and patting his back.

"I still haven't written my speech for Benny's wedding," he finally spoke.

"It's ok, why don't you go sit in the library and start writing it now."

"Ok, I'm gonna. How do you feel?"

"A little hangovery, but otherwise blessed."

"Blessed darling? Why blessed?"

"Because I slept last night beside my knight in shining armor." She propped herself up on her elbows and impressed a moist kiss on his cheek. "You go write, I'm gonna sleep a little bit longer then I'll get up and order us some dinner. I love you baby."

"I love you too," he returned as he ran his fingers down the length of her hair and kissed her neck, causing her to smile and her nose to crinkle as her sleep began to restore. He grabbed his notebook and pen from the bedside table and tiptoed into the library, gently pulling together its sliding oaken doors and getting to work.

Just as Kayiane had purported at times which found Rupert at an utter loss, crying his eyes out at the kitchen table in front of the only person in the world he let see him cry so deeply, he carried the burden for his baby bro the following Saturday, in the form of a physically manifested nervousness. At issue was that he didn't know what the fuck to make of people anymore. His presumption was that anyone he put his face up to, should they engage him kindly, was doing so in allegiance to some elaborately diabolical and really goddamn mean plot to again unravel him, upon arrival of a calculatedly inopportune moment. Could that moment come today? Too soon he thought. But still, the year prior's birthday party was supposed to be one of the monumental days of his life, as was the wedding. And he'd be addressing all-comers, as he did then.

He wrote what in my view was an unmistakably lovely tribute to his brother and his soon to be newlywed bride. But safe. So safe that it was a complete break from the chutzpah that even at his frailest, most mindblown moment Rupert had always maintained, prior to October, the notion that, because though people didn't know him, he'd kept himself a ghost for twenty years, as far as he knew they had generally liked him and enjoyed his presence. As he sat onstage during the nuptials, facing out at the attendants, into the unmistakable blessing of the sun; whilst afterwards he wound through the Connecticut countryside in a stretch limousine, approached the walkway of, lobby to, the inpouring of folks, these known people and faces, he looked at each of them and was so thankful that they were there to share this day with his little brother, and he couldn't so much as instigate himself into disliking the tiniest bit about 'em. He hated no one in fact, aside from himself. Hate himself as he did, he wouldn't have traded places with anyone, never would he have, and especially not on that day.

Shortly after the cocktail hour the moment of misdoubt arrived and Louise's older sister Grace delivered a poignant, stage worthy speech, layered and crafty, cute and intimate, not a supernumerary note, and she did it from memory, had very clearly began preparing her speech weeks or months before as to memorize its every participle. As she proceeded Rupert began to get exceedingly nervous, thinking that if he didn't immediately stop his nerves from further revolt he'd induce a panic attack. Mar gave his hand the 1-4-3 squeeze that he and his mother utilized to tell each other 'I love you' in silence and secrecy. Lunging to seize his water glass from the dining table he closed his eyes, imagined little baby dachshunds and giraffes playing badminton and drank it straight. The invited guests gathered in applause and Rupert opened his eyes, newly at ease. Breathing deeply as he stood he joined in applauding Grace for her contribution, hugged her and accepted the microphone. Without looking for them and as he reached into his inner-jacket pocket for his speech he locked in on his dad and his gramps in the crowd and took a prideful glance at Benny to his right before choosing a more self-affirmative, impromptu address.

"Thank you Grace, that was amazing, I kinda wish I had gone first. Thank you so much as well to our hosts,

Grace and Louise's wonderful parents Robert and Maria Elena for all the preparation and class you've infused into this thing, this is just amazing, the band is over there kickin' people's dicks right outta their pants, I was walking around during the cocktail hour Louise with your cousin Anthony, where is he, I see you brother, so awesome to meet you today, we saw this incredible painting by Walton Ford, go check it out upstairs around and to the back left it's the giant one in the corner with the spectacular orangutans. There's a fuckin' Wifredo Lam up there too, swear to Christ. Mom and dad, grandpa, aunt Miriam, you guys know how I feel about you already, Sauersteins and Lepores and Zilizikjians from all corners of the globe who made it up here today, it's a delight to see each of you, all my thanks and love, your presence testifies to how awesome a kid my baby brother is. My grandma Miriam, she'd be 100 this December, in Minnesota thinking poetic thoughts about this day, I love that woman so ridiculously much, the smartest, most soulful person I've ever known and so I wanted her to be on each of your minds, if just for a moment, on this life affirming day. Louise, thank you for accepting me into your family, and for the countless and ever-obvious positive effects you've had on my baby bro. Benny you could never do wrong in my eyes, you've done so well today, every day before it too, you are the epicenter of my pride in and love for this world, you have been since the moment mom and dad told me I should begin expecting you. My memories of childhood really are just memories of you, how we transformed that ¼ acre into our own fuckin' fantasy land, there wasn't a game in the known universe we didn't play together, if we hadn't played it it was cuz we hadn't invented it yet. Do you remember it all? Our urinary sword fights, *Harlem Globetrotters*, the luge courses and ramps we used to carve out of the snow in the backyard? I love you more than this earth baby brother, and I can't wait to see the fantasies that you and Louise, and your children, concoct in whichever ¼ acre you guys decide to put down home plate. Kiddo you've really been the big brother for a long time now, in every way other than that I had the blessing to watch from above as you grew into the kind and gracious man you are. Now, I look up to you in every way. Ladies and gentlemen, please enjoy this day to the absolute maximum capacity of your being, let's all raise our glasses and slam 'em back to, what is it, fuckin', 117 years? *Mazel tov* you guys, I love you both. *L'chaim* everybody. Drink with me."

The guests each took a slug before hollering and applauding, standing in solidarity until after Rupe had relocated Mar and had taken his seat next to her, according anyhow to the recount of his aunt Mary later in the evening. He certainly didn't see it, nor did he register the decibels of mad applause that his words had espoused. His hearing was flushed out in that moment, as he handed the microphone to one of the gorgeous ebony female back-up singers and locked in a soul-renewing hug with his beloved brother.

"Sri Lanka, and I have a friend there," Mar replied the following Tuesday, back in Gramercy Park.

Rupert was about to Google search it but to his surprise she was far better equipped when it came to answering the question "where would I have the best chance at swimming with a blue whale?"

"We're leaving on Thursday, I just realized I totally spaced on telling you that. Five days on Sri Lanka, a week in Colombia, back home for a night and then to Dubai to see my parents. Sound good?"

"Sounds amazing. You're sure you can do it?"

"Rupert, since we met have you once seen me do anything I didn't want to or for some reason couldn't do?"

"Fair enough. It's just that you always seem to want to do things for other people, so it's impossible to know if you're fulfilling yourself."

"Hunny, it's not as if this is a vacation for you and an indentureship for me. We're gonna have a phenomenal time together and I can't wait. Just shut the fuck up and come dance with me" (it was a Fats Domino and Thurston Harris kind of an afternoon).

"My fuck is shut darlin'." She lured him in with a wag of her tiny left pointer finger and they did the shake, the monkey, the mashed potato and the stroll until she sensed that the prime rib in the smoker which she'd rubbed up before Rupert woke up had hit a buck twenty-five in the center.

Just because Mar was a Communist and a philanthropist did not mean she was unwilling to enjoy the lavish lifestyle her parents' prowess afforded her. They flew privately from an airstrip in Scarsdale and after a 5-course sushi dinner, a viewing of Being There, refueling in Santo Porto, two joints, a fuck and a nap they found themselves in the back of an SUV en route to the seaside home of Mar's girlfriend Asheni.

As they got out of the vehicle Mar began bolting for the sea, where Asheni sat, crisscrossed and apple sauced, watching its ripples and redirections with some certain intent. Mar tackled her dear friend and smothered her with hugs and kisses. As Rupert arrived they were introduced and exchanged warm greetings.

"He's been pouting for three days, 'just tell me how, just tell me how'" Mar began mockingly as she and Rupert took a seat with Asheni on her blanket. "I told him I couldn't do it justice, not compared to how you tell it, and he just had to suck it up and wait. So would you please tell my big baby here the story?"

"I can and will," Asheni confirmed as she redirected her erudite eyes Rupert's way. "My great-grandmother, Rabia, whilst a little girl, spent placid afternoons on these Arugam Bay sands with her baby brother Abhiram. She was insatiably curious and independent minded, so I've been told, an artisan, scientist, civil activist and well-rounded out rabble rouser. When she was perhaps 5 and Abhiram 2 she was called upon by the sea, with the help of some schoolmates she began collecting uprooted seagrass and withered bay orchid stems, from which she reticulated fishing nets, keen and fascinated she'd become with snagging and inspecting the other-galaxial creatures perpetually cycling past. How I love them all, I often wonder if I love them as much as she did. Their efforts were rewarded immediately, as the first afternoon yielded them several newborn ocellated eagle rays and a starry triggerfish. On the second day they were part and parcel to the most horrific blessing in the centuries old diversiform history of our little village, written or otherwise. Great whites are not common to this bay, nor has, rather nor had a blue whale been seen, from dry land through naked eyes, for several generations. Murphy's Law, as it were. More quickly than her net could drop from her fingers and her jaw could drop to her collarbone my nan watched as four or five enormous male great sharks began engorging a poor darling blue like wolves on a watermelon. Blood stained the salt water in a round as wide as the Colosseum. They were too stunned to feel anything else as they watched, helpless as could be. And then into their lives, five or six feet long, premature and still cocooned in her amniotic sac, came beautiful Lochani, the girl with sparkling eyes. My grandmother and her brother scooped her from either end with their nets and ran to show their father. He immediately reinstated the local draft though this time to include children and adults alike, to begin excavation and filling of a pool that could house a baby blue comfortably until she was strong and wise enough to go at it alone in the deep. They had seal milk imported, 100 gallons a week at first and more and more over time, and the community hugged and kissed and loved that baby as if their own, which of course she'd become. This all happened 50 years ago, 50 years yesterday in fact. Lochani has birthed 9 calves right here in the bay. The law of the land is that if you're the first to see the baby you get to name it. After she gives birth she is typically gone with her baby for several weeks before resurfacing. Am I omitting anything essential?" Asheni asked herself.

"Even if you are somehow it's easily the most amazing story I've ever heard," interjected Rupert. "How often do they come around?"

"None of the babies do anymore, they've found their own villages I suppose, but if I'm to venture a guess Lochani doesn't ever stray more than 100 miles from this spot, and I see her typically twice or three times a week. Her favorite time to make an appearance is at sunrise."

"So you think I have a good chance of seeing her while we're here?"

"I wholly hope so Rupert but just let it be known that at times in the past she's been a bit skittish around strangers. You have a great energy though, I feel it will go as you wish. Are you guys hungry?"

"*Mata badaginiyi*!" Mar adorably employed a bit of her scant Sinhalese and Rupert grabbed up, shook out and folded the blanket on their way to the kitchen where Asheni's boyfriend Chathura was putting the finishing touches on their dinner.

The greatest physical benefit of his having found Mar was that once he was comfortably moved in and acclimated to his new life with her his sleep had improved dramatically. That night however sleep would not come. How could it, when there was even a remote possibility of a blue whale's presence a few hundred feet away? Trying not to disturb Mar he passed the time by air-practicing petting Lochani and fruitlessly Google searching 'how to endear oneself to a blue whale' with little feedback, until finally the black of their guest bedroom turned midnight blue and he made his move.

He went out through the bedroom's sliding door, still naked from his unrest, and headed for the mouth of the bay, walking out into the warm sea until his toes could no longer touch bottom whilst his eyes could survey from above. More than half an hour passed and as he grew tired from wading he scooped himself beachward, having to retreat nearly 50 feet because of drift. The moment he was able to toe the fragments and grains below he felt a pulsation, a pressure, and a singular wave rolled through that was at least three times as high and mighty as the ones which came before it. Semi-circling his body back towards the eternity of the sea he immediately sensed her nearness, shortly thereafter the water began rippling from her approach. Time then stood still and amidst the stillness Rupert floated back out a bit as Lochani got her immense left eyeball right up to both of the boy's tiny ones. They remained transfixed upon each other for several moments until Rupert found himself compelled to lap down and back beside her body, which, were it measured, would dismantle the standing record at 127 feet 9 inches of pure, pescatarian cutie pie.

When he reached her tail and turned back towards her far distant and unseeable face the moment became doubly miraculous, as he saw that he and the placid beast were not alone. Or rather, they were soon to be joined by the rest of the baby whose tail had already made it's complete way into the ocean water from inside of his momma.

"Mar!" he began yelling. "Darling please come see this! Mar darling a baby!" Though she'd continued to sleep after he got out of bed Rupert's voice boomed and he succeeded in rousing her. She woke their hosts and moments later he swam to shore for a rest as Asheni swam out to offer her love and encouragement. Six and a half hours later the baby boy was all the way out and receiving nudges and licks of love from his mother. Five minutes later they were gone.

"So what would you like to name him?" inquired Chathura.

"Grover."

"Really, Grover? That's the best you can do? Of all the names..." Mar was quick to express her distaste.

"Yeah Grover," Rupert interjected with playful rudeness. "There aren't that many boy names I like, there's Noddy, Spencer, Rambo, Benny, that's pretty much the list."

"Well Benny is your brother, Rambo is already Noddy's middle name..."

"Yeah and Spencer I wanna save in case I ever put a boy sperm in one of your lady eggs."

"Ok then my love, Grover it is."

"Thanks toots."

"You got it dude."

Put it just about anywhere else on the face of the earth and El Caño de Cristales would be the most visited waterway on said face. It is that gorgeous. The reason why most people haven't heard of it, let alone seen it, is because at the place from which one starts his trek towards it you can either go left into the global epicenter of cocaine production or go right towards El Caño. Mr. Emperius, Mar's overprotective father, assigned them each three heavily armed guardians and insisted they spent their entire stay wearing helmets and vests. They chose to take two days to walk to the river though a rapid pace can get you there in one. That first night Rupert had a terrible dream.

The two of them were deeply asleep in their king sized bed and woke slowly, calmly, in tandem. Mar sat up and said 'I need to show you something.' She levitated out from the covers and there above him she started to produce extreme heat, until she herself was fire as much as she was human. The building turned to ash and Rupert was left, paralyzed, sitting up on the bed, still somehow pristinely clean, fitted with sheets and rested atop the rubble which used to be their home. She razed Brooklyn, Queens, Central Park, Harlem. As she continued north she remained the same size though his field of view became enormous. Down went Yonkers, Valhalla, Mount Kisco. As the colonial on Timberlane came into view Mar began to crumble, the sight of which lurched Rupert out of the nightmare, his sleeping bag drenched from forehead to knees. As his mind grappled to secure a reality he turned on his head lamp to see that she was sleeping as peacefully as can be beside him. It took him two hours to regain some sense of calm, the result of the dream having been an assurance that she was not who she'd purported to be and ultimately would leave him, battered and bruised, if not charred.

Arriving in Dubai at what to their internal clock was 11:30 pm they made love under 17 showerheads and fell asleep. The following morning she gave him directions to a store down the road a ways so he could buy each of them a specific set of binoculars.

"I got it, Voltron Crop Placer Space Gliders. Be back soon," Rupert had written the correct name down but just adored busting Mar's ravishing chops. "I'm really buying two pair of $20,000 binoculars?"

"You sure are buddy, hop to it. We have a whole city to see before we meet my parents for dinner. You can write a $40,000 check to the ASPCA to level it out if it'll make you feel better."

Before he met Mar Dubai was a place that had repelled Rupert with its opulence; he never would have gone there without her. But he was a different man now, and he knew it. When he returned to the hotel she was waiting out front, left shoulder against a pillar and right foot swung over left. All the money available in this world and at that point in time not a penny of it was of his earning, but money is just an idea, it's not a thing of value, at least not appropriately so. Grandpa Giuseppe had legendarily called himself a multi-millionaire when his girls were young. Three million to be exact, one for each of his ladies. As Rupe grabbed Mar's hand and they began their walk upon completely new places he finally reconciled his grandfather's sentiment. And three million dollars was a lot of money back then!

Mar had been to the top of the Burj Khalifa before, though as a native of Dubai she was somewhat anomalous in that respect, much in the way that so too is a New Yorker who's visited The Statue of Liberty. The Burj (the Statue too) can be seen from so far away that it seemed as if they were walking in place. As they got close Mar slowed down.

"Alright I'm gonna go up on the roof of this building and you go up to the observation deck and we can make faces at each other, thanks to our amazing binoculars," came Mar's newest instructions.

Rupert fell into a swoon in that moment. he pulled her close and kissed her lips with such ferocity that they may have split were they not so adequately cocoa buttered.

"Goodbye Mar."

"Goodbye Rupert."

"I love you more than the earth."

I love you more than the earth plus 2. See you soon silly."

She looked back at him as they broke in opposite directions but not he at her. All around the outside of the hulking building men were hard at work tilling soil and planting a lovely array of date palm trees. It took half an hour until his turn on the high speed elevator ride to the observation deck, once there he located Mar with the binoculars in unexpectedly rapid style. They made faces at each other as planned, Mar's growing sillier and Rupert's tragicomically into stern seriousness. He mouthed her an apology and kicked out a window. As he jumped he got the taste of heroin and cocaine on his tongue and down his throat. He prayed that his ventricles would detach from his heart before his skull split. Still images of his life flashed as photographs several thousand per milli-moment. As he narrowed on 30 floors from the ground he realized he wasn't about to die and pummeled the rest of that distance wearing a hopeful and mischievous smirk. Eleazer and I laid ourselves to the ground and embraced.

My first thought was that I'd blasted down something like 10 or 12 feet into the tilled soil, loose as freshly ground coffee and as warm as a summer's worth of sun. Hundreds of microscopic lacerations sliced into my skin as I'd submerged, every edged granule garnering the efficacy of a samurai sword, passively, with no expectation or accomplice, through the speed with which I had met it. I began a crawling out, sensing as though following every inch of upward momentum I was able to muster I'd slip back down half, most or all of it. As I made it all the way up damp wind and motivated sunbeams offered love to the tips of my middle and pointer fingers. Feeling then the familiar and slender softness of Mar's fingers wrapping around mine, a raw and ancient instinctual power allowed her to turn excavation of my entire body into the uproot of a seasonal potato. She laid me out in the soil on my back and delicately examined my entirety for injury, including my hair and my glasses, which somehow still sat on my face. Her examination seemed to last an hour, she only made contact with my eyes during the moment or two she spent thumbing at their lids and every time I tried to talk she shut me firmly the fuck up with a butterfly's press on my lips with her salty, lugubrious cocoa flavored pointer finger.

Once she had gotten me to my feet she wanted to pull me in for a deep embrace, holding back because of the swell of bruises and trickles of blood bulbing out from my abrasions. Instead she grabbed me by my chin and offered my lips a swift kiss of furious sadness and love. She took my hand as have a billion mothers having watched their young sons allow sentient invincibility to get them near death. Any faster and we'd have been jogging, she kept a half pace ahead and yanked me the twenty or so blocks back to our hotel, neither of us saying a word until we were in our room with the door latched behind us. She drew a mineral salt bath so hot that I would've needed blow on it were it a cup of tea and reentered the bedroom where I sat at the edge of the bed, examining the absence stuck expression in the adjacent mirror. She walked around to stand in front of me, wagging a solitary ring finger and squeezed out a sweet susurration of 'come.' She undressed me and once again led me by my hand on a far more casually paced walk to the bathroom, supporting my weight as I struggled to get my right heel, which it turned out I'd pulverized a bit, up and over the lip of the tub.

Lowering to her knees beside the tub she reached behind me to take hold of a sea sponge, plunging it into the brew, welling up with tears once more as it purged cascades of water and suds from my forehead and foremost locks.

"Rupert, why did you do that?" was all in the world she wanted to know, struggling against her own purge, of heartbroken despair, at what should rightfully have happened to the only fellow she'd ever adored not an hour earlier.

"I'm just, I got too sad, I'm so sorry Marisol. I didn't know I was gonna do it when we left New York. I didn't even know I was gonna do it when we got here. I'm never gonna be a good man, someone you can be proud of. You deserve so much better. Either you were gonna realize that and leave me or stay with me out of pity, I couldn't handle either."

"So you jumped off the Jesus, tallest building in the world because you thought I was gonna tire of you?"

"I guess so," I felt like such a coward, a little boy getting his first real man dose of stern humility."

"Well dummy, I was never gonna. When you hit the ground it was like the stock footage of an atomic mushroom cloud."

"But please Marisol, why? You are incomprehensibly gorgeous and that's only like the 34th most endearing thing about you. You're a fuckin' saint among sinners. So why me?"

"Oh Rupert you really don't see any of it do you? You're kind, funny, gentle, thoughtful. And cute, and you're right, you are a good fucker. The afternoon we met in the park it was obvious I wasn't wearing a bra but you didn't stare at my tits once, not even when I feigned a look away to see if you'd take a peek. I love you for more reasons than there's time enough to detail. And, in about 7 and a half months we're gonna have a baby, incidentally When I sent you off to buy binoculars it was a ruse so I could take a pregnancy test."

Into my brain shot a holistically nirvanic rapture. I rose from my bathwater in a Phoenix' flash as she rose in turn, my wounds shedding all pique. Amid our embrace I thought about how in the coming months our hugs would grow top-heavy in deference to the sprouting of our child, evolving rhythmically in the world's most nourishing womb.

"Wow," I spoke softly into her adorable little ear, "I'm gonna, we're gonna, I'm gonna be a daddy, we're gonna have a little baby boy, or maybe even a little baby girl. I could eat a bathtub full of babies I'm so happy right now."

I called Benny from the airplane to tell him what I'd and we'd done but I couldn't possibly lay it on my parents prior to appearing in front of them in (primarily) one piece. Before I arrived I needed to reconcile the age-old debate over whether bad or good news makes for a better lead, here maybe there was a virginal duality between the two nuggets I needed to share. Suicide attempt? Grandchild? *Suicide attempt*? *Grandchild*?

"You guys, I have two things to tell you, both of which I guarantee you were not expecting to hear."

"Go ahead hunny, tell us anything you want, you always can," my mother assured instinctively, nervously.

"Are you ok kiddo?" my dad spoke softly and with a subtle quiver.

I went with grandchild first, a solid choice I'd say looking back. And so by the time I'd detailed both notables shrieks of declarative conquest had dead in their tracks morphed into Heaven-heard wails of dissociation on the part of my mother and soft-spoken, broken hearted murmurings of self-indictment from my father. We three cuddled up on the couch, me in the middle. I don't think they really knew what to say, really they just needed to hold their child. Typically the last to do such a thing my mom turned on the television and we shared an altogether necessary snicker as Joe from Impractical Jokers scoopskied potatoes. Benny arrived shortly after and joined us in reflection. I realized shortly thereafter that my parents and brother had always been my best friends.

In the morning I woke with an empowered impulse, to trek out into the woods to visit Morla and too many lost generations of friends, surprised and eager in spying my approach, introducing me proudly to their newest young. I had not thought about Hadi-Alim and Eleazer since my little free fall in Dubai. As my destination drew into view I was reminded of Hadi's promise that he'd call on me once more. Had I lost that privilege when I'd chosen to off myself? Or was he, like so many others, a big yellow liar? It wasn't visible as I climbed up and onto Morla though once I reached the apex of his shell there in front of me was the saddlebag I had designed for Hadi's use. Inside one of the notebooks was the story you've just finished reading, ending of course when I met with the earth in Dubai. Another was surfeit of anecdotes and guidance left, of my desire, for my eyes only.

The third contained a chronicle of his true gift to the world, his sack up, his finally mustering some of his own goddamn chutzpah. I'll share a little excerpt of it with you here:

Rupe in all those dead on arrival years before my decision to meet you there was one thought I had, obsessively, century after century, something I knew I could do that would make the world a better place. Just kill all the bad guys. The only thing that changed as entire eras waved goodbye was the definition by which I identified exactly who those guys were. To save you from the bore which would be another one of my history lessons, the long and short of it is that the right brand of bad guys arrived around the time the Greeks defined megalomania. You were so close in your fever dreams my boy. As I see it, there are 1,111 men and 6 women alive today whose control over all the rest needs to cease should this world of yours ever be one of peace and fairness. So that will be my contribution. Please, by all means, write a conclusion to this tale, go through the cock-in-the-ass process of publishing it, if that's your choice. It'll be of great interest to many, may even stop someone from a wanton leap, might also inspire one. But you must know that the true reason I came to you was so that when our time came there would be someone to remember Eleazer and I. Surely the population wouldn't be able to wrap its head around my fuckin' plan or the reality of Ellie and me, and more to the point my plan can only be executed if no one (but you) is aware of it. Let me mention also that it occurred to me my plan's only a stopgap in inevitable global slavery, unless of course there are some other god type dudes and chicks out there, and they happen to be likeminded. As it were, the superdust I used on you, long ago in your wayward wood, wasn't the only tincture in my possession. When in 2031, the incidentally same year the last of my victims will die brutally, publicly, biblically, the UN giggles their way through the Multinational Megalomaniac Tax Imperative while the global press completely spaces on covering it I hope you'll think of me fondly for a sweet second. It's gonna tax 75% of all personal capital above 1 billion dollars American, keeping the new generation of megalos at bay. They'll be a docile bunch by then anyhow, their alienness exposed, neurotic, defeated, charitable even, down to the most miserly Scrooge among them.

And yes, of course I know what you're thinking, what possible moral justification can I have for murder. For starters, that's not exactly how it's gonna go. The majority of them are gonna kill themselves when their crimes are brought to light. I guess I have two defenses, the first being go plot me on a spread sheet of world leaders and I'm way at the bottom, up against other gods an 1100 headcount is puppy balls in a bucket. But fuck all of that anyhow, cuz I don't have a species, so I don't hafta abide a moral code either, at the very least I'm unaccountable by circumstance. As for the folks Eleazer ate, he was a fuckin' lion, lions kill and eat shit. And randomly, before I forget, don't worry kiddo, it didn't hurt a bit when we transmogrified.

I'll share a little bit of his letter to me too. From the looks of it it was the last thing he wrote, the characters wrinkle from the unsteadying of his hands, and I can only presume that the sporadic smudging was created by big, bubbly teardrops:

I know things are gonna go well for you the rest of the way. You've changed way more than you realize. I hope I've given you some things to think about, to be proud of and to strive towards. Just as imperfect men have caused you pain, your indiscretions and viral self-esteem and abuse have led you at times to disrespect and disregard the feelings and existential sanctity of others. Take that basketball coach for example. Sure he was a bit of a homer, a nepotist even, but he wasn't anti-Semitic. Should you run into him on the street, destitute, alone in the universe, suck his cock and buy him a beer, if that's what he needs and he asks nicely enough. And Apollonia, just like you, and like everybody else, she was trying to figure life out, battling her own demons, her treatment of you was harsh but often accurate and borne of frustration, because you never reached or more to the point tried to reach the potential that everyone you've ever met has seen in you. If she was alive today I'd like to think that all it would take for you to outright love and forgive her is a hug and an apology. Life is a trillion-piece puzzle of huddled zebras, almost too difficult to try getting through, and everyone carries around his or her amniotic sac, draped over their strongest shoulder, stuffed up with pain and regret a fist or two more with every sunken experience, each plotting to find the path to a simple, reasonable armistice of the soul on a blank map of the stars. I can promise you, every little crumb of peace you offer up out there will kill off an equivalent morsel of hate. But you need to go all the way with it Rupert. Even occasional malice on your part nullifies all your precedent kindnesses. As you go forward, please, put yourself in the other guy's sandals before you judge and condemn. Presume that what everyone you encounter did in the precedent moment was lose everything they'd ever had, and proceed from there. There are so many wonderful experiences in front of you yet, go get 'em if you want 'em. And pleasures you can continue or return to, cooking, playing music with people, zoological intrigue, finally reading *The Canterbury Tales*. I just hope that the peace you feel now, and the heightened levels of love you're gonna feel in a few months when you hold your little daughter will relieve you of all regret, all the perceived suffering, each bit of which has imbued you with wisdom and strength. So, Rupert my boy, my second call on you is to urge this simple action: as you wake with every newborn sun to feel the power of a lion and a god inside you, keep an open mind to the real possibility that everyone else has got one of each inside of them too.

For Grandma Mary and Grandpa Norman

Credits

Song Lyrics Used:
Ch.2 opening, excerpted from the song *'Hey Babro'* off of the 1969 album Alias Pink Puzz by Paul Revere and the Raiders.
Ch. 2 bedroom scene, lyrics excerpted from *'It's Late'* written by Brian May and off of the 1977 album News of the World.
Ch. 3 opening, excerpted from the Antoine 'Fats' Domino song *'Ida Jane'* released in 1959.
Ch. 4 opening, excerpted from 'Get You Off' from the eponymous album by The Go, released in 1999.
Ch. 5 opening, excerpted from *'A Natural Man'* by Bobby Hebb, original date of conception unknown.
Ch. 6 opening, excerpted from *'Manic Depression'* off of the Jimi Hendrix Experience album Are You Experienced?, released in 1967.
Ch. 7 opening, excerpted from *'Radio-Friendly Unit Shifter'* off of the Nirvana album In Utero, released in 1993.
Ch. 8 opening, excerpted from the standard *'Nobody Knows You When You're Down and Out'*, original release date unknown.
Ch. 9 opening, excerpted from *'Momentarily Sane'* off of the 2006 album Dear Independence by The Blue Van.

Cover Artwork courtesy Beatrice Kern
Cover Design by Melissa Secondino

Thank you to Mom, Dad, Josh, Damian, Sophia, the Otts and the Reynolds.

Made in the USA
Middletown, DE
19 October 2018